MECHANICS OF LOVE

Love on Madison Island 3

MEKA JAMES

Finding love
where it's
least expected!

Happy reading

Meka

�֎ Created with Vellum

It's never too late to live your best life!

This story nearly did me in. I've never struggled with a book from start to finish as much as I did writing this one. It was 100% a group project with the wonderful Wordmakers. They are the writing ass writers who wouldn't let me fail! Talking out plot points. Suggestions given. Belief I could do the damn thing when I had all the doubts in the world. And for calling me on my bullshit (especially you Tasha L. Harrison) with the tough love y'all know I need. There was no way I would have gotten to the end without their constant and total support through my actual writer's tears.

Extra shout out to Coralie Moss and Amelia Foster who managed to not block me from their DMs with all the crying I did. Seriously I owe you two a drink or three for all the hand holding.

The Write Owls who stayed up late nights dragging me along until I got to the finish line.

Randi Love who was probably as sick of my opening chapters as I was. K. Sterling, Felicia Grossman, Deana Birch, and Ali Williams, y'all are rock stars for reading and cutting down the forest so I could see the trees.

Thanks to Tera for dealing with my extra neediness with this manuscript. And to Ms. Williams for giving it to me straight and making sure everything was in line.

Cover design by Kylie Sek of Cover Culture
Illustration by Tamara Davies

Edited by: Tera Cuskaden
Sensitivity read by: D. Ann Williams

Follow me on Bookbub for up-to date information about future releases

CONTENT WARNING

This story contains discussions of infertility, caring for an ailing parent, and infidelity.

On a less important note this story is a slow burn, and I do mean SLOW. But there will be a Bonus Booty extended HEA.

IRENE

MADISON ISLAND THIRTY MILES.

I sighed with relief when I saw the road sign. My two-day road trip from New York to home was nearing an end. When I'd packed my bags after the last fight with Derrick, I'm sure he'd expected me to only stay at a hotel for a few days. To take some time to "calm down." He hadn't bothered to call until after he'd gotten served with the divorce papers. I tightened my grip on the wood grain steering wheel and mentally forced any tears to stay put.

"Come home and stop with the dramatics." His condescending voice taunted me. Whenever I'd called him on his bullshit, I was always being dramatic. Blowing things out of portion. It was always me. But not this time. Not when he'd paraded—

I shook my head and sat up straighter in the plush leather seat of my Audi. I was done giving my energy to a man who didn't respect me. I'd mourned the time I'd wasted, but no more. After realizing he had zero intentions of apologizing—not that he ever did without there being a "but" included—I'd gotten the bug to get farther away. I longed for simpler. A place where I could almost remove the mask and relax just a little bit more.

Almost.

As I settled back, I laughed quietly to myself over the fact I'd taken the car he loved the most. Was it petty? Sure. But it was purchased during the marriage, which meant it was half mine. And it wasn't like either of us drove much in the city, but status, it had all been about status. Like having a professional and sophisticated wife. Along with other women to warm his bed. The car was part of my severance package.

I leaned against the headrest and daydreamed about what being myself would even look like. Hell, did I even know? I'd been the reflected version of whom everyone expected me to be for so long...

A large branch laying across the road came into view. I yanked the steering wheel to the side, but not quickly enough to avoid it completely. My low-sitting car ran over it, tossing me upward like I'd gone over a speed bump too fast, and a cloud of dust bellowed up from the side as the sound of my tires on the dirt shoulder squealed in my ears.

The back end fishtailed before I managed to come to a screeching halt. I placed my hand over my rapidly beating heart and glanced in my rearview at the limb, now shattered into pieces. The stretch of road leading to Madison Island was basically no-man's land, but fuck, they still should have people out to clear hazards from the roadways.

After a few calming breaths, I eased back onto the road. Derrick's voice taunted me. He'd have something to say about not paying attention, and somehow the branch being in the road would have been my fault. I blew out a long exhale and did a full body shake to get rid of the remaining nerves and negative thoughts about my soon-to-be ex-husband. Sitting up and rolling my shoulders back, I attempted to give eagle eye attention to the road ahead just in case any more of the beautiful mossy oaks decided to lose additional pieces.

I pushed down on the pedal, forcing the car faster, only instead of accelerating as it should have, the fine piece of German engineering—as the salesperson had called it—sputtered most unceremoniously, and the dials on the dash went haywire.

"What the hell?" I pressed the gas again. The engine tried to rev in response, but it came out more of a sputter as it jerked forward. "Great. Just fucking great." I managed to maneuver to the narrow shoulder.

"Now what?" I turned the car off then cranked it up again. It started, but when I pressed the gas, even knowing nothing about cars, I knew the sound it made wasn't a good one.

"Damn it!" I muttered as I hit the service link button and waited for it to connect. Why couldn't I even take time away in peace without shit falling apart around me?

"Good afternoon, Mrs. Moore, how can I be of service today?" The female voice spoke over the speaker.

"Yes, the car won't go. It makes some weird noise, and I think I might need a tow."

"Were you in an accident?"

"No, it just stopped."

"Are you in a safe area?"

"I'm in the middle of nowhere for the most part, but yeah, I'm fairly safe."

"Okay. One moment."

There was silence for a while, but I could hear the faint sounds of clicking as the agent worked.

"Thank you for your patience, Mrs. Moore. I have contacted the closest wrecker service. They say the estimated time to get you will be 20-30 minutes. Is that acceptable?"

I rolled my eyes, not that she could see. What option did I have? Not like if I said no, they could somehow make the driver warp speed or something. I relayed my acceptance and declined her offer to stay on the line with me until they arrived. I needed the moments of peace.

I hadn't told anyone I was coming for a visit. It had been a minor inconvenience with the office for me to take a sudden vacation, but I'd covered for Dr. Joyce plenty over the years, especially with his stints in rehab. He owed me. Besides, it was only two weeks. Maybe. Regardless, I knew there would be questions. From my parents, and especially from my girls. The time alone would give me a chance to make sure my answers to the inevitable questions were in place and delivered with practiced ease. Regina and Cynthia were a lot easier to dodge virtually. Too much time around them and I knew they'd start to see through, though maybe that wasn't such a bad thing.

I was tired of pretending my life was perfect.

My phone dinged, indicating I had a new text message. I pressed the button on my steering wheel, then commanded it to be read: *You need to be home by 5 today. We have dinner plans.*

The robotic voice fit the tone of my husband perfectly. We hadn't talked since he called to tell me he'd gotten my "ridiculous papers," but he expected me to just show back up and pretend as if everything were okay. I sighed and rested my head back against the headrest. Of course, he did, because pretending all was well was what I excelled at. He'd be pissed when he found out I wasn't going to be there to play the role of the dutiful wife. That particular role was over for me.

The car continued to make an awful noise as it ran, but I needed to keep the AC going. April in coastal Georgia meant high humidity, and I'd be sweating all too soon; I didn't need my edges curling up. Besides, the only time one was permitted to perspire was when working out, but even then, one glistened, they didn't sweat. At least, according to my mother.

The sound of a big engine got my attention. I sat up and squinted at the sight of an approaching vehicle. As it got closer, I could tell it was the tow I'd been waiting for, though I expected to see it coming in my rearview, not in front of me. There was absolutely nothing along this stretch of road from the direction the truck came other than Madison Island. I turned off my car then stepped out as the driver stopped and did a U-turn in the middle of the two-lane road so they could back up in front of my broken-down car. The logo on the door pulled a deep groan from my throat. *Martin Autobody*.

All the talk from Cynthia and Regina about how the woman I'd deemed my high school nemesis now ran her father's mechanic shop and worked wonders on their cars ping-ponged through my head. Not to mention Remi had been instrumental in getting Regina's food truck. Somehow the woman who'd never been a part of my friend circle seemed to have wormed her way in, and I wasn't sure how I felt about it.

Remi Martin, the woman who, with a few choice words or dismissive glances, had the uncanny ability to make me question all I believed to be important. The clothes and other material things I'd put so much importance on, she'd disregarded, and her lack of caring had always irked me. But it'd been that same aloofness that had drawn me to her.

I had the momentary thought it might not be her in the truck but was quickly proven wrong when the driver hopped down. My first secret crush. It'd been over twenty years since Remi and I had said much to each other. Sure, I'd seen her in passing around town when I was home for visits, but we'd never done the whole catch-up thing. There hadn't been any need. Or rather, I'd kept my distance to avoid her unknowing rebuffs and quiet judgments. But here she was, in a set of dirty blue overalls with the top half tied around her waist and a white tank top with the unfortunate nickname clinging to a figure she'd always hidden. Oversized, baggy clothes had always been her go-to. Except during gym. The memory of the secret peeks I'd try to take as we'd changed for class popped unwanted into my mind.

She'd also fully embraced the tomboy look where her hair was concerned. Wasn't quite the total low cut with line-up, because she did have tight curls on top, though I'd have to say Derrick probably sported more hair than she did. And I was sure he probably spent way more time on his. Being well groomed was all part of his façade.

When she laid eyes on me, she laughed and shook her head. "Irene Johnson."

I didn't bother to correct her by adding the Moore to my name. Damn, she looked good despite the less-than-flattering outfit. Flawless skin, amazing cheekbones, full lips, and dark, serious eyes that had always seemed to bore into me. It'd taken one deep look from her... No, I stopped the thought before it ran away to places I couldn't handle currently. Remi had been the source of many of my teenage fantasies. But she could barely stand me, so my defenses were activated.

I rolled my shoulders back and lifted my chin. "Nice to see you, too, Remi."

She drew together what were surprisingly well-shaped brows. "Is it?"

"Isn't that the typical greeting when you see someone you've not been around in a while?"

"Only if you mean it, otherwise, why lie?"

Same attitude from high school. Blunt without a care of how her words came across. Was it really that hard to pretend? To put forth basic politeness? The multitude of fake smiles and air kiss greetings I'd perfected, given, and received over the years flipped through my head. No, Remi didn't do pretending. And her brutal truth was a hard thing to combat when one's life was full of make-believe.

As she turned her attention to my car, appraising it with open appreciation, clearly for her, the answer was yes. She whistled through her teeth. "The Audi TT RS with a two-point five-liter turbocharged engine giving it three hundred ninety-four horsepower. Zero to sixty in three point six seconds." She moved around the side to the back. "Oh, the sport exhaust. I bet it sounds like a beast on the road. It's... a...beauty. What's wrong with it?"

I didn't have a clue what most of what she said was. I did, however, pick up on the fact she was impressed, and that made me stand a little bit taller. One of the many reflexes I'd picked up from my mother. "How am I supposed to know? It was going, then it wasn't."

She rounded the car, easing past me as she continued to check it out. "Did you run out of gas?"

I planted both hands on my hips and frowned at her. "Did you just ask me if I ran out of gas? Is that the mechanic equivalent of did you power it on?"

She lifted one shoulder but didn't answer. Instead, she tilted her head and simply stared at me, waiting.

"No, I didn't run out of gas. Aren't you just here to tow it to a certified place, not play diagnostic on the side of the road?"

"Crank it up," she ordered, completely ignoring what I'd said.

It'd irked me to no end when she'd do that in high school. She'd either pretend I hadn't said something, or act unbothered by my words. Other people cared about what I'd had to say, and what my opinion of them was. Other people wanted to be like me, to have what I had. Everyone but Remi Martin. Which had made me want her attention in the worst way.

"No. Look, I know Regina and Cynthia sing your praises,

but really there is nothing you can do for me here other than put it on your truck and take it to a service location."

I was annoyed enough that the damn car had died on me. She wasn't helping by keeping me out in the heat longer than needed by trying to do something I was fairly certain she wasn't qualified for. I didn't know much about cars, but I did remember how much Derrick talked about certified this and certified that. I drove, he handled everything else. Or rather, would call for the concierge service to come take care of it whenever work was needed.

"Suit yourself." Remi headed back to her truck, pulled a lever, and after a squeak, and a thud, the back slowly began lowering to the ground. She went about dragging chains toward my car then dropped to her knees to peer under it. "Did you run over something?"

I pushed my sunglasses up to the top of my head. "For goodness sakes, Remi, stop with all the damn questions."

She laughed again, which only served to annoy me more, then flipped onto her back, not caring one bit about laying in the dirt. The muscles in her arms flexed and tensed while she worked. I inched forward to squat down, placing my palm on the side of the car to help with my balance, in an attempt to get a closer look. Though my attention was more on her than what she was actually doing.

She sat up, brushing against me in the process, which nearly knocked me on my butt. With quick reflexes, she caught my arm to keep me from falling backwards. Her grip was firm and hot, and I wasn't sure which stunned me more, her touching me, or my near fall. Our closeness brought back those fluttering inklings of excitement I'd tried to chalk up to teenage curiosity at the time.

Only they'd never gone away.

She pulled us both to standing. "You good?"

I couldn't find the words and could only nod my answer.

She didn't release me right away. Instead, her dark, intense eyes continued to bore into me, the heat of her hold radiated up my arm, causing me to swallow the dryness in my mouth.

She tilted her head, and a frown furrowed her brow, but she finally let go and dusted off her hands. "You're leaking fluid, so you may have punctured something. Hence why I asked if you ran over something."

Her quick swerve right back to business jolted me out of my odd stupor, and I wiped at the spot on my forearm, which now sported an abstract dirty handprint. Without waiting for me to reply, she went back to her truck, and my car lurched forward before it was slowly pulled onto the flat bed.

I watched it, instead of giving too much attention to the woman with me. "A tree branch."

"What?"

"A little ways back, there was a tree branch in the road."

"Why didn't you drive around it?"

"Why is that any of your concern?" I shot back.

She shook her head and headed for the driver's side of her truck. "Go around and hop in."

"Hop in what?"

Remi looked at the cab of her vehicle then climbed in. She couldn't be serious.

2

REMI

I watched Ms. Snooty in my side view mirror. She stood gaping at me as if I'd grown two heads or something. Her dismissive attitude to my questions wasn't an unusual reaction. Both professionally, and with our personal history. Most people expected men to know the what's-what about cars, especially the men I'd been sent out to retrieve.

I'd had my fair share of comments about my boss being wrong to send a woman out to do a man's job or some other such nonsense. Most of the time I didn't bother to correct their assumptions on either front and simply did what I needed to do.

With Irene Johnson, I really held it back. She'd always had an idea that she not only knew better, but that she was better than me or others she deemed beneath her, and I had little to no patience to get into a pointless argument with her. My non-reaction was the best reaction where she was concerned. It'd served me well when we were in school, no reason to change what wasn't broke. She wanted her car towed, I'd tow it and be done.

"I don't have all day," I yelled out my window.

"Is it even clean?" She gestured up and down her body. "Because this outfit doesn't accessorize well with motor oil and grease."

I pinched the bridge of my nose. Yup, same old Irene. Appearance had been everything to her. I used to wonder if she even owned jeans, let alone a pair of sweatpants. Every day she'd be dressed like she was having lunch at a country club or something. I never quite understood how she, Regina, and Cynthia were friends because those two were way more down to earth, but somehow, they made it work.

I hopped out of the truck and took stock of what were sure to be designer clothes she was worried about getting dirty. The pastel pink pants clung to the curve of her hips and stopped mid-calf. The white lace blouse, complete with floppy bow at the neck, looked more like a doily I'd see on my grandmother's table than on a person, yet Irene wore it. And wore it with pride and...wore it well. Beneath the lace, the cami hugged her flat stomach and slender waist. Both of the light colors worked with her dark complexion.

She stood with her arms crossed and her hip cocked out as if she was serious about not getting in. Why didn't I let Tony just take the call when he'd offered? Sure, he'd gotten stuck once, but damn I was regretting giving him shit over it now. Just my fucking luck I'd end up with the bitchy woman who for some reason couldn't seem to leave me in peace when we were in school. She'd always had something to say from how I'd dressed, to who I'd hung out with. It didn't fucking matter. No matter what I did, she always seemed to be there. If I'd sneezed too loud, wannabe Queen Bee was there with some snide comment or another. And now her bad driving was inconveniencing my day.

"Look, you have three options." I held up a finger. "One. Get in the damn truck." I put up a second finger. "Two. Call someone to come get you." And I counted off with a third.

"Or three. Walk. So, what's it gonna be? Because I have work to do."

There weren't many people who tested my patience the way Irene Johnson did. She forever had an uppity attitude thinking she was somehow better than others because she'd have designer clothes and went to fancy places on vacations. Or, hell, the fact she went on vacations.

Irene started to speak, but stopped, and instead strolled past me, trailing a soft scent of what was probably an expensive perfume behind her. The same sweet aroma that had me holding onto her for longer than I should have. I flexed my fingers, trying to work out the tingling memory of how soft her skin was beneath my palm. She stretched up on her tiptoes and peered inside the cab of the truck. I definitely had a thing for legs, so I couldn't help but notice the way her calf muscles flexed with the action. I couldn't deny she was a beautiful woman—back then, and now—but she was wholly too irritating. And too straight.

"Do you have a towel or anything? These pants are light, and I don't want to end up with some smear across my ass."

I had to stop myself from glancing down, and that fact irked me. "Your ass will be fine. So, are you getting in or what?"

She frowned at me, squaring her shoulders. "You don't have to be so hostile. We can't all walk around in stained dungarees and combat boots. Some of us care about how we look."

I released a long, audible exhale. Before I could say anything, she held up her hands. "I'm getting in."

She gripped the steering wheel and door to hoist herself up. The pants she'd been so concerned about pulled tighter across her ass with the motion. And this time I did look, it was a nice one. I shook off the thought as quickly as it came and rolled my shoulders.

"If you are so concerned about getting your butt dirty, why are you about to slide it across my seat? Just walk around to the other side." Not that her pants would get dirty, because despite her thinking I rolled around in filth, I kept both my truck and shop as spotless as possible.

With a soft oof, she made it up then stuck her leg out. "There is dirt on the other side, and these are six-hundred-dollar Jimmy Choo. My pants can be dry cleaned, my wedges can not."

Right...that made perfect sense. The sooner I got us back to town, the sooner I could be done with Irene and get on with my day. I waited until she'd moved over before I joined her. The scent of her perfume mingled in the air. Not overpowering, but enough to take notice. In all the years I'd known the woman, I realized this was probably the longest conversation we'd ever had.

"Shit. My purse. It's in the car."

"It'll be fine until we get back."

"But my phone is in it."

"Do you need to make a call right this moment?"

"No, but..."

"Then you'll be fine 'til we get to the shop."

I checked my mirror before pulling back onto the road. Irene huffed loudly, but her attitude didn't bother me. She'd be fine for the twenty-minute ride.

The few minutes of blessed silence didn't last nearly long enough. "Wait. You said shop? As in yours? You can't fix my car."

I cut my eyes over at her briefly. I actually could fix her car. I'd spent ten years in Atlanta working at the luxury vehicle garage. I'd made it up the ranks to lead mechanic before Dad had gotten sick and I'd had to return to Madison Island. Not many people in town drove high-end cars, but I'd outfitted the place so I could handle all repairs since I had my certification. It was the biggest and only real improvement I'd made to Martin Autobody.

"If you want to have it taken to a dealership, you'll have to figure that out on your own. You get fifteen miles of complimentary towing."

"That seems like a scam. You're driving me farther away from an authorized repair place and then I have to pay? What sense does that make?"

I came to a stop in the middle of the road and turned to face her. "If you want me to drive you to Savannah instead, I will do that. You get your fifteen then it's two bucks a mile for everything over. Plus, a fifty-dollar convenience fee for my return trip."

"What the hell? That's highway robbery."

"I don't make the rules. You can take it or leave it. But you're eating into my day, and I have actual customers waiting on me to fix their cars. Madison or Savannah?"

"Fine. Madison. But I can't believe you wouldn't offer me some sort of friend discount."

We were in a brief stare-down as I processed her statement. Slowly, I tilted my head to the side and frowned. "When have we ever been friends?"

She twisted her lips to the side and turned away. We didn't speak for the rest of the trip. Once we got back to my shop, I backed the truck up so that I could unload her car into one of the parking spaces. A small puddle of black liquid ran down the surface of the bed. She had a fairly substantial oil leak. Because there was some still coming out, she might not have engine damage. However, I wouldn't know for sure unless I checked under the hood, and that was something I doubted she'd let me do.

"Hey, Boss. Need me to clear out a bay for ya?" Devon yelled from the garage door.

"Nah, the lady wants to take it elsewhere, we were just the rescue."

Irene pulled a large leather bag from the passenger side. I had no doubt it probably cost as much if not more than the shoes she'd been so concerned about. She ran a hand across her butt, attempting to look behind her. "Do I have any stains?"

I glanced down at her ass, and I may or may not have admired it for longer than necessary. "Nope, looks good."

Her lips turned up in a smile. The first pleasant expression to grace her face. "Thanks."

I untied the top of my overalls and slid my arms in before zipping it up. "My pleasure."

"Do you mean it?"

I grabbed the paperwork from the truck and chose to ignore her question. "Just need your signature here and here." I pointed at the two places on the paper. "You can wait inside if you want until whoever comes to retrieve you. And there are paper towels you can put on the chair to save your ass from any other potential dirt." I turned and headed toward my building when I heard her quick stomps gaining on me.

"Good to know you're concerned," she commented after falling into step with me.

"About?"

"My ass."

I cast another quick glance down then laughed. "You're concerned. I'm simply being accommodatin'."

"If you say so. But, about my car."

"What about it. You want it at a dealership, it can stay here until you get that sorted out. And I'll be friendly by not charging you a storage fee."

"You really do that?"

I shrugged. I never charged for cars being parked on the lot, but for her I'd make an exception.

"Anyway. It can't be left outside."

"It'll be fine."

She grabbed my arm, and an electric zing shot through me. "That's an eighty-thousand dollar car. It can't be left outside like some budget compact."

I pressed my fingers into my eye to stop the twitch that had started. "Maybe if you hadn't treated your eighty-thousand dollar car like it was some jacked up, off-roading truck you wouldn't be in this situation."

She pushed her designer shades to the crown of her head, stepping closer. The perfume that had been wreaking havoc on my senses the entire car ride once again teased me as she stood close. "Remi, cut me some slack here. I didn't run over it intentionally. I simply didn't see it in enough time to miss it completely." Her dark brown eyes seemed to be pleading with me.

I peered up; her shoes gave her a couple of extra inches on me, but it didn't matter. A height difference wasn't a deterrent to me standing my ground against unnecessary bullshit. "I realize you expect to be catered to and coddled, but that's not how I rolled then, and I'm not inclined to do so now."

She took on her signature defensive stance. Arms crossed and chin turned up ever so slightly, allowing her to quite literally look down her nose at me. "I'm asking for a reasonable accommodation."

"Reasonable? Really? And where am I supposed to put it?"

"Your guy there said something about clearing out a bay."

"First, to do that means I'm down a spot to do the work for my actual paying customers. Secondly, I don't think you fully understand the severity of the possible damage to your car. It's not meant to run without oil. Attempting to crank it up and drive it unnecessarily would do more damage. Leaving it where it is, is the best option until it can be towed to the dealer and deposited in their garage for service."

Irene closed her eyes and relaxed her posture. "So, you're not simply being difficult because...well, because?"

I looked her up and down. Put together, not a hair out of place. Picture perfect as always. Not that I'd expected anything different from the woman who seemed to bend the world to her will—for most people, at least—but the years had been good to her.

"No, Irene. I'm not in the habit of being difficult out of spite or for any other reason. That was more your deal. What this is, is me actually being somewhat cordial and trying to save you from further damage and extra repair costs."

Irene sucked in a breath and readjusted her oversized bag on her shoulder and pulled her shades back in place. "I wasn't aware it was that bad. I'll defer to your expertise."

With nothing left to discuss, I continued to the shop, leaving her to her own devices to find a ride and leave me in peace. Though the latter was something she'd always had a hard time doing.

3

IRENE

REMI'S COMMENT ABOUT NEEDING TO BE CATERED TO AND coddled stung. Though it wasn't the first time I'd heard some variation of that. High maintenance. Uppity. Bougie. All words that meant the same. But that was what was expected from a "lady of social standing," and I always did as expected. *And look where that had gotten me.* But with Remi, her near disdain for everything I represented, her disapproval, had always affected me in a different way.

I glanced back at my disabled car and all I could hear in the back of my mind was Derrick lecturing me about not thinking things through. And how I should have stopped throwing a tantrum and simply returned home like an adult so we could "discuss" things, which meant he talked, and I was supposed to agree. Because that was what a good wife did according to him and my mother. Smile, don't argue, and keep the peace by being amicable. But after two years of therapy, I was reclaiming my voice. Or rather, finding it for the first time.

I took a smidge of pleasure in knowing he'd have to be the one to make up some random ass excuse for my absence. I sure as hell had had my share of times when I'd had to do the same for him whenever it came to my functions. Because that, too, was expected of me.

How could I have expected him to attend the wedding of one of my closest friends? Or the grand reopening of the other's bakery? Or the benefit dinner for the hospital my office was affiliated with. His job as an investment banker at the a firm in New York was highly demanding and stressful, who was I to think he should have made time in his schedule to be there for me? I was only the wife. Low priority.

Yeah, he was going to be pissed when I called him back to let him know I wasn't even in the damn state. Though a seed of guilt over disappointing him, over not fulfilling my obligations, tried to grow. *No, no, no.* I was done with that life. Him being pissed was no longer my concern.

The scent of charred wood and smoking meats made my stomach growl. I hadn't stopped for lunch because I'd been so over driving and ready to get to my destination. I debated on whether I should go eat or wait until I got to my parents' house. I ran my hand over the curve of my hips. Ribs sounded great, but I'd be doing at least forty-five minutes on the stair climber to work them off.

Waiting it was. I headed inside the auto shop. As I crossed the threshold, it dawned on me I wasn't sure if I'd ever been in this building. I'd not had a reason to. Even after I started driving, Dad handled whatever maintenance my car had needed. Had he used Remi's dad? I pondered the question as I settled into the black vinyl chair, which looked like it belonged more in a diner somewhere than a repair shop.

But like her truck, the place was clean. Older, showed some wear, but it was neat and organized. Bright even. Not as nice as the customer lounge at the dealership, but also not dirty or dingy as I would have expected it to be. The odor swirling around was a mix of motor oil and old school Pine

Sol. I groaned quietly. She'd not bothered to correct my assumptions about the cab of the tow, instead she'd let me act like a spoiled brat, and I'd been too embarrassed to walk the behavior back. *So much for changing.*

Voices mixed with the squeal and clanks of tools carried in from the garage area as they worked. Through the glass I could see everything and what stood out was just like in high school, Remi was the only female among a group of males. And she fit right in. They talked, possibly joked around even as she smiled and laughed at whatever the guys were saying. The younger one was thin, kind of pale and had freckles. His sandy-brown hair was hidden mostly behind a green bandana, but peeks of it curled out and touched his collar. The other guy, the one who'd yelled out, seemed older, but not much. From where I sat, I couldn't see any gray mixed into his black hair. His complexion was lighter than mine and he sported a neatly cropped goatee.

And then there was the woman of the hour.

With Remi, what you saw was what you got. And that was something I couldn't relate to. If she didn't care for some-thing...for someone, you knew. No pretense, no faking it. And secretly I envied her that. I'd secretly envied her for a lot of reasons. She glanced in my direction, and even from the distance her eyes, her look...she threw me off, and I was already frazzled enough. I turned my attention away and dug my phone from my purse. Another voicemail waited for me, again from Derrick. One I'd listen to later, I had more pressing matters at hand.

I clutched the device as I went through my mental Rolodex on who I could call. A Tuesday early afternoon. Why didn't this town have a fucking ride share service? Or a damn rental place? Either of those would make life so much easier. My choices came down to Cynthia or my mother. My impulsive trip seemed like a good idea at the time, but I was quickly remembering why I rarely acted rashly.

Deciding it would be easier to deal with my mother sooner rather than later, I opted to call her. As I waited for someone to answer the house phone, I went through a script of what I could say when the question of why I was in town came up.

"Johnson residence." The warm voice of Patrice, our long-time house manager—a term Mom thought sounded better than housekeeper or maid or cook—came over the speaker.

"Hello, Patrice, it's Irene. Is my mother there?"

"Miss Irene. Good to hear your voice. Yes, your mother is out on the veranda. One moment."

I heard faint sounds as she made the trek from most likely the kitchen to the enclosed and air-conditioned veranda. She loved sitting in there, looking out over her garden, but staying cool while she did so. No glistening for Vivian Johnson. More faint sounds as Patrice informed my mother who was on the phone.

"Irene, darling, this is a surprise."

"Hello, Momma. How are you?"

"Good dear. Having a light lunch. Not that I don't enjoy hearing from you, but shouldn't you be at work?"

I took in a short breath at the subtle dismissiveness of her question. "I took some vacation time."

"That's lovely, dear. Where are you and Derrick going?"

I sighed and prepared to launch into my speech, but she spoke again.

"What did you do this time?"

I closed my eyes and massaged the low thrum starting at my temple. I really should have stopped to eat. "Why would you think I've done something?"

"Your unladylike heavy breathing. You tend to do that

when you're attempting to break the news about a transgression."

I readjusted in the chair, correcting my slumped posture even though she couldn't see me. "I didn't do anything. I came to town as a surprise but had a little car trouble. Can you come pick me up? I'm at Martin Autobody."

"Where?"

"Martin Autobody." I repeated my location slowly. "You know, the one and only mechanic shop in town."

"Why in God's name are you there?"

The door separating the garage from the lobby opened, and Remi strolled in. I kept my eyes on her as I answered. "Because, Mom, I told you I had car trouble and I needed a tow. Can you come, or should I try Cynthia?"

This time she did the "unladylike" breathing. "No need for dramatics. I'll come fetch you."

I ended the call and massaged my forehead. That word. *Dramatic.* I don't know how it'd never dawned on me before, but I'd married my mother. No wonder she and Derrick got along like thieves. A stubby plastic bottle of water appeared in my line of sight. I noticed the neatly trimmed and surprisingly clean nails before I glanced up to see Remi.

"Thank you."

"Don't mention it. Your ride on the way?"

"Yes, my mother will be here to get me... Well, whenever she arrives."

Remi strolled back to the high counter and pulled out a second bottle from the mini fridge. She uncapped hers and drank it down in one gulp before tossing the empty container in the blue recycling bin. "Well, we usually lock up for lunch about this time."

"Is that your way of asking me to wait outside?"

She unzipped her coveralls and once again tied the top half

around her waist before she settled against the smaller desk, crossing her legs out in front of her. I tried not to stare too much at the way her breasts pushed upward when she folded her arms over her chest. Easy, relaxed, and a cool, nonchalant sexiness. Being trapped in the cab of the truck with her had set me more on edge. All I kept thinking about was how she'd touched me. I'd had to stop myself from staring, her side profile was striking, and I'd wanted to reach out and trace along her jawline. She'd always been distractingly beautiful, and time hadn't changed that.

She narrowed her oval-shaped dark brown eyes as if she were debating on really making me sit outside or not before she pushed to standing. "Nah, you can stay."

Remi turned her head and whistled down the hall. A jingle and what sounded like nails hitting the linoleum floor got my attention. She kneeled to greet the animal that appeared from a back room. A medium-sized dog with a beautiful, smooth, tan coat. She'd had a dog in here the whole time, and I hadn't had a clue. He had to be the world's most well-behaved animal.

"Hey, boy. Need to go out?"

Her voice went up a pitch in that cutesy tone people used when speaking to their pets. The animal flipped onto his back, revealing a white undercoat, and she gave his belly a few rubs before pushing to stand. He responded by flipping over and giving his body a good shake.

"He's beautiful."

She opened a drawer and pulled out one of those retractable leashes, clipping the end to the leather collar. "You like dogs?"

"Why do you sound so surprised?"

She looked me over again then lifted a shoulder. "Never pictured you as the type."

I held my purse tighter against my body and resisted the urge to go pet the sweet-looking animal. "Why not?"

She chuckled quietly. "That question coming from the woman who was worried about getting her expensive pants dirty? I don't exactly see you risking dog drool, fur, or being out with a pooper scooper."

I loved animals, but unfortunately never owned one. First, my parents were against it, Mom thought they'd be too messy and smell up the house. Later, Derrick was against them for nearly the same reasons. It was one of many discussions that weren't really a discussion at all with him. More like I spoke, he shot it down, and that was the end of it.

"Not every dog drools excessively or loses fur. As for the 'pooper scooper,' I'm sure there's someone that can be paid to handle that. Isn't that why dog walkers exist?"

Her only response was to shake her head before she started to exit out the door with her animal in tow.

"What's his name?"

I half expected her to keep walking as if I hadn't spoken, but she stopped and turned to look at me. "Axle."

I stood and slowly walked toward her. We were close, and the hairs on my arm tingled at the memory of her earlier touch. She smelled of motor oil and cinnamon. A weird combination, but one that wasn't as terrible as it probably should have been. I couldn't stop myself from inhaling deep as I peered down at the animal to avoid staring at her. "You named your dog Axle?"

She unhooked the leash and pushed the door separating the two parts of the building to let him trot out. He stopped to let each of the guys give him attention before he plopped down in the band of sunlight just outside the bay. "Yeah. Like the axle that rotates the wheels of your car. Supports its weight. He's a garage dog; he needed a name to fit. He adopted this place, and subsequently, me." She glanced at her pet, and a half-smile lifted the corner of her wide set mouth. "Try not to steal anything."

Before I could retort her comment, she exited through the door. The two guys outside looked toward me as she spoke. One lifted his shoulder while the other headed to a small sink in the corner to wash his hands. The trio walked out, and Remi gave me a parting glance as she lowered the garage door.

4

REMI

With any luck, Irene would be gone by the time we finished lunch, and other than her luxury car sitting in my parking lot, I could forget she was even in town. After he did his business, Axle made a beeline to the back of The Shack, where I was sure my cousin Al had left scraps for him no matter how many times I said don't feed my dog human food.

Waiting until after the lunch rush meant the place wasn't as packed, plus, we liked to stay open in case customers popped by while on their break to get their cars. We didn't eat barbecue every day, but with it being close, the location was convenient, and honestly, who could turn down free food.

The guys had already settled at their usual table, with Al sitting shooting the shit with them. After I placed my order and grabbed my sweet tea, I went over to join them.

"So, apparently there's a fine machine over there I need to come take a look at," Al said.

I took a sip of the sweet liquid perfection. Not too sugary, not too bitter, and ice cold just how I liked it. "Yeah, it's a sexy car. Bit of a letdown being an automatic. Well, paddle shift, not true manual, but I'm sure she could still fly when out on the open road."

A soft smile pulled at the corner of my lips as I thought about getting behind the wheel of the Audi and just going. I had no doubt it would be an exhilarating ride. One I'd never know, but that didn't stop the daydream. My joys in life were simple. I liked my animals, my job, and cars. The latter a passion I could thank my father for. The man who'd wanted a boy but had to make do with the girl he got instead. Once he came to terms with his disappointment, he realized I had an interest in what he was doing. I spent more time in his way—as he'd called it—watching him work instead of jumping rope or playing hopscotch. After a while, he made "the best of a bad situation" and started teaching me what he knew, and I never looked back.

"Who does it belong to? Another tourist coming in to stay at Cynthia's bed and breakfast?"

I quietly thanked the cashier when she dropped off my order before I answered my cousin. "Not quite." I took a bite of my sloppy pulled pork sandwich. Juice and sauce ran down my fingers as the sweet and tangy, well-seasoned meat hit my taste buds. I didn't care how much I ate here, every bite was delicious.

"I think the boss knows her," Devon piped in.

I shot him a look as Al leaned forward, resting his large forearms on the table, his interest clearly piqued. "What makes you say that?"

"Because boss was fussin'. She doesn't do that with the tourists. She's always, you know, polite and shit with them. With this chick, not so much. At least from what we could see from the garage."

Tony nodded as he cleaned the meat from the rib bone. I gave them both a death stare that they promptly ignored. I'd worked with these guys for years and never knew them to be so aware of their surroundings as they apparently had been while I was dealing with Irene.

"An ex? Old fuck buddy??" Al asked in a huffed laugh.

I sopped my fries in the barbeque sauce before shoving them in my mouth to keep me from saying things that were none of their business. An ex? Not even close. And I didn't do fuck buddies. Shutting down the juveniles I worked with, and encouraged by the one I was related to, needed to be done sooner rather than later. I cut my eyes at the men at the table while taking another drink of my tea. "She's just someone I went to high school with."

"That's mighty vague, cousin."

I raised one shoulder. "It's the truth, so not sure what more you want." I leveled my gaze at Devon and Tony. "And why the hell are you two being so nosy? Because if you have that much time to pay attention to me, you ain't workin'. Which is what I pay you to do."

They exchanged shit-eating grins. "Boss, come on now. How could we not pay attention? She was fine as hell," Devon offered up as commentary with Tony wholeheartedly agreeing, nodding so hard he looked like a bobblehead.

I finished my food, then drained the last of my drink before wiping my mouth. "That's Doc Johnson's daughter, but more importantly, she's Vivian Johnson's daughter, and that apple didn't fall from the tree at all." A collective silence fell over them. I picked up my metal tray and gave them one last glance. "Lookin' is barely advised where Irene Johnson is concerned." Though I'd failed to heed my own warning. I'd looked and enjoyed the view. Too much. Tall, with legs that went on for days, and soft curves a person could lose hours exploring. I mentally scolded myself for the thought. For a few reasons.

Doc Johnson was a nice enough man. Friendly, and if some

of the old rumors were correct, too friendly at times. But Ms. Vivian Johnson was lukewarm cordial at best, depending on who she was around. She paraded around town with an air of authority and self-importance that her daughter absolutely inherited.

When I stepped out of The Shack, I turned my face up to the sky, letting the sun warm my skin as I gave my body a good stretch. Like usual, Axle was curled up on the sidewalk, doing what he did best, sleeping.

"Let's go." At the sound of my voice, he hopped up, shook, and trotted beside me back to the shop.

As I got closer, my attention drifted to the parking lot, where Irene pulled a suitcase from the trunk of her car. I lifted my chin in her direction before raising the garage door to get back to work. Luckily, it was a light day, and dealing with Irene hadn't set me back too much. I only had to finish off the last tune-up and oil change for the second police cruiser, check the status on the tire order I'd placed for Olivia Lewis, and do the brake job for Mr. Hubbert.

If all went well, I could actually get out early. I stopped in my tracks after getting Axle settled in the back office again. Irene stood in my lobby instead of being off my property. "I thought you were leaving."

"I am. And I can't keep Mother waiting too long, but I thought you should have my number."

"For..."

She easily strolled toward me, a soft sway to her hips, holding a business card between her fingers. "Just in case. If something should happen to my car. I've already taken one of yours from the desk, though it only has the office number on it, no cell."

I managed to hold back the eye roll over her once again thinking something terrible would befall her Audi if it spent one night in open air. I took the offered piece of paper from her and slid it into my back pocket without bothering to look at it. "Why would I make my cell number available to anybody walkin' through those doors by puttin' it on my business card? Those who need it, have it. For everyone else we have a phone out in the garage as well as in here, so calls aren't missed."

Irene adjusted her purse on her shoulder and a half-smile pulled her lips to the left. "Fine." She said the word almost as if she were annoyed I didn't offer up my personal number. There was zero reason I could think of that she'd need it. Or want it. "Regardless, mine is on the back of the card. Feel free to use it."

She held my eye contact for a moment before turning on her heel and sashaying out the door. I took another chance to appreciate her retreating backside. The guys weren't wrong in their assessment of her looks. Irene Johnson was what many would consider to be an attractive woman, myself included. But, unlike them, I knew her. And looks could be hella deceiving. Though someone had been able to look past her attitude, if the rock on her left finger was any indication.

IRENE

FOR MOST PEOPLE, RIDING IN COMPLETE SILENCE WITH your parent could have been an indicator of trouble. But not for my mother. When she drove, or really even as a passenger, she required complete silence for concentration. Small talk was only necessary at dinner parties and fundraisers. In the car, talking wasn't needed, nor was music. I was surprised she came herself instead of sending Patrice to fetch me. Considering she pulled up in a sleek, brand new Mercedes E-Class, I suspected that had a lot to do with why. She never kept a car longer than two years, regardless of how little she actually drove them. But Dad indulged her luxuries.

I sat, stared out the window, and ran through what I would say to my parents as well as my husband, unsure of which beast would be the hardest to tackle. As she took the turn down Newton Street, my chest constricted a little. We drove down the tree-lined street until it dead-ended at the stately Colonial with its perfectly manicured lawn and rose bushes. She loved those damn championship roses.

Mom pulled around the house to park in the four-car garage, which was hidden from view. She exited the vehicle with the grace of an aristocrat and ran her hands down the front of her cream-toned sheath dress with its fold-over collar that helped to show off her "elegant" neck. An outfit she deemed to be casual wear, for sitting around the house.

One must always look their best and not be caught out unawares by surprise guests. That particular life motto was in direct contradiction with its good manners to always call before simply arriving at someone's home. A rule I'd broken, and I was sure she'd make comment on at some point.

Her hair being more gray than black these days was the first indication of her seventy-four years. From a distance, the "lines of experience"——because Vivian Johnson did not get wrinkles——were hardly noticeable in her near flawless dark skin. The same complexion she'd graced me with.

The heels of her nude pumps echoed on the epoxied floor. "Take your bag to your room, then meet me in the lounge. We can discuss the reason behind this surprise visit." My stomach chose that moment to growl. "And I'll have Patrice fix you a light plate." She entered the house, calling for the other woman.

I wheeled my suitcases into my designated guest suite. Avoiding Derrick could no longer be put off, so I plopped down onto the bed and pulled my phone free.

"It's about time," he snapped, after answering on the second ring. "Where the hell have you been and why weren't you answering my calls?" I tried to speak, but he started up before I got a word out. "You know what, never mind. It's not important. You need to get home so we can go to dinner. Enough of your tantrum."

I took a deep breath, straightened my posture, and squared my shoulders. "No."

"What the hell do you mean, no? Irene, I don't have time for this. I let you have a few days, and now we need to get back to our lives."

Let me...he let... I don't know why I expected him to be even remotely ashamed or apologetic of his behavior. He never had before. He'd simply supplied me with a host of excuses dealt out with a side dish of gaslighting. And I'd let him. I forgave, got over, and turned a blind eye to every other infidelity, so how could I really expect his attitude to be any different?

"I'm at home."

"The hell you are. I'm here now and you are not."

"Not the condo. I'm in Madison. So even if I wanted to play dutiful, happy wife for you, I couldn't because I'm not in the state. Besides that, I served you with divorce papers, Derrick. There is no getting back to our lives."

There was a stretch of silence. My heart raced, and I almost felt sick to my stomach. But there was nothing I could do at this point. Even if I wanted to, and that was a mighty big if, there was no way for me to make it back on time.

"Are you kidding me? This tantrum of yours has gone to damn far. You stole my car and drove it all the way to fucking Georgia. If that wasn't bad enough, you know what this dinner means. How important it is for me. I can't believe you'd be so damned selfish."

I was selfish? He'd gone and gotten his latest mistress pregnant, but I was the selfish one? Anger boiled in my belly, and I nearly choked trying to stuff it down. *What's done is done, nothing can change it now...* The words he'd spoken replayed in my head. As if the bomb he'd confirmed once confronted wasn't majorly life changing and damn near soul destroying. He'd been against having kids because it'd upset *"our"* life-style. Then after I...I forced out a breath. I had enough eating away at me without that particular trip down memory lane.

So many thoughts, comebacks, rebuttals swirled in my head. But years of dealing with Derrick I knew he'd wouldn't hear any of them, just like he'd once again ignored the fact I wanted a divorce. Derrick's first priority was always Derrick.

"I'm sorry. But you should go get ready. Tell them I'm not feeling well. That I've come down with something. I'm sure they'll understand."

Even with all that he was putting me through, I still attempted to placate him. To provide him with a reasonable cover. *Remi would never.* I jolted at the thought. Remi…being close to her. Riding in the small, enclosed cab of her truck, interacting with her, even if she was as impatient with me as usual, it'd been the bright spot of my fucked-up day.

"Oh, and Derrick. I didn't *steal* anything. It's called marital property."

He grumbled under his breath before clicking off without so much as a goodbye. I dropped the phone onto the bed and flopped backward to stare up at the ivory and gold coffered ceiling. I didn't know which was going to be worse, spending two weeks with my parents, or getting rid of a man who refused to accept a woman would dare leave him.

I pushed myself up from the light blue down duvet and took a few cleansing breaths. Walking in circles, I shook my hands, attempting to rid myself of the jitters and my well-established impulse to call him back and apologize. I'd spent the last week telling myself it was over. Hell, if I were being honest, my marriage had been a sham for at least the last ten years, and we'd only been married for thirteen. Though he probably only suspected it to be two, and that was because I'd moved into the guest room.

I pressed my fingers to my eyes and puffed out my cheeks, muffling a squeal. I couldn't keep thinking about Derrick when my mother waited for me downstairs. With a final shake of my body, I donned a new set of armor to face Vivian.

I found my mother sitting ankles crossed, perched near the edge of the charcoal-gray wingback chair, sipping on tea.

Spine straight as a rod. I couldn't think of a time where I'd seen my mother be relaxed. Even when at home with just us around. It'd been something I'd admired when I was younger. My mother was a vision of poise and grace, something I'd wanted to live up to. But in the last few years, I'd wondered if she too wore a mask, giving off what people expected to see. Was what I saw the real Vivian Johnson, or was there more to her?

A small serving tray sat beside the other chair with a plate of finger sandwiches and a salad. My mind wandered back to the delicious scent of the barbeque coming from the smaller building on Remi's lot, and my mouth watered for that instead of the offering in front of me. But I'd eat it with a smile.

I took a seat, mirroring my mother's posture. She smiled at me and set the cup down on its matching saucer with a soft clink. I bit into the watercress sandwich and prepared for the interrogation.

She folded her hands in her lap, and I knew we were about to begin. "Are you ready to explain this little trip?"

I chewed slowly as the truth I wanted to scream played out on a megaphone in my head. *The son-in-law you love so much cheated on me, though, sadly, that was nothing new. Only this time he'd gone and gotten one of them pregnant. And in true Derrick fashion I wasn't supposed to be upset about this revelation. I was supposed to smile and show up for dinner parties. Laugh at stale jokes his partners told and be a proper wife dangling from his arm just like you taught me.* But I would say none of those things.

I took in a breath and let an easy and well-practiced smile spread across my face. "There's been some stuff going on at work. You know Dr. Joyce." I made the drinking motion with my hand. "The practice has been having some rough patches because of his indiscretions, so I decided to take some time off and evaluate my options."

Her lips turned downward, and she scrunched her nose while waving her hand as if to rid the air of my comment. "Uh, that man. So disheveled and unkempt. You should have left years ago and started your own practice."

I smiled at her approval before picking up the small salad plate. I knew there was a "but" coming, or some reference to Derrick, so I chewed slowly, waiting for it to come.

She retrieved her cup, taking a dainty sip. "Then you didn't call because this is some sort of surprise for your father?"

Every opportunity he got, my father dropped not-so-subtle hints about me moving and taking over his practice. Unlike my mother, who aspired to the high life I currently lived, he seemed to thrive in Madison, whereas my mother always appeared to simply make do.

"Yeah..." She arched a brow at the word, which I quickly corrected. "Yes, Mom. Though nothing is a done deal. With... everything going on, I have been considering caving to Dad's demands. But just considering. There is a lot to weigh."

"And Derrick is on board with this? I mean, darling, it's not that I wouldn't love to have you closer, but New York. Park Avenue. I know your father is rather eccentric with the idea of passing down Johnson Family Medicine to a Johnson. Your brother went into law, and you are a Johnson-*Moore*. Dr. Michaels is perfectly capable."

It wasn't missed how she stressed the Moore of my name. I chewed my next bite and swallowed it down around the lump in my throat and against the rage and frustration clawing under my skin. Park Avenue, that was more bragging rights for her. Sure, like most parents, my mother wanted the best for me. Sadly, the best appeared to be the life she'd wanted to live. It was a big drop from wife of a thoracic surgeon to wife of a small-town family doctor.

Dad still consulted, went to conferences, kept up on the

latest breakthroughs, but his hands had failed him, and adjustments had to be made. His insistence on me taking over was always funny, considering he was once the "new doctor" in town when my parents relocated before I was born, and he'd taken over for the previous physician. But all that was history. Dad had it in his mind the office was his legacy, and I was meant to carry it on.

"Mom, I'm only considering my options."

Satisfied, my mother set her cup back on its saucer and rose in one fluid motion. "I won't ruin your 'surprise' to your father by calling to let him know you're here. But do finish eating then clean up before dinner. We shall dine as a family tonight."

I was forty-four years old, and I'd basically just been told I was not allowed to go out tonight. No matter how politely the statement was delivered, the punch remained the same. And as always, I nodded and offered up a "Yes, ma'am" before she strolled from the room.

❧ 6 ☙

REMI

I TOSSED MY KEYS ON THE CONSOLE TABLE BY THE DOOR AS Hemi weaved between my legs, her usual welcome home greeting. The fluffy Birman purred softly as I picked her up. "Who missed Momma?" I cooed, carrying her to the room. Axle made a beeline for his large bed located under the TV, plopping down as if he was worn out after a hard shift. The day had gone smooth as usual after the interruption that was Irene Johnson.

I deposited Hemi on my bed, then unzipped my coveralls and stepped out of them. A hot shower was calling my name, but first I needed to go check on Pop and relieve Aunt Evelyn. She and Al had moved to Madison after Uncle Joe died. She'd wanted to be close to the last bit of family she had, and my cousin Al had been struggling to get his footing and had been in and out of jail. She'd hoped the smaller town would aid in keeping him out of trouble, and so far, it'd been exactly what he'd needed.

After tugging on a T-shirt and a pair of gym shorts, I slid my feet into my slides and walked the three houses down to my childhood home. The small two-bedroom one bath shotgun-style house wasn't much, but it'd been enough. And despite my father's declining condition, I was determined to do what I could to keep him in it. Even if that meant living on the same street instead of closer to town like I'd wanted when I'd returned to Madison.

Although Pop could be on his own, Aunt Evelyn insisted on sitting with him "just in case," and after his fall, I appreciated her presence even if Pop didn't. Plus, I think she wanted to show her thanks for helping Al since for whatever reason she attributed me for his newfound success. I entered the house and saw my dad's sister sitting on the sofa knitting, the evening news playing on the small flat screen TV.

"Hey, Auntie. How was he today?"

She pulled her glasses from where they were perched on her nose and folded them so they hung around her neck on the beaded chain. "Remi, love. He was the same old cranky bastard he is most days. But for the most part all good. He's restin' in his room." She started packing up her supplies in the satchel she carried with her nearly everywhere.

I leaned in and gave her a kiss on her feathery-soft skin. "Let me go say hi, and then we can do dinner."

She pushed herself up from the couch, shaking her head. "I'd love to, baby, but I'm meeting with my bridge club tonight. Though I did leave you something in the refrigerator." She lovingly patted my cheek. "You really need to learn how to cook."

I laughed. "Why would I do that? Between Al's BBQ and your home cooking, I stay well fed."

She made a harrumph noise as she stretched, groaning. "Lord, I done sat too long."

"What are you making this time?" I asked, gently taking the satchel from her hand as I walked her out the door.

"A blanket. Lucille's grandbaby is having a baby."

I placed her knitting supplies on the passenger seat and

closed the door of her old Ford Taurus. "Don't take the ladies for all their money tonight, Auntie.

She let out a dry laugh, and her dark brown eyes crinkled at the corners. "Baby, I make you no promises on that."

With a parting kiss, she lowered her form into her car. I stayed outside until she drove off before heading back inside. There was rustling coming from the back, and I quickened my steps to make sure Dad was doing okay. He was sitting on the edge of his adjustable bed.

"Hey, Pop."

"Did I hear your aunt leavin'?"

"Yup. It's card night at the community center."

I resisted the urge to help him when he gripped the handles of his walker and slowly heaved his hulking form to standing. Randal Martin had always been a proud man and didn't like showing weakness, and he sure as hell didn't like showing it in front of me.

"I don't know how many times I done told both y'all, I don't need a sitter."

I moved into the hall to clear a path for him. "Well, too bad. You've had one too many falls. The last one left you so bruised we thought you might have broken your hip. Again. And you were stuck for hours. You didn't want the medic-alert necklace, so you got Aunt Evelyn instead."

Ideally, I would have loved to have a full-time in-home nurse, but they were expensive, and Medicare only paid for someone to stop in twice a week. They'd cover more if he was in an assisted living place, but I couldn't do that to him. At least not yet. I was sure the time would come when I'd not be enough as his condition worsened, but I'd take care of him for as long as it was feasible. Even if he seemingly resented me for it.

He collapsed into his easy chair, his breathing slightly labored and a soft sheen on his forehead. "Y'all two just love this. Bossing me around and shit like I can't care for myself. Got cameras all in my damn house. Alarms on my bed. I mean, damn, I ain't no damn child."

I ignored his rant and headed into the kitchen to pull the food containers Auntie had left and heated up portions while he continued to fuss. Witnessing the change in him hurt, even if I'd never let him know. He'd always been strong and opposing at six-four and over two hundred pounds. He used to be a force to reckon with until the Parkinson's slowly started stripping that away. No longer being able to work had been the biggest blow and had turned him into the perpetually cranky person I encountered most days.

I set both our plates on the coffee table then grabbed his TV tray, raising it so it was on level to keep him from having to bend. Once he was situated, I settled back on the couch with my own food. Pork chops, okra, and mashed sweet potatoes. I flipped through the channels until I settled on MotorTrend.

We ate in silence other than him making random commentary on the show. After we finished eating, I cleaned up, fought with him to take his meds, then made sure he was settled before finally heading back to my house.

Neither of my four-legged dependents bothered to even look up, much less greet me when I entered. Axle was asleep on his oversized dog bed, and Hemi was sleeping on top of him. I made sure both their bowls had food, then took the much-needed shower I wanted.

As the water heated, I scrubbed my hands down my face. It had been a long day made worse thanks to fucking Irene. I liked to give people the benefit of the doubt. High school was a long time ago. People grew and changed. Most anyway. But not her. She'd come across exactly the same. Belittling, self-centered, and self-serving. And all of it wrapped up in an annoyingly attractive package.

I stripped free of my clothes, tossing them in the hamper, and stepped under the heated spray. The forceful pelts beat against me, each hit acting like a pressure point to relieve the stress. I closed my eyes and took a few deep breaths, taking in the light lavender scent of the aromatherapy shower disc, trying to let the release of the day happen. Only the calm wouldn't come. Instead, my thoughts swirled around one particular pebble in my shoe. Despite my best intentions in the past—and apparently present—with large doe eyes, plump lips, and a tight ass, fucking Irene Johnson was invading my headspace.

I tilted my face up to the water, hoping in vain for relaxation. Snatching down the handheld showerhead, I adjusted the spray to the pulsating bursts. Back pressed against the cool tiles, I closed my eyes and took slow, deep breaths as I directed the water down the center of my body. I cupped my breast, pinching the nipple as the alternating pulses beat against it. It stiffened in response, and I pinched harder, keeping the pressure on until the tingling sensation started.

A low moan rumbled in the back of my throat as I trailed my hands downward. I thought about soft skin and warm fingers, touching me, teasing me, accompanied with soft kisses from lips that probably tasted of cherry. I widened my legs and cupped my pussy, pressing my palm to my clit, sliding up and down before making a V with my fingers and letting the water tap against my sensitive nub.

The showerhead was worth the cost. The alternating pulsing beats of the water acted like rapid fire flicks of a tongue, and I shivered from the stimulation. I drew circles around my clit, tilting my hips up to get maximum impact from the water. My mouth hung open, and I pictured large brown eyes pleading for something, her biting the corner of her lip, unsure of what she was after. My fingers worked faster as phantom scents of sweet sugar cookies filled my senses.

The dam broke free as the disjointed images cleared and a face to my fantasy came into view in my mind.

Fucking Irene Johnson....

After getting clean and slipping into my pajamas, I stalked to the kitchen to retrieve an ice-cold Coke from my fridge, a pack of chocolate chip cookies from my pantry, and carried everything over to my couch. Getting off in the shower had the opposite effect I'd been after. Not a full twenty-four hours, and she was once again the splinter under my skin I couldn't get out. I settled into soft suede and kicked my feet up on the industrial designed coffee table. Home was my place of solitude. Or should have been.

It wasn't much bigger than my childhood house, but it had been gutted and completely re-imagined. A tranquil place. I pulled up the monitor app on my phone to check on Pop, then, once satisfied he was doing okay, flicked on the large flat screen hanging on the wall, popped the cap on my soda, and settled in for another quiet night.

IRENE

It was no big surprise that Derrick hadn't called again. And he wouldn't. No, he'd expect me to. I was supposed to call and apologize for my behavior. Not this time. If I held my ground, eventually he'd get the picture. I hoped at least.

As I eased my father's Lexus into a parking space, I shook off the worry. I had two weeks to decide what I wanted to do. Or rather, spend that time donning the proper armor to break the news to my parents that I was divorcing their "charming" son-in-law and returning to my roots.

The bell above the door dinged when I entered. Regina's bakery was alive with activity. I inhaled deep at the scent of coffee and cookies. Just a Bit of Sugar was back from the brink of destruction. A blaze couldn't even keep the place— or the force behind it—down. Luckily, that bastard ex-employee of hers was behind bars and would be there for a while. Not only had he stolen from her, but he'd set her bakery on fire as an act of retaliation for having him arrested. His audacity still made my blood run hot.

But from the ash she rose anew, stronger than before and

with a new man by her side as an added bonus. Shame weaved through me. Keeping up pretenses had kept me from being here when Regina had needed me most. I'd come for a weekend, but that wasn't long enough. I'd missed so much. But no more.

"Irene?"

A wide smile spread across my face when I laid eyes on my friend as she approached me with arms open. Her long, red dreadlocks were piled high on top of her head, secured with a colorful scarf that matched the bright green scrubs she wore. Her makeup was impeccable as always, with the color selections fully complementing her warm brown skin tone.

"In the flesh." I settled into her tight embrace.

"Why didn't you call? When did you get in?" She led us to a small corner table.

"Yesterday. It was a last-minute decision." The familiar pang of guilt coiled around me as the lie rolled off my tongue. They deserved better than that.

She sat back and crossed her arms. "Really?"

"Why do you sound so shocked?"

"Oh, I don't know. I figure if you were taking an impromptu trip anywhere it would be somewhere more exotic than Madison Island."

I ran my hand down my ponytail and let the strands fall against my shoulder. "True, true. But I decided to give my passport a rest." A change of subject was needed before she interrogated me too much. "Where's your mama?"

Regina smiled. "Finally understanding what the hell retirement means after everything." She waved her hands around. "With the working conditions we had while we were rebuilding it sort of forced her to let go and unwind more. Don't misunderstand, she still be here gettin' on my nerves, but not as much." She rolled her eyes but smiled.

I envied the relationship Regina had with her mother.

Mama Charles was warm, friendly, and treated everyone like family.

"You want something?"

I shook my head. "I'm good, just wanted to pop in and see you and find out if I can pull you two away from your mens."

A small ping of jealousy shot through me. It wasn't that I wasn't happy for my friends. Both Cynthia and Regina deserved to have all the love and happiness they'd found with Marcel and Alec. I just wanted a little taste of it. Both those men adored my friends, and I wanted to know what that was like. Really experience it. To the outside world, Derrick was *the* catch. Good looks. Excellent career. He was a smooth talker extraordinaire. And he had turned on the charm during the dating phase, but I'd quickly gotten a peek behind the curtain once he realized he had me and the effort could stop.

"Well, I'm free. Alec is actually out of town, so we can hang at my house. And Marcel will be okay for a few hours."

She'd already whipped out her phone and was firing off a text. The device chirped before she even managed to put it back in her pocket, and mine started ringing right after.

"Hey, lady," I answered with a smile.

"You're in town? What the hell?"

"I had some time off, so I figured, what the hell, go see my girls."

"I like the sound of that. Vito's?"

I was probably biased, but Vito's was the best New York-style pizza to ever grace my lips, even after years of living there. My thoughts wandered back to the barbecue I'd denied myself yesterday. I was taking control. Becoming the person I wanted to be. Or was trying. I'd taken a big step when I'd started therapy, then a bigger one by leaving. "Yes, extra sausage and mushrooms."

"Got you covered."

NEVER BEFORE WAS I nervous about walking into Regina's house. Part of me wanted to cave. To break down and tell them everything, but I knew I wouldn't. At least not all of it. Dr. Adams told me to trust in my relationship with them. But there was only so much I could dump in one night.

I rang the bell, and it was Cynthia, not Regina, who greeted me with a squeal and a tight hug. Just being around them made things better. Life made sense when I was with them, and I was typically my most authentic self in their presence.

"I still can't believe you just showed up." She shut the door behind me.

I followed her to the kitchen. "I know I should have called, but like I told Regina, it was sort of spur of the moment."

"Well, whatever the reason, we're happy to see you," Regina said. "Load up, and we're taking this party to the living room."

I reached out to touch the silver strands of Cynthia's hair. It'd grown since I'd seen her last and she wore it slicked back and tucked behind her ears. "Tired of the short?"

She shrugged. "More like getting tired of driving to Savannah to get it trimmed since you know I'm not stepping foot inside Crown of Glory."

I nodded and said nothing. Cynthia's relationship with her mother was next level dysfunctional and Mrs. Marshall still worked at the only salon in town. After fixing my plate and pouring a generous amount of wine, I joined the two women who meant the world to me.

Regina wiped her mouth after taking a large bite of her slice. "If you got in yesterday, why didn't you call?"

I knew the question was coming. She'd held back when

we were at the bakery, but now I had to face the inquisition. "Truthfully, I was tired. I had car trouble and had to get towed." I stopped for a sip of chardonnay. "And you know how traveling takes a lot out of me. By the time I got to my parents I just wanted to shower and go to bed."

"Whew, I understand that. The drive from Portland to here was a lot," Cynthia commented.

It'd been just over a year since Cynthia had picked up and moved back to Madison after losing her job. She'd started over from scratch and now had a thriving B&B.

"But look how well that worked out," I said before shoving a bite of Caesar salad into my mouth. I pointed my fork toward Regina. "And you. I was there earlier, and the bakery is doing better than ever. Plus the food truck. You both are doing the damn thing with sexy other halves to boot."

They both smiled and nodded. I was damned proud of both of them. Pulling themselves up, Regina literally from the ashes, and continuing to forge their way. Living life unapologetically. I wanted that. I was determined to follow in their footsteps in that regard. My thoughts drifted to Remi and our interaction yesterday. A small thrill had gone through me when she'd checked out my ass and seemed to enjoy doing so. Well, as much as I could tell. She didn't give a lot expression-wise, but I got the inkling there was more than her being accommodating. Or maybe it was wishful thinking.

Regina took a drink and then tipped her glass toward me. "Hey, we're just catching up with you. Like you haven't had yourself a fine piece of man all these years."

"For reals. Derrick, with his Rick Fox-looking ass... Gurl, please. You ain't doing bad yourself," Cynthia agreed.

I took a big gulp and forced it down past the bitterness lodged in my throat. Their comments pulled me from my wandering musings and toward everything I was trying to temporarily escape. Derrick was the distinguished gentleman, a smooth talker with a killer smile. And a serial adulterer. And a workaholic. Or at least that was the excuse I gave whenever they questioned me. He was busy, I was upset he wasn't giving me enough attention. Because everything had to be about me. Or so I presented. But it was an excuse easily believable for why he wasn't around, and why I'd be upset sometimes on the rare occasions I let it slip he wasn't the be-all and end-all.

"What happened?" Cynthia asked.

I paused. *Shit! Did my face give away something?* "Nothing. Why do you ask?"

They both frowned at me, and Regina pulled her perfectly arched brows together. "You said your rental needed a tow."

The change of topic gave me a bit of whiplash, but I'd take it. "Oh, right. Sorry. Not a big deal. I was on the way into town, ran over a stick, and it messed up something. Remi towed me. All is well."

Cynthia sat forward in her seat. "You called Remi?" The slow manner in which she spoke the words relayed her shock.

"No. I called roadside assistance; they sent her." And her toned arms, serious eyes, and husky voice. I stabbed at my salad and shoveled more in my mouth, glancing around the room and trying to rid myself of more of the wayward thoughts. "So, you said Alec is out of town?"

"Yeah, some training thing. He'll be back in a day."

The wistful smile that tugged at her lips warmed my heart. "Nothing much has changed. The house is still very much you. What'd he do with all his stuff?"

She lifted a shoulder and darted her eyes to the side. "Um...storage."

Cynthia waved her hand at the wall. "The artwork. That's his. But don't give her too hard a time; it can be rough moving into an established house. Especially when the original occupant is stubborn, set in her ways, and is reluctant to change." Cynthia raised both eyebrows as she stared at Regina.

My other friend rolled her eyes. "I asked him to move in, didn't I? That is a pretty big fucking change. He has half my damn closet, and an entire dresser. And he turned my guest room into a pseudo playroom with all that video game nonsense. We can't all be Marcel, who was ready to throw out everything if you'd asked." Regina gave her a pointed look before dragging her attention back to me. "Your dad convince you to move back yet?"

I moved to collect our now empty plates. "Not yet, but that doesn't mean he has given up trying."

And I fed into it even if I wasn't sure if remaining in medicine was what I wanted. I'd never considered any other career besides following in my dad's footsteps. He loved being a doctor and had talked plenty about how much he hoped one of us would take it up as well. With my brother out of the running, I'd stepped in to fulfill my dad's dream. Shedding my husband wasn't the only life change I'd been contemplating.

"You have to stop back by the bakery tomorrow, Momma wants to see you."

"Can do. I'll pop in before I go check on my car."

Cynthia twisted to look at me. "Wouldn't the rental place take care of that? You got the extra insurance, right?"

I pulled open Regina's refrigerator to grab a bottle of water. "Either of you want one?" They both shook their heads. I uncapped it and took a long drink before responding to Cynthia's question. "It's on me since it's my car. I drove."

"Drove, drove. Like from New York to Madison?" they both asked.

I could only nod.

"Well, so much for spur of the moment," Cynthia

muttered before taking another drink from her glass. I tried not to wince at the rightful snippiness of her statement.

The two of them exchanged a look before Regina pulled in an audible breath. "Okay, what's up? You've been acting squirrely for a while now."

"What are you talking about? I'm the same old me."

"Bullshit. This is us," Cynthia chimed in. "Something's off. And has been for at least the last year."

I squeezed my hand around the plastic bottle. Here was my opening. A chance to say everything—no, some of the things—I'd been holding in for so long. I took a deep breath. To give them a peek behind the curtain. "I'm getting a divorce."

"Wait! What? When...how...what?" Regina asked, glancing between me and Cynthia.

What did I say? That he stuck his dick in any welcoming wet hole? That I spent years letting him gaslight me? They deserved it all, but I couldn't make the right words come. I wasn't ready to fully admit how much of a fraud I'd been.

"We got to the point where we wanted different things in life."

Not a complete lie. I wanted different things. Respect being the biggest one, and he didn't seem inclined to make the sacrifice in that regard. They both moved so they sat on either side of me, wrapping me in their arms and acceptance. Meanwhile, guilt clawed under the surface. I needed to tell them more, tell them the entire sordid tale about my sham of a life. And I would, but for tonight I needed them to just hold me and tell me I'd be okay.

8

IRENE

Dad picked up his English muffin and slathered on a heaping amount of strawberry jam. "You should stop by the office today. I would love to reintroduce you to the staff. Get you reacquainted with the place."

Mom sipped her coffee and gently shook her head. "Melvin."

"What? Why is it so wrong for me to be happy one of my children followed in my footsteps? I just want to pass down the practice I've worked hard building."

I reached over to lay my hand on his arm. "I have a few errands to run, but I will stop by."

Mom pursed her lips but said nothing. We finished breakfast with general pleasantries. Mom discussed the plans she and the community board had for the hospital fundraiser event. She'd chaired that particular event for as long as I could remember and had slowly taken over the Founder's Day celebration as well. My mother excelled at throwing parties and accepting praise for a job well done. She was a shark in a small pond, and she liked it that way.

I excused myself and returned to my room. After getting

my laptop set up, I stared at the spinning cog on my screen waiting for the call to connect. I was glad that Dr. Adams offered a virtual option since my impromptu trip interrupted our regular appointment. The screen went from black to filled with Dr. Adams's smiling face. I liked Dr. Adams and hoped that we could continue the virtual sessions after I moved. *If I moved.*

"How are you today, Irene?"

"Good and you?"

She readjusted at her desk. "Well, can't complain."

What was there to complain about? A question I'd asked myself a lot over the years as part of the excuses I'd made for Derrick, but more for myself. A sexy, well-off husband. A well-established career in medicine. Living large with a pent-house apartment. Trips all over the world whenever we wanted. Sure, he cheated, but wasn't the tradeoff worth it? I held back the scoff that threatened to break free.

Dr. Adams folded her hands on her desk. "When you called to change your appointment, you said you'd gone out of town. A little R&R to think about next steps?"

"Something like that. I drove home, to Madison. I needed a little simplicity and to put a bit more distance between me and Derrick."

"Is he still not handling the divorce well?"

This time I did scoff. "He won't even acknowledge I served him with papers. And it's not because he's so invested in saving the marriage, but more to save his bank account. Because I may have been a fool for far too long, but I wasn't fool enough to let him omit the fidelity clause of the prenup."

A small smile lifted the corners of her mouth. "You weren't a fool. We've been over this. People stay in situations for various reasons that make sense at the time. You have grown from your initial set of reasons, and that is part of life."

I bit the inside of my cheek as I digested her words.

Change didn't happen overnight. It happened when you were ready. Words Dr. Adams constantly reminded me of when I grew frustrated with myself for continuing to spin my wheels because I was too afraid of the unknown. Too afraid to admit I'd found it easier to fall in line rather than do the work needed to figure it out on my own.

"I told my friends I was getting divorced."

Her eyebrows shot up. As much as I loved and trusted Regina and Cynthia, opening up to them remained my hardest fought battle. I'd always presented myself as strong. Independent. Confident. When the truth was, I was none of those things.

"How did they respond?"

I huffed a breath. "Supportive. Curious. But sympathetic. All without me telling them the why."

"What made you hold back? If you told them about the divorce, why not go all in?"

I rolled my eyes. "Because I still feel like a fraud due to all I've held back. Plus, it'd been enough of a blow that I'd driven home and not spoken to them. I wasn't prepared for what will be rightful anger when they find out how much I've kept to myself. They are both the strong independent woman I pretend to be." And nothing proved that more than my cowardly actions last night.

༄

As promised, I was back at Just a Bit of Sugar to see Mama Charles. If there was one person I didn't want calling me on my shit, it was her. Regina's mom mothered everyone, and I loved her for it.

"Ooh, Doctor City Slicker. Looking as stylish as eva," Mama Charles said as way of greeting. She eased her large form from behind the counter with her arms wide. "How you been, baby?"

I settled into her motherly embrace. "I'm doing good. How are you? Regina said you're actually acting like a retired woman now." I glanced over her shoulder and smiled at my friend.

She turned and shot Regina a look. "She just trying to get rid of me, but I ain't going nowhere." The loving smile on her face acted like a cozy blanket.

"That's because you don't know when to stop meddling and let me be," Regina fired back.

"Child please. Even when I go, I'm gonna hang around and haunt you just because."

Regina simply shook her head and smiled as she continued to check out the small line of customers. I knew my mother loved me. I never doubted that. And I loved her. But I wished she was warmer, more nurturing. I wished our relationship could be as relaxed as the one displayed before me. She'd wanted grandchildren, but my niece and nephews couldn't dare call her grandmother. She was Mimi instead. Unlike Mama Charles, who seemed almost allergic to formal greetings and monikers, choosing instead to make every stranger feel welcome.

"Look, I won't hold ya. When Gina told me you'd stopped by I just needed to lay eyes on my other girl. But I'm sure you got stuff to do."

"Yes, Daddy wants me to get 'reacquainted' with the office." I did air quotes around the word he'd used at breakfast.

She gave a full-body laugh, her impeccable curls bouncing with the motion. "Ya daddy is antsy to get you back here, but with that high powered husband of yours... Well, but I get the desire he has." Her eyes glazed over as she glanced around the rebuilt bakery.

I squeezed her hand and ignored the comment about Derrick. "The place looks amazing. And so glad that asshole is behind bars where he belongs!"

"Don't even get me started on that. Can I get you somethin'?" She was already walking back to the counter before I had a chance to answer. "You have to try this new cupcake Tricia made. Lavender and Earl Grey. I wouldn't have thought it would be good, but this old dog can admit when she's wrong."

Regina already had one out of the case and held out for her mom. I took the offered dessert knowing it was zero use in arguing with the woman in front of me. We both moved toward the end of the counter, out of the way of the other customers. I bit into the sweet confection. The royal icing was a sugary delight, not too overpowering. The vanilla cake was light and fluffy. The flavor combination was divine, but that was not surprising. There hadn't been a single dessert I'd had from Regina's place that I wasn't in love with.

I nodded, licking icing from my lips. "Oh, yeah, with things like this, plus y'all's tried and true. The next generation will keep the place going strong."

"I'm so proud of my girls. And I don't just mean my kin. You and Cynthia as well." She reached up and cupped my cheek. "You all have done so well for yourselves. And the way y'all have stayed friends... It warms my heart. Especially seeing how y'all rallied with all of this." She waved her hand around the bakery.

I smiled despite the guilt that never quite let me have peace. Good, bad, or ugly, we were there for each other, and the fact I'd held back so much from them made my lies by omission burn my throat. "Thanks, Mama Charles."

"How long you here for?"

"About two weeks."

"Oh, good. You come 'round for dinner. I'll tell Albert and we'll do it up big."

I glanced at Regina, who just shook her head. Arguing with Mama Charles got you nowhere fast, so I did as we all were accustomed and agreed. "I'm going to head out. I need to stop by Remi's to check on my car then go see Dad."

"Oh. Remi. Bless her sweet soul, coming back to take over for her daddy. Never 'xpected that man to retire. I'd have thought Randal would have stayed working 'til he killed over with a wrench in his hand." She pursed her lips and shook her head slow like she was thinking of more but didn't want to say. "Guess that's the theme goin' on. Y'all leave, live, but come back where you should have been all along."

I smiled at my friend. "Yeah, well we can't all be like your daughter. Knowing what we wanted and sticking to it."

Mama Charles nodded. "Yeah." She leaned in close. "She's a good one, but don't let her know." She shot a playful glance in Regina's direction.

"I'll take the praise, even though I've had my moments." She reached across the counter to squeeze my hand. "Oh, here take these." Regina started filling two of her signature boxes with cookies. One strictly snickerdoodle, the other an assortment.

"I don't need cookies."

She sealed them both with the bakery logo stickers and placed them in a bag. "The small box is for Remi. She loves snickerdoodle, but not sharing with her guys. The other is for them."

"And why am I taking these to her?"

Regina arched one of her perfectly shaped brows. "I know you. And I know how you are with her. Take the damn cookies and play nice."

Mama Charles planted her hands on her hips and frowned at me. "Reny, you be misbehaving?"

"No, ma'am. I'm always on my best behavior." I leaned to kiss her cheek and shot my friend the bird, but took the bag of cookies.

On the short drive, I thought back to what Mama Charles had said, coming back to where I should have been all along. Regina had always known Madison Island was her home, her place. Meanwhile, Cynthia, she couldn't get away fast enough. Me...I'd been indifferent. I'd wanted to know what life was like outside of the island. I'd wanted the freedom to explore my wants, my sexuality, without prying eyes that would judge me. *As they'd judged her...* The gossiping, the whispers, the looks, and Remi had handled it all with her signature don't-give-a-shit attitude.

But what if I'd stayed? What if I'd acted?

My thoughts wandered back to that day in gym. I'd lingered, waiting for her to come in. I put my hand over my chest, remembering how my heart had raced. She'd gotten so close, invaded my space, challenging me and my reason for being there. I'd wanted something to happen that day, but I couldn't act. And for once I'd been at a loss on what to say. No snide remark or witty comment. Her closeness had scrambled my brain as she'd peered at me. Her dark eyes had turned me to jelly, and she'd simply smirked and walked away. And I'd fled the locker room.

Mama Charles was correct, I was back. I was wiser—or at least trying to be. And I wanted to act on what I should have long ago.

9

REMI

"Head's up, Boss."

I peeked around the hood of the Dodge Charger and frowned at Tony. He thumbed toward the lobby, and I couldn't stop the groan. After yesterday, I didn't want to lay eyes on her again so soon. It had to be some sort of weird, cruel twist of fate that I'd hold any sort of attraction toward the annoying woman currently drumming her fingers along my counter.

"Thanks." I peeled my black latex gloves free and tossed them in the trash before I pushed through the door. "What can I do for you, Irene?"

"Good afternoon to you as well, Remi. Are you this unpleasant with everyone, or do I get special treatment?"

"I'm not unpleasant. I get to the point because I know you're not here for a social call. So, it would be nice if you got to yours. I'm down a person, which means extra work."

She glanced toward the window. "Someone sick?"

"No, someone gave birth."

"But you work with men." She realized her comment no sooner than she'd said it. And a hazy shadow crossed her face. "Well, congrats to him and his wife." She diverted her eyes and started digging around in her purse, her movements causing the distinctive bag from Just a Bit of Sugar to rustle with the actions. "Here." She held a key fob out to me.

Our fingers brushed when I took the offered device. Fleeting contact, but one that felt like a static shock making me hyperaware of her. I stepped back, putting more space than just the counter between us. "Why are you giving this to me?"

She pressed her knuckles to her lips briefly. "Thought you might need it. Just in case."

"First your number. Now your keys. What am I missing? I figured you would have contacted a tow to get it to the dealership. Especially since you were so concerned about it being left outside."

She drew the corner of her lip between her teeth while she slowly ran her thumb across her wedding rings. "Or is your husband taking care of it?"

She balled her left hand into a fist and closed her eyes briefly before her posture changed. Whatever temporary moment she'd experienced went out the window. Back rod straight and haughty chin in the air.

Irene shook her head. "No. I simply got a bit busy yesterday, but I'll take care of it."

I lightly tossed the fob in my palm. There was something in her demeanor, her attitude shift, though it wasn't my business. I opened one of the drawers and pulled free a notepad and rubber band. "Is there anything else?" I asked while jotting down her name on the paper then wrapping it around her key.

"No," she said the word, yet lingered. Finally, she took in a deep breath. "Oh, and these are for you." She held out the small distinctive green plastic sack.

mech__2I __ 3

I took the bag and peeked inside. "You brought me cookies?"

"Actually, Regina sent them. She was under the impression they might act as some sort of peace offering."

I set the bag on the desk. "And you don't think you need to make peace?" I couldn't say I cared one way or the other, and despite me wanting to maintain the less is more approach when dealing with Irene, the statement about the peace offering and how she phrased it made me ask.

She adjusted her purse on her shoulder and leveled her gaze at me. "Why do you have such a low opinion of me? High school was a long time ago. And maybe I could have been nicer..."

"You think this is about high school? Regardless of what you might like to think, I haven't been holding a twenty-plus-year grudge against you over some unimportant bullshit like your opinion on how I dressed or who I hung out with. Didn't care then, don't care now."

I rounded the counter and took stock of her. Dressed in another expensive outfit to which she undoubtedly knew the cost of each piece. The army-green romper showed off her long, toned legs, the thin gold belt accentuated her narrow waist, and I was sure the matching gold wedges were just as costly as the other pair she'd been so concerned about. *And that damn perfume...*

She was a pretty package, but her better-than behavior, the condescending nature in which most of her words were delivered... It was that I had a hard time looking past. Most people grew and matured with age, but she seemed frozen in time. The same rich girl who was only concerned with the material things in life.

"Then why are you always so hostile?"

I huffed a sardonic laugh. "Hostile? Really? No, you get back what you put out."

61

"What does that mean?"

"Do you ever stop and listen to the words you speak and how you say them? Because if not, you should. I take people as they are, when they are. So, what you're getting has nothing to do about then and everything to do with now. My opinion of you isn't low, Irene, it just isn't as high as the one you have of yourself."

She opened her mouth to speak but pressed her lips together instead. Irene cut her eyes over at the bag then returned her attention to me. "Yes, I guess those are a peace offering then."

I shook my head and scratched at my hair. "That's not how it works."

"And why not?"

"Because *you* don't mean it. You have to want to make nice, not drop off cookies our friend made you bring, that you yourself 'well actually'd' me on in order to distance yourself from the gesture." I turned and headed back to the garage and paused after I pushed the door open. "Tell Regina I said thanks for the cookies."

"Lover's quarrel?" Tony asked when I entered.

I narrowed my eyes as I pulled a new pair of gloves from the box. "Don't make me fire you."

He barked out a hard laugh. "I'm just sayin', she hasn't moved." He jutted his chin back toward the lobby.

Sure enough, Irene remained in the same place until she noticed us, which prompted her exit. I shook off Tony's comment about a lover's quarrel and got back to my clutch job. Being a small-town mechanic wasn't a glamorous job. But it was good, honest work that I enjoyed. There was peace to be found under the hood of a car or beneath a chassis. Lover's quarrel...no, that was something Irene and I would never engage in for a host of reasons. Her seeming lack of respect for people she deemed beneath her station was near the top of the list. Followed closely by her status as a married—to a man—woman.

I HESITATED before ringing the doorbell of Marcel's house. I looked forward to weekly poker, but with Irene in town, and after dealing with her earlier in the day, I paused, preparing myself in case she was here visiting Cynthia. Irene's friends were now also my friends. An overlap I'd not had to deal with before. But we were adults, and as long as she kept her bullshit to a minimum, I could be cordial.

"Remi." Cynthia greeted me with a tight hug; a warm affection I was still getting used to. "The guys are all in the kitchen getting set up." She shut the door behind me.

"Are you joining us tonight?"

"Ha. Not likely. You sharks don't need to take both our money. Marcel loses enough as it is. I have the food ready, and y'all can have at it. I'll be hanging with Regina and Irene. They're going to help me get rooms ready for guests tomorrow. Oh, but Regina did bring you an extra treat."

Since I'd helped Regina get her food truck, she'd been supplying me with all the sweets I wanted even after I told her it wasn't necessary. She'd said it was the least she could do for the time and effort I'd put in. I finally relented because I could only turn down delicious sugary goodness so many times before I caved.

The B&B Cynthia had opened had been doing well. The new business brought visitors to our small island, and that was always a good thing. The number of roadside assistance calls I'd been sent out on had increased. The shop held its own, but every little bit helped.

I smiled and nodded. It was a low-stakes game, with the pot never hitting more than a hundred or two, but it was about the shit-talking fun of it. "Fair enough. But the offer stands. And we'd go easy on the newbie."

She laughed. "Right, like y'all went easy on Alec?"

I put my hands up in mock defense. "Hey, not my fault he had too cocky of an attitude to go with a total crap poker face."

"Hey, are you talkin' about me?" Alec said soon as we entered the kitchen.

"What gave me away? The cocky part?" I took in the familiar faces and noted the absence of Irene. There was something to be said for small miracles. Her visit to the shop had been enough of a disruption; I wasn't in the mood for her to get poker night off to a bad start.

"Is she wrong? You are a tad cocky, Chief Hodge," Regina said, winking at him.

"Just the way you like me."

She lifted the corner of her mouth in a half-smile and looked him up and down. "If you say so."

He slid an arm around her waist and placed rapid-fire kisses to her neck and cheek with her trying to push him away. The other guys seated at the table laughed. Our weekly poker night rotated houses so the same person wasn't always stuck with the cleaning. Not that we didn't pitch in at the end of the night.

My friendship with Marcel had morphed into one with his wife. Unlike Irene, Cynthia and Regina had never bothered me, but I wouldn't have called us friendly back in the day. But things change. People changed. Hanging out with Cynthia led to me hanging out with Regina more, and they were great. Funny, caring, and non-judgmental. And with Regina and Alec being a couple, he'd been absorbed into the mix. My inner circle had expanded despite my mostly introverted ways.

The doorbell chimed, and with me being closest to the entry I offered to get it. Any tiny slivers of hope that I'd not have to deal with Irene again today evaporated. The smile on her face momentarily faltered, but I did not miss the way her eyes seemed to travel the length of my body before she spoke.

"Remi, hello again. Wasn't expecting to see you."

I stepped to the side to let her in. "I can tell."

She'd changed from the romper she'd worn earlier in the day and now wore a sunshine-yellow one-piece jumpsuit. Her obsession with fashion and name brands made me roll my eyes, but at the same time, I had to reluctantly admit she wore everything well. Every piece was cut and designed to show off her best features. The drape of the collar teased hints of cleavage I couldn't stop myself from being curious about. Her hair tumbled down around her shoulders with one side tucked behind her ear, and teardrop-shaped earrings dangled just below her lobe.

As she moved past me, a soft trail of honeysuckle and vanilla tickled my senses, once again making me acutely aware of her. She turned on her heel just as I started to follow, stopping short, causing me to nearly run into her. I expected her to step back, but she didn't. Instead, she rolled her tongue along her glossy bottom lip before pulling the corner of it between her teeth.

"You look nice, Remi."

I couldn't figure out if she was being genuine or facetious, but for the sake of not letting her get to me, I went the benefit of the doubt route. "Thank you, Irene. You look good yourself."

She seemed to inch closer, or maybe it simply felt as if she were crowding my space thanks to her height, the way her perfume short circuited my brain, and the way I was still reeling from the fact I'd gotten off thinking about her. A coy grin twisted her lips. "Do you mean it?"

She'd challenged me with a similar comment when we'd been discussing her ass, and I'd chosen to ignore her then. I couldn't figure out her endgame, and it probably was not advisable to feed into whatever it was, but I'd never let her get the better of me before and wasn't inclined to start now.

I stared into her expectant eyes and lifted one shoulder. "I wouldn't say it if I didn't."

Her grin broadened, and she opened her mouth as if to speak but was cut off by Cynthia.

"Hey, Remi, who...y'all okay?"

Irene finally moved back, gave me one last odd lingering glance then turned to answer. "Yeah, we're good."

❧ 10 ❧

IRENE

WHY COULDN'T I HAVE JUST SAID SORRY? I'D SPENT THE better part of the day thinking about what Remi had said, and it'd stuck with me. Painfully so. The point of me going to therapy, making changes in my life, was to become someone new. To be the authentic me. But being around Remi had always scrambled my brain, and I hated it. I couldn't seem to figure out how to not be bitchy around her. And if that wasn't bad enough, my awkward attempts at flirting were.

Remi...oh Remi, she'd looked good. Really good. The white slightly baggy jeans and dark blue short-sleeved Henley. My eyes had zeroed in on the top button being undone. I'd wanted to run my fingers through her hair and just... But I could see the distrust of my compliment. The look on her face had told me as much. Full lips downturned, eyes narrowed.

"And the aliens landed."

When I tuned back in, I glanced up to catch Regina's gaze in the rearview.

"Hey, look who's out of her daydream. What's going on with you?"

I shook my head. "Nothing, just a lot on my mind."

Cynthia turned in her seat. "The divorce?"

Regina eased her small SUV onto the private drive that led to the Blue Bird Inn. I stared out the window at the solar lights that lined each side to light our path and chewed the inside of my cheek.

"This place brings back so many memories," I said as we filed out of the car.

"Yeah, it does, but good ones. And I know she'd be proud of me," Cynthia agreed.

Just like Mama Charles was everybody's mom, Cynthia's Aunt Drea acted as everybody's auntie. She never minded us teens hanging out on her property, being up late and making noise at all hours of the night. Our teenage years, such a simpler time I wished I could go back to.

These were my friends. More than that, they were my sisters. I'd been there for them. When Cynthia was scared, pregnant, and left home at eighteen. And again when she was taking care of her aunt after the cancer diagnosis. Regina, losing her husband and mother-in-law. Helping her hold it together for her son's sake. Supporting her through the worst time in her life. Then all the business with her bakery.

They'd trusted me enough. Had no problems showing their weakness and being vulnerable in their truth. I owed them the same respect. I wanted to give them that. I needed to give them that. And my years in therapy had been working up to this. Living my truth. It was time.

"I went through menopause ten years ago." I spoke the words low as we entered the foyer of the large, restored Victorian.

Both turned and looked at me, then at each other, then back to me. "Aren't you the lucky bitch? I'm so damn ready to be done with all that shit," Regina said before she pulled her brows together in a frown. "Or not."

I sucked in a deep breath and released it slow. "You have Darnell."

Like when I'd told them about the divorce, a collective silence fell over them. I didn't make the statement to throw it in her face she had a child and I didn't. But the way her expression changed, that was how the comment landed. She pressed her lips together and shifted her gaze to Cynthia. And my good friend guilt took over because I'd dropped that bomb in the worst possible way. And I heard Remi in the back of my mind again.

"Regina, I didn't..."

"It's okay. I get it. I think. With your high-end lifestyle, I assumed you were like Cyn, and kids weren't part of your plan."

I shifted my attention to Cynthia. Growing up with her parents and their resentment over her existence, Cynthia had known early in life she'd never want children. Getting pregnant at eighteen by the love of her life hadn't changed her mind. Something she'd trusted us with. An anvil settled in my stomach. It wasn't an unreasonable assumption considering, and I couldn't even get mad at her for stating it. I nodded. "I know. And that's on me."

Cynthia held my hand. "This calls for ice cream."

We trailed behind her up to the third-floor owner's suite with Regina holding my hand and lightly rubbing my arm the whole time. Cynthia directed the two of us over to the soft leather sectional while she pulled out the tub of ice cream and a bottle of wine.

My heart beat erratically and my stomach churned. But I'd opened the door so there was no closing it. Not with these two. And as nervous as I was to pull back the curtain, at least somewhat, I didn't want to keep hiding from them.

"We're supposed to be getting your rooms ready," I commented, taking the bowl from Cynthia.

"They can wait, and honestly, I can do them in the morning. First guest isn't arriving 'til eleven."

I scooped a spoonful of the creamy butter pecan, letting the coolness melt on my tongue. "So...where to begin?"

Regina squeezed my arm. "Wherever you want."

"First, I want to say I'm sorry. To both of you." I glanced at each of them. "You both deserved the same level of open honesty from me that y'all have given."

Cynthia laid her hand on my shoulder. "We're family, Irene. And families have ups and downs. And they damn sure have secrets."

"Exactly," Regina added. "We've been friends for a long-ass time. We know by now you share when you're good and damn ready and not a minute before. Now, did I think it'd ever take you ten years for something that is apparently really serious and hurts you so much? No. And I won't lie to you, knowing you kept closed lipped for that long... I might be in my feelings a bit."

She paused and put her attention on Cynthia, who nodded in agreement. "But we can discuss all that at a later date. And we will discuss it." Regina tilted her head and pursed her lips. Her "I mean business look," and I knew there would be a reckoning at some point. "For now, however, we're here to love you and get whatever is going on off your chest. Because I get the feeling there's more."

They were both letting me off easy, at least for the time being. At some point they'd take me to task, and I'd deserve it. Until then, I'd let them see what was behind all the glitz and glam they believed my life to be.

I took another bite. "Always thought I had time. First, I needed to finish school. Then my residency. Then it was getting established in my job." *Not to mention trying to convince Derrick.* I sucked in a shaky breath. "And honestly, I wasn't even sure I wanted kids or if I was supposed to have them, you know."

That was the hardest part to admit. It hadn't been until I was unable to have kids that I really evaluated whether I'd wanted them in the first place. Or if it had been a matter of wanting something simply because you couldn't have it. Which made me feel like a horrible person when I stopped to think about all the women who suffered with infertility and wanted a child more than anything. *Selfish. Self-centered.* Maybe Remi was more right about me than I cared to admit. *No...I'm changing my ways.*

When I'd missed my first period, I'd actually been a little excited about the possibility despite how pissed my soon to be ex was thinking I'd followed through on my threat to go off my birth control. Then the world bottomed out and he had been pleased like a problem solved. The memory of his reaction hit me hard, and my chest constricted.

Regina squeezed my hand. "Is that why... Is that bastard leaving because of the menopause?"

A hard, nervous laugh sprung free, making both of them jump. I covered my mouth and muffled an apology. I shook my head. "No, he..." I stopped. I wasn't ready to admit to how much I'd actually put up with over the last two decades from a man everyone seemingly thought walked on water.

"Gina, you were right. Not having a period is a major perk. Having a husband who stuck his dick in any and every willing vagina, not so much."

Both their mouths fell open.

Cynthia speared her ice cream with her spoon. "That bastard! I will never understand. Divorce is right fucking there."

"Prenup with a fidelity clause," I said with a shrug. "For him, it was quite literally cheaper to keep me. And I fucking let him." I released a long sigh and set my unfinished dessert onto the coffee table.

Regina twisted so she faced me. "If I'm reading between the lines here, the cheating isn't recent? It started because of the menopause?"

I pressed my lips together and shook my head. I couldn't meet their eyes. "We were still dating the first time. In hindsight, I probably should have never married him. But, in theory, he was the ideal man, and I could lead the dream life everyone expected." I ran my thumb over my ring. "Anyway, Derrick was under the impression that fidelity was a mere suggestion, not a requirement for marriage. Only where he was concerned, of course." I clasped my hands in my lap, letting my shoulders drop as I avoided both their gazes.

"Uh-huh. No. What is this?"

I turned to stare at Regina and internally braced for the "you brought it on yourself" or "only a fool stays" beratement.

"That man got you fucked up. That body change right there." She circled her finger in my direction. "You are not small, and you will not let his actions make you feel small. You hear me?"

"That's the damn truth. We will get angry. And we sure as hell can get petty. But you, ma'am, will not waste another minute wondering why. Or what did you do. There is no excuse for his behavior," Cynthia agreed. "Ol' busted ass. Done pissed me right off. Cheatin' on you. On you!"

Their outrage brought a smile to my face and lightened the burden just a bit. And letting them focus on that gave me cover to keep the rest at bay for just a little while longer. I knew I had my part to own in all of it. I'd enabled his behavior by letting him get away with it for so long. First, he'd used the excuse of me working too many hours while I was in my residency. It'd been the beginning of the downfall, but I'd been all too eager to ignore the truth.

And for what? I had nothing to show for it other than heartbreak and embarrassment. I picked up my glass of wine. "Anyhoo, I served him with papers, which he's basically refusing to acknowledge. But I'm serious. So, this should be fun." I drained my drink in nearly one gulp.

Regina frowned. "If it's about money, wouldn't it be cheaper to let it go rather than spend more on lawyers fighting?"

A near hysterical laugh burst out of me. They both just stared as I worked to calm myself and catch my breath. "I'm sorry. I'm sorry. I know it's a legit question, and the fact you have to ask it is on me. I've spent my entire relationship with Derrick portraying him one way." I inhaled deep as I refilled my glass. After taking another long sip, I cleared my throat ready to continue. "Truth is, Derrick Moore is an anaconda in a three-thousand-dollar suit. That man would rather squeeze the life out of me than admit defeat."

Cynthia sat up straighter, and her lips were pressed into a hard line. "That is a metaphorical statement, right? Because if that man has put hands on you on top of everything..."

My eyes went wide, and I sucked in a sharp breath while shaking my head frantically. "Oh, god no. Sorry. It's more about him protecting his image. He's never... The hits I took were all emotional I guess you could say."

Both of them visibly relaxed. Regina gathered up all three bowls and carried them to the kitchen. "So, you have a fight on your hands. But you won't be doing it alone. You know that, right?"

I needed their unwavering support because explaining to Vivian Johnson I was walking away from my marriage was not going to go over well. "I do. And I appreciate you both. So much. Even if I've been terrible about showing it. But I've been in therapy, and I'm going to do better."

Cynthia inched closer and wrapped her arms around my shoulders. "We'll get through this, Irene. And when it's all said and done, we'll throw one of those new trendy divorce parties or take a long vacation."

"Or both," Regina added.

I laughed and leaned into my friend's embrace. "I like the sound of that. I guess if there was an upside to all of this, it's that I'm considering moving back."

Cynthia's arms tightened, and she started bouncing us up and down. "Silver fucking lining for sure."

"Yup. Just gotta find a place to live because I can't stay with my parents for too long."

Regina laughed and nodded. "I hear that. I love Momma, but I'd go bald living with her. Let me check with Remi..."

"What why?" I asked, cutting her off as I sat up.

"You g'on have to get over your issues with her. Remi is good people," Regina softly scolded.

"I know. Y'all are all buddy-buddy with her. Meanwhile, she barely gives me a lukewarm response."

Cynthia shook her head. "Tell me something. What did she ever do to you? I have never understood your problem with her. Far as I could tell, she kept to herself and didn't bother nobody. Hell, she's still that way."

Regina settled back on the sofa and crossed her arms like she was waiting for the answer as well. But I had no idea how to explain it when I couldn't fully understand it myself. We were different people. She was blunt, matter-of-fact, and just too much her. Too honest and too comfortable in who she was, which had scared the hell out of me. And too damn beautiful. She was too much of everything that I wanted.

"I don't have a problem." Soon as I said the words, they

both hit me with their "that's bullshit" expressions. "We have clashing personalities, but I'm trying to be nicer."

They both still looked unconvinced. "Are you?" Cynthia challenged. "Because there was some energy between you two at the house."

"There was no energy. I was actually being polite. Complimented her outfit and everything. Besides, Regina, if you think I have such an issue, why would you even bring her up?"

"Because she has a rental space Marcel completed for her a while ago," Cynthia answered. "But I'm not sure it's your speed."

"What is that supposed to mean?"

"Um...exactly what you think it does." She gestured between herself and Regina. "We've been to your parents' house and to your penthouse in New York. Remi's loft space, major downgrade."

Regina nodded. "Now that you say that, Alec was going to rent it before he moved in with me, but yeah, there are a few others around town. Just check with Dana over at the realty office."

I bit the inside of my cheek and kept back any retorts. High maintenance. Materialistic. Snobby. Just a few of the words used to describe me over the years popped into my head. I couldn't entirely blame them. I liked the finer things in life, and I'd liked low key bragging about them over the years. Again, I couldn't be offended they'd think I'd turn my nose up at Remi's rental. I'd spent my entire life basking in the material things. And it wasn't to say I still didn't appreciate and want them, but I'd finally let it sink in there was more to life than what you owned. Something Remi had always made painfully clear when my attempts to impress repeatedly backfired.

Her comment from earlier sprang back into my mind. "*I*

take people as they are, when they are. So, what you're getting has nothing to do about then and everything to do about now." Finding out who I was and what I wanted meant changing who I'd been. They expected me to continue my lifestyle, but simpler sounded so much better.

❦ 11 ❧

REMI

I PULLED ON THE DOOR, DOUBLE CHECKING TO MAKE SURE the lock was engaged, and the building was secured for the night. Not that I worried about break-ins, but it was an old habit and one that gave me final peace of mind at the end of the day. Rolling the kinks from my neck, I strolled toward my bike, adjusting my backpack on my shoulder. Devon was still taking days off to be with his wife and newborn daughter. I understood his want and desire to be with his first child, and I gave him the time he'd asked for. But damn if it didn't make work longer for Tony and me.

Irene's gray Audi sat in the same place. She'd called to check up on it as if it could grow legs and walk off but made zero mention of when she'd be removing it from my lot. Though I'd take a phone call over her walking in to distract me in person. Sighing, I pulled my helmet on, buckling the strap under my chin. Like with the door, I gave the protective gear a little shake, making sure it was in place before I fired up my bike.

I revved the throttle just to listen to the purr of the engine of my 1970 vintage Ducati. The beautiful machine was

77

my pride and joy. It was a lucky find at an estate sale. The guy had no idea what he had and had thought it was just an old piece of rusted junk his grandfather kept. I may have lowballed him a bit, but he'd been all too eager to get rid of it.

Fixing it up had been a labor of love. Now, simply looking at it gave me an endorphin rush. The vibrations between my legs were damn near erotic. The power, the control, the freedom of barreling down the road with the wind in my face gave me the euphoric feeling of peace and calm. I laughed quietly, trying to picture Irene on my bike. She'd probably be too worried about messing up her hair or getting her designer clothes wrinkled.

I paused. Why the hell was I thinking about her in the first damn place? She was getting under my skin. Again.

Shaking off the thought, I pointed my bike in the direction of town. One of the things I missed the most was being able to go out for long rides to clear my head. Something I needed desperately of late. I didn't take it out often because cruising through the streets of Madison didn't inspire the same level of enjoyment, but it was a small sacrifice to make. I needed to be close in case anything happened to Pop. Which meant hour-long drives on stretches of road, leaving the noise and stresses behind me were a thing of the past. At least for the foreseeable future.

Auntie was a help, but she wasn't getting any younger and had her own things to do. Al pitched in as well, best he could around his work schedule, but at the end of the day, Pop was my responsibility. I parked my bike in the little space not really meant for parking, but I'd claimed as my personal reserved spot all the same. The bell dinged when I entered the bakery. Off to the side, a group of high schoolers were huddled around two tables they'd pushed together.

A few other locals milled about, and those who looked up from what they were doing gave polite waves of acknowledgment. Including Chief Morris, who offered up a subtle nod in my direction before returning his attention to his grand-daughter, who was trying to eat the wrapper of her cupcake. He may not have held the job any longer, but it was hard to think of him as anyone other than the chief. And I was sure it'd be the same whenever Sheriff Parker finally decided to retire.

And then, sitting in a pair of the club chairs, chatting and looking over something on a laptop, were Cynthia with Irene. I'd gone years rarely running into that woman, yet now she seemed to be everywhere. Part of me wanted to continue on to the counter, get my order and go, but ignoring the duo was out of the question. I wouldn't be rude to Cynthia in that way.

I was temporarily saved from the awkward what-to-do situation when Ms. Charles came bursting through the swinging metal doors, arms wide and grin wider. "Well, Remi Martin. As I live and breathe."

I laughed quietly at her greeting. I didn't stop in often, usually choosing to head directly home after work, but if you heard her tell it, she'd not laid eyes on me in ages. "Good evening, Ms. Charles." I returned her embrace, juggling my helmet and trying not to wince when she undoubtedly squeezed too hard. They were huggers. The whole lot of them.

"How's your dad?" she whispered before stepping back but holding on to my wrists.

Not many people knew about Pop's condition, and I preferred it that way. I'm sure if they did, they'd be well meaning, maybe even want to help. But that'd drop off soon and I'd be left handling everything anyway, so it was much easier to cut out the middle part. However, since Aunt Ev was friends with Ms. Charles, she was aware, but as far as I knew, she hadn't said a word to Regina.

"He's good."

She squeezed my free hand and nodded. "I'mma do some cookin' this weekend and send it by way of your auntie, okay."

"I appreciate that."

"Hm-hm. And don't think I haven't noticed your absence, I'mma start taking it personal if you keep not showing up for my invites out to the house. I want you to promise me right now you comin' to the next fish fry."

I knew the elder woman meant business as she peered at me over her glasses. I hadn't avoided out of disrespect, but I'd rather deal with people in small doses, and I'd heard Ms. Charles threw some legendary get-togethers. But she'd also been there to help out with Pop at times. Especially when she'd had more time on her hands while the bakery was under reconstruction.

"I'll be there, I promise."

She clapped her hands together. "Good. We're plannin' something for my other girl's return." She pointed at Irene, and I clamped my lips together to keep the groan from escaping.

How had I walked into that one? Of all the events, I'd promised to attend one in honor of *her*. I glanced at the woman in question whose eyes seemed to sparkle as her focus was solely on me. "Can't wait." Our gazes lingered as a silence blanketed the moment. Finally, I tore my attention away and faced Ms. Charles. "Is my order ready?"

"Yeah, Gina was finishing up when I came out here. You know I've told her she should sell those things, but keeps them special just for you." There was a twinkle in her eye when she said that.

"What's that?" Irene asked.

"Cookie sandwiches," Cynthia answered. "Regina makes them with the snickerdoodle, which is Remi's favorite." She smiled up at me when she said that. "And fills them with her cannoli cream. I tried one, and it's divine. Super rich, but divine. A Remi special."

Irene settled back in her chair. "I've been friends with her for thirty years and she's never created me a special dessert." She pushed her pink tinted lips into a small pout.

"That's because you don't eat sweets like Remi. Plus, she refused to take my money for finding the food truck, so I pay her in cookies," Regina said, coming to join the conversation with my bag of goodies in hand.

"I told you it wasn't a big deal, but I'll never turn down your treats." Ms. Charles took my helmet before I could set it on the table. "You gonna take her for a spin?" I teased while carefully placing the cookies in my backpack.

"I'm all for trying new things, but I think I draw the line at metal between my legs."

"I don't know, Ms. Charles. I think you'd be pretty badass on a bike."

"Don't go encouraging her bad behavior, Remi," Regina scolded. "Next thing you know her old behind will be trying to take lessons or some nonsense."

Ms. Charles pursed her lips, frowning at her daughter and I stifled a laugh.

"Whatever. I ain't that old, but there's only one thing I'm ridin', and it hasn't failed me in fifty years."

"Momma!"

The older woman shrugged, seemingly pleased with herself for mildly horrifying her daughter. When she went to hand me back the helmet, Irene stood and grabbed it instead.

She stared at me directly. "Can I take her for a spin?"

I frowned and glanced at Cynthia and Regina, who appeared to be as shocked and confused as I was by Irene's question. "Do you know how to handle a motorcycle?"

A slow smile spread across her face as she held my helmet out to me. "Nope. But you could take me for a ride."

I twisted my lips and narrowed my eyes at her. "Could I?" I closed my fingers around the lip of my head gear, but she didn't release.

"Yes." She held on for a moment longer before finally letting go.

Again, Irene's friends glanced at her, then each other with scrunched faces. Ms. Charles, however, had a look of interest with an arched brow and a smirk on her face as she watched both me and Irene. She'd been giving off strange vibes, and I had no idea what to make of them. But her comment, as demanding as it came across, unfortunately played into my earlier rebellious thoughts. To have her on the back of my bike, pressed against me... Nope, wasn't going there.

I cleared my throat and locked away any lingering errant notions. "Well, I'll keep your gracious willingness to *let* me take you for a ride in mind. I'll see y'all later."

I exited and did my best not to search for Irene through the window as I secured my helmet. I didn't want to know if she was tracking my movements, even if I could almost feel her eyes on me. After sliding the visor in place, my hidden gaze betrayed me as my eyes snapped upwards when I cranked up my bike and found her staring in my direction. I had to be getting soft in my old age for Irene to get to me as much as she'd been lately. I'd had much better defenses in my younger days.

When I walked in the door, both my loving companions greeted me. Axle immediately started sniffing at the bag in my hand; they always expected treats.

"No goodies until I'm sure y'all didn't wreck the place with the wild parties I know you throw while I work to keep you both in a life of luxury," I cooed, kneeling to give him a good scratch behind the ears. Hemi rubbed herself along my back before she moved to sit her fluffy ass on my backpack. I picked her up and placed her on the floor. "Can you not?"

After getting everything put away and the food bowls filled, I headed down the street to check on Pop and relieve Aunt Ev.

"Whew, honey. He is in a foul mood today," she said as way of greeting when I entered the house. "He ain't eaten all day, turned his nose up at everything like a damn toddler." She twisted her lips to the side and shook her head.

From her body language and the way she jammed her stuff into her bag, I could tell it had been a rough day. "You should have called me, Auntie. I would have come home early." And I sure as hell wouldn't have made a pit stop.

"It wasn't nothin' I couldn't handle. Besides, you workin'. I know you got too much on your shoulders right now. You should be out doin' stuff you young folks get into."

I laughed and kissed her cheek. "Auntie, I'm forty-four."

"And?"

"And I haven't the slightest clue what 'young folks' get into."

She swatted at the air. "You know what I mean. Look at your friends. They all the same age as you, and all got themselves new boo thangs." She rested a weathered hand on my cheek. "There is more to life than work and an occasional poker game."

"I know, that's why I have Axle and Hemi."

Her deep frown made me laugh hard.

"I'mma disown you."

I kissed her cheek. "No, you won't. I'm your favorite."

I knew she meant well, but with everything else going on, even attempting casual dating was low on the priority scale. And even if I wanted to, the pickens had always been slim to none on Madison Island. Which was partially my main driving force for leaving as soon as I could. On top of the fact, I'd never been good at casual. However, I was genuinely thrilled for my friends—though calling them that still felt odd at times—and the new relationships they'd found.

Cynthia and Marcel reconnecting after decades apart. Regina and Alec... That man had even moved to be with her. A rare thread of envy weaved through me. My last relationship fizzled when I'd decided to move back to Madison. She'd had her career, and unlike Alec, she hadn't been willing to make a life change just because I had to. It'd hurt, but she'd been honest and upfront, and at the end of the day, that was all I could have asked for.

Regardless, I enjoyed spending time with the four of them. I'd been more than welcomed into their extended family unit, and while it'd taken some getting used to, I looked forward to the get-togethers. But their path was not mine.

My aunt had her well-meaning hopes for me, but I didn't see myself falling into the same situation. After she'd left, I made my way to the kitchen. Pop had refused to eat all damn day. Shit. If he'd turned down my aunt's good cooking, I knew there was only one thing that would tempt him. I set about putting eggs on to boil for the tuna salad. It'd always been his favorite, and if he turned it down, I knew without a doubt it was a bad day and the depression had gotten worse.

Sighing, I worked diligently to get the food prepared. My thoughts strayed to the usual. How much longer could I keep taking care of him without more professional, full-time help? Would I be able to keep him in the house? As it were, I was running two households, and while the business, plus my side hustles were doing well, medical bills... I placed my palms on the counter and stretched. That was a worry for another day. For the time being, I had it handled.

I plated up his sandwich and headed down the hall to his room. He sat in his chair staring aimlessly out the window. It pained me to see him like that. I'd take his cranky moodiness over the despondent listlessness any day.

"Hey, Pop, I made you dinner." I tried to put as much enthusiasm in my voice as possible. "Tuna, bread lightly toasted just how you like it." I set the plate down on the small side table. "Auntie said you hadn't had much of an appetite today."

He harrumphed a noise but picked up the plate and took a bite from the sandwich. A small victory. I tinkered around the house until he finished, and once I was sure he was good for the night, I headed back home. Auntie's comment played on repeat during the short walk. There had been moments I missed companionship. I wanted someone to talk to at the end of the day who would talk back. My animals were great, and I loved them, but there were times, especially when Pop had a bad day, where I craved the physical connection from another human.

I wanted to be able to lay my head on their breasts while they stroked my hair and told me it'd all be okay. However, being a realist, taking the situation for what it was, that's how I functioned. And I knew regardless of what I wanted, it wasn't in the cards. But sometimes...sometimes I wanted to be able to pretend things were better than they were.

❧ 12 ❧

IRENE

"THIS IS A PLACE TO EAT, NOT A WORK SURFACE." MY mother spoke as she glided into the room.

I closed the lid of my laptop and suppressed the eye roll. "Sorry, I was checking a few work emails."

She eased into the chair across from me and poured herself a cup of coffee. I straightened my posture on instinct, and the slight smile that pulled her lips to the side let me know she was pleased with the correction.

"Is the office falling apart without you?"

"Not quite."

I broke off a piece of my muffin to buy time while I ran through my options. Did I tell her I was looking at the steps needed to transfer my medical license? Was I ready to get into the divorce talk? I dismissed that idea as soon as it entered my head. Breaking that news to my mother was not how I wanted to start my day.

My mother quietly fixed her plate, loading it with various fruits and a side of Greek yogurt. I wanted to share with her. In the years when she'd inquired about me having kids, each time the "you're not getting any younger" comment came I died a little on the inside. But instead of telling her the truth, that her son-in-law didn't want them, and later I couldn't have any, I made excuses about our lifestyle. Used strange acronyms like DINK to support that excuse and she bought into it since she lived vicariously through me. She was so proud of all I'd achieved.

"How are you spending your day?" I inquired.

"The committee members for Founder's Day are stopping by. We have to start planning." She glanced at me over the rim of her mug. "Do you want to sit in? It could be fun, the two of us planning the event."

"Mom, you have a whole committee."

"True. But you have experience putting on more elegant affairs."

"The occasional dinner party does not make for elegant affairs, Mom."

"You sell yourself short." She gave another half-smile before clearing her throat. "Are you ready to tell me what's really going on?"

I did my best to keep my expression neutral. "What do you mean?"

She thoughtfully chewed her next bite all while keeping her eyes on me, waiting for me to answer. Her look was a stark reminder that Vivian Johnson could never be accused of not being acutely aware of things going on around her. Dad had been happily distracted with talk of me considering taking over the family business; Mom, however, wasn't so easily deflected.

"Nothing is going on. I told you and Dad at dinner, I'm simply weighing my options. Looking for possible change. Nothing more, nothing less."

"And how exactly would your marriage work, darling? You can't have a meaningful relationship with him living in New York and you living in Madison. Because we both know as lovely as Madison Island is, it's not a place meant for a man like Derrick."

Or a woman like her. At least that was what I felt were the unspoken words. My parents had been part of the high society life in Buckhead before Dad developed arthritis in his hands which prevented him from doing surgery. I'd never been clear on whose decision it'd been to pack up and move to Madison, though I had my suspicions that it'd been my father.

"Yes, Mom, I'm aware. Right now, it's more of a scouting mission. Nothing has been decided."

"I understand, dear, and I didn't want to rain on your father's parade at dinner, but logistics. It doesn't seem like you've thought that through. Which is why I get the distinct impression there is more you aren't telling me." She kept her gaze on me as she took a sip of coffee.

My first thought was to answer that there was a lot I wasn't telling her. But I wasn't sure I was ready to have the discussion. It'd been hard enough with Cynthia and Regina, and they expected less from me than my mother did. The illusion of happiness and perfection. I'd learned the art of it in the confines of the house I now sat. It was what we did. We might not have been the wealthiest people on Madison Island, but we'd lived as if we were. We had the biggest house on the biggest lot. Both my brother and I had to finish top of our class. Took family vacations every summer and holiday break without fail. Mother wanted us to be the Joneses that everyone else wanted to keep up with.

And I'd not outgrown that idea.

"Why do you think I'm hiding something?"

She arched a brow while slightly inclining her head to the side. "I didn't say hiding; I said not telling me everything. For you to phrase it that way must mean you are hiding something."

I massaged the low ache in my temple. "Mother, by nature of me being an adult, don't you think I've been afforded the right to be honest with you at all times. It's not like I'm a teenager and still have to sneak around. Not that I did that," I rushed to add.

She finished her breakfast and readjusted in her seat, crossing one elegant leg over the other. "Not ready to tell me. Understood." She pulled in a sigh. "Irene, let me counsel you on this. Before you make some sort of rash decision based on emotion, think about all you've built, all the time you've put in over the last twenty years. Then you need to decide if whatever is going on is a point of no return. Or if this is simply a rough patch. A midlife crisis."

Rash. Dramatic. Overreacting. More words consistently used to describe me. I was in fact an adult, and it was beyond time I was truly honest with my mother. Mostly. I straightened my posture and dug deep for the confidence I was good at portraying even when my insides were jelly.

"I'm divorcing Derrick."

If uttering those three words weren't enough to make me want to vomit, the prolonged silence from my mother would do it. I waited for her to speak while crafting a series of proper responses.

"I can only assume this spontaneous trip home is a result of said pending divorce."

I nodded. "Derrick and I were in need of some distance."

She reached forward and covered my hand with hers and squeezed lightly before letting go. A bit of comfort that was unfortunately short lived. "My earlier words remain true." She picked up the bell from the table, rang it twice, then rose with grace, smoothing down the front of her yellow linen dress before exiting the room.

I don't know what I expected. A hug maybe? Some sort of comfort, assurances like I'd gotten from my friends that things would be okay. Anything other than my mother's same logical and near cold reaction, which basically told me I should reconsider.

Patrice strolled in moments later and began clearing the dishes. "Are you done, Ms. Irene?"

"Yeah, I am more than done. Thank you." I picked up my laptop and headed to my room.

My mother's message weighed heavily on my mind. "A rash decision based on emotion." I scoffed. Yes, picking up and going to a hotel, that was rash. Driving from New York to Madison, also rash. Serving my husband divorce papers after years of infidelity and disrespect. Not so much. Sadly, however, the fact remained that even though I was sure I wanted out of the marriage, needed out of the marriage, my mother's indirect directness had me almost second guessing. But I'd thought long and hard about my actions.

I'd lived the life others wanted me to live. It was my turn, even if I had no fucking clue who I was or what I was doing. I'd stumble or walk of my own accord. First step being a place to live. And I knew the perfect location.

Cynthia and Regina were right, old me would have turned her nose up at the idea of living on that end of town. Where commercial met residential. Not much of Madison could be considered lively, but the area with the shotgun-style houses... It seemed to be its own world within the town. Or maybe it could have been the mystifying mind of me as a teenager. The life there seemed to be vastly different from the one I'd led.

And it'd been where *she'd* lived.

I thought about the last time I'd seen Remi and had to cover my mouth to stop the snort that erupted. Regina and Cynthia had looked at me like I'd grown a second head. Me, on a motorcycle, but I'd been able to play it off as trying new things. Which wasn't far off. But it was the driver that made me open to the idea.

Seeing her in the unflattering coveralls was somehow adding to her appeal, but to throw in the biker's jacket—I thought I'd spontaneously combust when she'd walked in. There wasn't much room on motorcycles, so I'd have to be pressed against her, holding on tight...a thrill zipped through me at the idea.

Everyone around me would probably think I'd gone off the deep end, but I wanted different. I wanted to learn how to live authentically me. And I wanted to be as close to Remi as possible. I couldn't think of a better place to do both.

❧ 13 ❧

REMI

"HEY, BOSS. MS. JOHNSON'S HERE TO SEE YOU," DEVON hollered.

I rolled the dolly from beneath the Ford Focus I was working on. Sure, I had a lift, but the times I wanted more solitude, even from the guys I worked with, I went old school and worked under the car. And solitude was what I needed more than ever. But so much for that. There was only one Ms. Johnson who could be asking for me. Sure enough, after I'd pushed to standing, I peered through the large glass to see none other than the thorn in my side. Dressed like a spring bouquet in a sleeveless floral print sundress. Vibrant colors and trouble making legs on full display.

I blew out an exaggerated exhale while peeling the black latex gloves from my hands and tossing them in the trash. She was the last person I needed to deal with after the phone call from Aunt Ev letting me know Dad was having an even worse day. Crankier than usual and refusing to take his meds. Again, refusing to eat. I'd offered to come home, but she'd told me not to since his nurse was there. He seemed to have more bad days lately and I was doing my best, but his care was getting to the point it was beyond what I, Aunt Ev, and the twice-a-week in-home nurse could handle.

"Maybe she's here about her car finally," Tony offered up.

"I could only be so lucky."

She'd spent the last week calling me every other day it seemed to check on her damn car, yet none of those calls ever mentioned her getting it moved off my damn lot. I was almost really considering charging her a storage fee. But at least she hadn't come by, which I'd been thankful for.

Devon slid past me, entering the bay as I walked into the lobby. "What do you want, Irene?"

She pulled her full, glossy lips into a beaming smile. "Good afternoon to you, too, Remi."

She stepped closer to the counter, running her fingers across the surface before rubbing them as if she were trying to get crumbs off. I shoved my hands into the pockets of my coveralls and balled them into fists, trying to not give into the irrational annoyance her simple presence caused me.

"I'm looking for a place to rent, and Regina told me you might have an option."

"There's no way Regina would have told you that." Regina and I got along. She knew the history I had with her friend. There was no way in hell she'd inflict Irene on me in such a way.

The subtle tilt of her head and lifting of her chin. Haughty Irene. "Why would I lie?"

"How would I know? You aren't exactly the most logical woman I've met."

"I'm a doctor, of course I'm logical. It's part of the job."

"Then explain why you pitched a fit about where I'd take your car, then be all worried about it being out in the elements yet have made no plans to move it elsewhere."

She whipped her head to glance out the window at the dark gray Audi, which now sported a yellow coating of pollen.

"I've had a lot on my plate with preparing to relocate. And since my parents had an extra car I could use, that one hasn't been a priority. Besides, it's not like it's in the way."

"According to you."

She blew out a forced breath and ran her hand along the side of her head, smoothing the already tightly pulled strands that made up her high ponytail. "You're getting off track. I'm here because I want to see your rental. Cynthia said it's a converted loft that Marcel did."

Moving back? The mere thought of that sent a stabbing pain behind my eyes. Fuck, that's right. Ms. Charles had said as much when I'd agreed to attend her next fish fry. Why that hadn't connected fully before now was me probably trying to block out the information. Avoiding Irene had been easier when we didn't operate in the same circles.

Handling the occasional run-in was one thing, to see her every day... I shook my head. "No."

"What do you mean no? Have you already rented it?"

I shook my head again and leaned back against the desk. "Nope. Just not renting to you."

She pulled her brows together into a deep V, stormed around the counter, invading my space, and planted her hands on her hips. "And why the hell not? I have excellent credit and would make an amazing tenant."

I tried to ignore the way her intoxicating scent coiled around, beckoning me in like one of the come-hither hands seen in cartoons. Standing at my full five-five height, I still had to tilt my chin up to meet her glare. "Because I don't want to, Irene. And let's be honest, you don't want to rent from me. You do remember where I live, don't you?"

A small flicker of remembrance flitted across her face. Either from recalling that I didn't exactly live on the "good side of town" in comparison to where she came from. Or from the snide comments she'd made as a teen about my family's modest home. I'd never been ashamed of who I was or where I came from, no matter how damn hard she'd tried to make it so.

"Great. Now that we have that settled, I need to get back to work, and you apparently have house hunting to do."

I'd moved around her to return to the bay when she spoke again. "I'm fairly certain that denying me housing is some form of discrimination."

I tightened my grip on the pull bar of the door and rolled my shoulders, attempting to get some of the mounting tension out. "Why?"

"Because it's the law. A person cannot be denied housing based on gender, race, or sexual orientation." A smug grin tugged at her lips when she said the last part.

"First, I'm not denying you housing for any of those reasons. You simply annoy me. I don't want to deal with you and whoever is attached to that." I pointed at the large diamond on her left hand.

She followed my line of sight and curiously placed her right hand over it, as if I were planning to steal it or some nonsense. It was that sort of attitude I didn't want to deal with.

"Secondly, it's a garage apartment. Meaning you'd be too damn close to me. Besides, why are you so insistent? There are plenty of other places you can rent. The beach. Main Street. Staying with your parents. Hell, you could rent a room from Cynthia. Why are you intent on being around me?"

That was the biggest issue needling under the surface. The delay in her moving her car and now trying to rent from me. Irene's actions almost came across as intentional to keep herself in my path, and I could not figure out why.

She clenched her hand around the strap of her purse. "Because it's temporary and because it's on that side of town, the rent will be less since it's not exactly the most desirable location." She pressed her lips together and tightened her grip on the strap as an almost grimace danced across her face so quickly, I probably imagined it.

I huffed a sardonic laugh at her dig. "And yet you insist on coming." I massaged my temples. "You know what, if it means getting you to leave, fine. I close up shop at six; meet me at six thirty."

Shoving the door open, I exited the lobby before she could say anything else. I kept walking out the bay and around to the back of the building to take a minute. I pressed against the brick wall and leaned forward, resting my forearms on my thighs. What did I do to deserve this much frustration in my life? I could not understand why the universe seemed so fucking intent on punishing me with the likes of Irene Johnson.

A low groan rumbled in the back of my throat when the sound of heel clicks echoed in my ears. "What else is it, Irene?"

She stopped short as I pushed myself to standing. "Are you okay?"

Her face registered a shock, and near concern, and that's how I knew I was stressed beyond belief if I actually thought she'd be concerned about anything to do with me. I pressed my fingers to the corner of my eye in hopes of stopping the twitching. Having to figure out the shit with my dad was enough; compound that with Irene Has-To-Get-Her-Way Johnson and I was close to losing the razor thin bit of patience and civility I struggled to hold on to.

"I'm fine. Did you need anything else?"

She shifted and adjusted her oversized bag on her arm and stepped closer. "Um, sorry. You just look a little stressed."

I cocked my head to the side and arched a brow. "You don't say."

She crossed her arms, the action pushing her breasts

upward so the rounded tops peeked out over the top of her dress. "I mean other than the prospect of being an unwilling landlord."

I cracked my neck. "I'm good. What did you need?"

She stepped closer, placing a hand on my shoulder, and gently rubbed her thumb back and forth. The move was unexpected, yet oddly comforting. "Are you sure you're okay?" Her tone was soft, soothing in a way that made me want to lean in for more.

The deep breath I pulled in was a mistake as it filled my senses with that damn perfume. The distractingly distinctive smell which seemed to linger long after she'd gone. Tormenting me with things I shouldn't want but craved all the same. Looking into her eyes and seeing something that almost mimicked true concern nearly did me in.

She'd caught me at a rare moment of weakness, and that fact unsettled me to my core. I inched away and rolled my shoulders back. "Yeah. Did you need something?"

Her face fell and she pressed her lips together and cleared her throat. "The address. I don't actually know where you live."

"Right. You have something to write on in that bag of yours?"

She dug around for a few minutes before pulling out another business card and a pen. I scribbled down the location and handed it back to her. I shouldn't have been surprised with how pleased she looked with herself. She never managed to leave me be in high school, and it seemed not much had changed.

14

REMI

PART OF ME HOPED SHE WOULDN'T SHOW UP. AFTER IRENE had left the shop, I'd been kicking myself for not standing my ground. There was no reason I needed to rent to her. I still had no idea why she'd been so damned insistent, but I had no doubt that once she saw the apartment was beneath her high standards she'd go on about her way. *I needed her to go about her way.*

Axle's ears perked up. Moments later the sound of a car door closing rang out. So much for not showing up.

"Well, boy, it's going to take a lot of Rocky Road this evening," I grumbled.

The lazy beast had no concern for my plight as he stretched to reposition himself on the couch. The piercing sound of my doorbell rang out, and I mentally prepared myself to deal with my unfortunate prospective tenant.

When I opened the door, she pulled her glossy, pink-tinted lips into a too-wide smile. She certainly took great pleasure in getting on my nerves. And looked too damn good while doing so.

"Hello again. I'm all ready for my tour."

"I'm sure you are." Axle jumped up and trotted over to the door, sniffing at the interloper on my porch. To my surprise, she actually kneeled down to pet him.

"He really is a sweet boy, isn't he?" She glanced up. "Why are you frowning at me?"

"Didn't expect you to actually touch my dog."

"Isn't that what you're supposed to do with animals?"

"For most people, yes."

She rose gracefully, with a soft smirk on her face. "I told you before, I liked pets."

"Yes, you did. But I thought that was in a 'they're cute from a distance' way."

"Well, take that as lesson one."

"For?"

"Getting to know me. I know you have your opinions, but I'd say some of them are wrong."

"And your opinions about me? Am I also wrong about those?"

She paused. "You'd be surprised to know what I really thought about you."

"I'm pretty sure I know."

Like the night at Cynthia's house, she eyed me up and down before a sly smile once again graced her full lips. "I'm pretty sure you don't."

We stood in a stare-off, and I debated on whether I wanted to keep going down this path. There was something with her, but I couldn't put my finger on what. And I wasn't sure I wanted or needed to expend the energy trying to figure it out.

Disappointed he was no longer getting attention, Axle left us and went back to his spot on the couch.

Irene glanced over my shoulder before returning her attention to me. "Are you going to invite me in?"

"Uh...no." I slipped my slides on and stepped out, forcing her to move back. Though not by much.

"Not even going to offer me a water? Try to sweeten the deal to sell the place?"

I chuckled low. "No. If I recall, you came to me. I would rather not rent to you, but I don't trust you not to file some sort of complaint somewhere over made-up discrimination bullshit. So, I'm not trying to sweeten anything. I'm pretty sure you and your other half won't want to move in."

She pressed her lips together and spun the ring around her finger so the diamond faced her palm. She was really too much with that damn thing.

"It'll just be me."

Interesting. I briefly wondered about who left who, but I wasn't about to ask. It was her business, and I was not her shoulder to cry on. Instead, I shrugged and headed down the steps with her close behind me. We didn't make it far before my phone alarm went off.

"Shit. Give me a sec, I need to go help my dad."

"Is everything okay?"

"He fell," I called back over my shoulder. It took me a few to realize she'd followed me. "What are you doing?"

Her long strides kept up easily with my shorter ones. "You said he fell, which means he might be injured."

Of all the people that would be around and find out about Pop, it was her. I did my best to keep his illness on a need-to-know basis. I'd even found him a specialist in Savannah. Doc Johnson was capable, but this was my dad, the only parent I had, and I needed to do everything in my power to keep him around for as long as possible, despite the rocky nature of our relationship.

Irene remained hot on my heels as I entered my childhood home. "You don't need to be here. I can handle it. Pop?"

She didn't stop and stayed in step with me. "I'm a doctor, Remi. I can help."

I had no time to fight with her. She followed me into the house and down the hall toward his room. I found him trying to pull himself back up, but since he'd refused his meds all day his tremors were worse which meant he couldn't keep a grip on the handrail. Irene went to the left to take that arm, while I put the other around my neck and she helped me get him back onto the bed.

"What happened? Are you hurt?"

"Who's dis?" he questioned, keeping his attention on Irene, who picked up his overturned walker near the foot of the bed.

She flashed him a gentle smile and thrust her hand forward. "Irene Johnson."

He grinned back, covering her hand with both of his shaky ones. "Johnson. Johnson. As in Doc Johnson?"

"Yes, sir."

"He still driving that Lincoln? Whew, that thang was pretty."

She glanced at me, and I slowly shook my head.

"No, sir. Not anymore."

"Huh. Damn shame. I loved working on that car."

"Pop, are you okay? How's your hip? And how did your walker get so far away?"

He finally released her hand and frowned at me. "I told you I don't need that damn thang."

"You hittin' the floor because you're being stubborn proves otherwise," I shot back.

"Watch your tone. You actin' up, and in front of company."

I pinched the bridge of my nose and took in a steady breath.

"Mr. Martin, can you lay back for me? I just want to do a

quick check if you don't mind." She spoke softly to him, with a pleasant, almost genuine smile on her face.

"Nope. I don't mind at all. And a gal as pretty as you can call me Red." He again grinned wide as she helped him slide back onto the bed.

Clearly, in a past life I'd fucked up and it was coming back to bite me in the ass now. My ailing father who spent more time pouting and being a cranky old man was attempting to turn on the charm before my very eyes, and with Irene-fucking-Johnson of all people. He wasn't arguing or fussing about not needing care. He'd given both my aunt and his nurse hell all day, and here he was being compliant.

Rocky Road with extra marshmallows. That's what I was going to need at the end of the night after dealing with both of them. I settled into the chair by the window while she did a cursory check of his side. He winced a few times but assured her it was nothing. I had to admit, despite her normal attitude of superiority, Irene put on a wonderful bedside manner. She spoke kindly, smiled, joked around, and was surprisingly gentle with him. There wasn't a hint of condescension to be found in her tone or body language. She even managed to get him to take the meds he'd refused all day.

"So, you and my girl?"

I perked up at that question. "No."

"Why not? She's pretty. Nice. A doctor. All in all, I'd say she's a catch."

She had the nerve to look at me, and the smug smile that was her norm pulled across her lips. "Thank you, Mr. Martin. I am a catch."

I pushed out of the chair. "She's been caught, Pop. Are you good now?"

He hit the button on the side to raise the electric bed. "Yes. I'm going to the living room to watch the game. You and your girlfriend can stay if you like."

I considered correcting him, but he was calm and not agitated so I let it go. "We're good. But let me help you to the living room before we leave."

"Irene can help me."

She held out her hand toward him. "I'd be happy to."

What twilight zone was I in? Irene grabbed his walker, and the two of them headed out of the room with me being left behind. After she'd gotten him settled, she joined me outside on the porch.

"You still want to see the rental?"

"Yes."

I nodded as I gripped the railing and pulled myself up to standing. We walked side by side for the short span back to my house.

"Parkinson's?"

I gave a curt nod.

"When was he diagnosed?"

I briefly debated on not answering, but there was no longer a reason to be evasive. "About six years ago." I blew out a breath when we stopped outside the door of the apartment. "Thank you. For helping with him. But I need to get something straight, whatever issue you have with me, he's not a part of. Am I clear?"

Her eyes went wide. "I would never... Taking care of a loved one isn't easy. And I commend you. Honestly. I remember when Cynthia was taking care of her aunt. Do you have any help?"

"My aunt. Sometimes Ms. Charles, and a nurse comes twice a week. But outside of that, my business is mine."

"Have you thought about—"

"Look," I snapped, cutting her off. "I appreciate your help, but the rest is not your concern."

She put her hands up in defense. "Sorry. I wasn't trying to...sorry."

"Okay."

"Okay. And you're welcome." A smirk pulled at her lips again. "So, you're not immune."

"To?"

"The whole parents being in your dating life."

I huffed a laugh. That was a swerve, but I'd take it if it meant not having to discuss my father's condition or his care with her. "Actually, normally he never asks, but he's not quite himself."

"Then what you're saying is, I should read a lot into him calling me your girlfriend?"

I frowned and shook my head. "No. That's the furthest thing from what I'm saying." I unlocked the door and stepped to the side to let her walk ahead. "And why would you want to, anyway? Nope, scratch that, never mind, there are a multitude of reasons why we don't need to have this conversation." I held my arm out, indicating she should go inside.

Only she didn't. Not completely anyway. Instead, she moved into the small space of the opening, once again crowding me. "I wouldn't say multitude."

I scrubbed my hands down my face and tried my best to ignore the warm vanilla scent coming from her. She smelled delicious, like a sugar cookie, which was tapping into my sweet tooth on more than one level. "Irene, what do you want from me? Like, what is all this? You insisting on trying to rent from me? The fact you're trying to push whatever conversation because of an off-the-cuff comment from my father. What do you want, Irene?"

She bit the corner of her lip before a slow grin spread across her face. "To be friends."

15

IRENE

I WASN'T SURE IF I SHOULD HAVE BEEN AMUSED OR offended by the look of shock—horror possibly—that took over Remi's face. I shoved my hands into my pockets to keep from reaching out to touch her. Our proximity set off flutters in my stomach. I was thankful for the ruffled fold of my romper, it hopefully hid how my nipples hardened under her gaze.

"Why do we need to be friends?"

I crossed my arms and regarded the woman in front of me. Having met her father, the intense eyes I enjoyed looking at I now knew came from him. I wondered if her defined cheekbones came from her mother. Who was her mother? When they'd moved here, it'd been only her and her dad.

I made a mental note to ask Regina or Cynthia about it covertly. They hung out, so maybe Remi had confided in them. "Because you're friends with my friends. We'll be seeing more of each other. Don't you think putting our differences aside and starting fresh would make sense?"

The scrunch of her brows deepened before a half-smile replaced the grimace and she shook her head then turned to walk up the stairs to the apartment. I probably should have kept my eyes down, but I didn't and was rewarded with a nice view of her ass as the material of her fitted black joggers stretched with her movements.

The narrow passageway reminded me of the steps to reach Cynthia's owner's suite at her B&B. When I got to the top, I pressed my lips together as I looked around. It was bright, thanks to the two windows on the side wall and the sliding door at the front, which led out to the balcony. That was a nice feature to have, a place I could sit out in the morning and have a cup of coffee. And I had to admit, the view wasn't terrible.

The neighborhood I'd imagined as a teen was nothing like the one I'd driven through to get to Remi's house. It wasn't as tree lined and suburban feeling like most of the town, but it was still cozy. The houses may have been closer together, but they were all well-kept and colorful. They reminded me of the homes I'd admired in New Orleans.

"As you can see, it's not huge," Remi stated, interrupting my thoughts. "Open concept area with your living room and kitchen." She moved toward the door against the far wall. "Your bathroom, and it has a stack washer/dryer."

She stepped out of the way when I moved closer to take a peek inside. It was small in comparison to the one I had in New York, or hell, even the guest bath at my parents' house. But it was also nicely appointed. The walk-in shower had tan tiles with a blue mosaic accent band. The sink vanity was the same light gray as the kitchen cabinets, and I appreciated that there was storage, even if it was minimal.

Could I really downsize this much?

"Bedroom?" I asked, pointing at doors across from the staircase.

Remi nodded. "There's actually two." She stopped and

looked me up and down. "Though for you, I suspect the second will act as a closet."

The rooms were about equal size, but she was correct that one needed to be my closet because the ones included were decent for the average person's wardrobe. I had no shame in admitting mine was anything but average sized. And I would still need to pare down or put some in storage to make it fit.

"Would you mind me putting in a closet system?"

Remi crossed her arms and leaned against the doorframe. "You're really considering movin' in?" The shock in her tone couldn't be missed.

I adjusted my purse on my shoulder. "Yes. I mean the space is small, and a little simple. But with some decor, a bit of color on the walls, I can make it work."

She blew out a slow breath and rolled her neck from side to side. "I do not understand why you're so insistent on this."

"And I don't understand why you're so insistent on not renting to me. Honestly, are you in the position where you can turn down guaranteed money?"

Remi didn't speak. She didn't have to. I wanted to swallow the words back no sooner than they'd jumped free. I knew she saw me as the spoiled rich bitch, and my comment played right into the persona. Yet the follow-up apology that I knew I needed to speak wasn't as forthcoming.

"You've insulted my neighborhood, yet insisted on viewing my property. Then you imply I somehow need your money as if I should be grateful you're being so generous and playing some sort of savior. And you had the nerve to say you wanted to be friends. No thanks. I'm good." She didn't yell; hell, she didn't even come across as angry. But the even keel of her voice had the ability to cut deeper than I'd have thought possible.

She turned and exited the room, heading down the steps and leaving me to deal with the foot I'd stuck in my mouth. I took a few calming breaths and mentally ran through a list of things I could say. When I got downstairs, I expected to find Remi waiting for me, but she wasn't. I closed the door then made the short walk around to her front porch. After a moment's hesitation, I knocked.

The wait seemed to be forever, and I started to think something else happened with her father. As I turned to go back down the street, she opened the door, frown firmly in place, and a large bowl of ice cream topped with mini-marshmallows in her hand.

"You're still here."

"We didn't discuss rent or deposits."

She scooped a generous spoonful of her treat into her mouth while shaking her head. "No need." She spoke around the cold dessert, blocking her mouth with the back of her hand.

"I misspoke. For that, I apologize."

Her eyebrows shot up as she took another bite. "Misspoke? Is that what you call it?"

A nervous energy hummed under my skin when faced with her unwavering scrutiny. She peered at me with a mix of disinterest and unbridled annoyance. She was blunt, unbothered, and had a way of challenging me but also putting me in the box of whom she thought I was. And I'd played the part.

I was supposed to be doing better. Why couldn't I keep my foot out of my damn mouth when I was around her? I easily slipped into what I was comfortable with. It was better, familiar, almost safe. But it was also a fucked-up way of being and a damn setback.

I sighed and rolled my tongue along my bottom lip. "No. It was rude." I sighed again. "And I'm sorry."

"Huh. That sounded painful." The dismissiveness of her tone was nails on a chalkboard.

"Do you have *any* give?"

"What do you want, brownie points for an insincere apology that you gave in hopes of getting what you want? It's like the cookies. You have to mean it, Irene."

I pressed my lips together and thought back to her comment from the first day. Not about the past, but everything to do with my attitude of the present. "You're right. I was out of line, so can I have a do-over?"

She finished the last of her ice cream. "That almost sounded sincere."

I bit the inside of my cheek and pulled in a long breath. How much did I want to fight with her? Fight for...hell, I didn't even know. The disinterest rolling off Remi reminded me of the twenty years of Derrick making me feel like my presence was in his way unless he wanted or needed something. And I was done being that person, the one always made to feel in the wrong.

I stepped closer. "You know what, Remi, for a woman who claims she doesn't hold a grudge, you are pretty un-fuck-ing-moving at every damn misstep. You're not the only one going through shit. Did you ever stop to consider that? Yes, what I said was wrong, and I apologize. Sincerely. I know I stuck my foot in my mouth. But you...you aren't perfect, either, Remi."

A weight settled in my stomach, and I needed to rethink and recoup. She stared at me, blinking slowly. Her lack of words was almost as bad as her giving me hell.

She set her bowl on the console table and wiped at her mouth. Her eyes narrowed as she tilted her chin up to glare at me. "I never claimed to be perfect. I'm a simple woman tryin' to live my life. That's it. That's all I've ever tried to do. And yet you... Why can't you just leave me to it? What do you want, Irene?"

I swallowed hard, my mouth suddenly dry. We'd been here before. Her daring me. Taunting me. My heart rate increased, and a low buzz started in my ears. The warmth surging through my body had little to do with the temperature. I sank my teeth into my bottom lip trying to formulate words. My attention focused on her mouth, and I wanted nothing more than to know what it'd be like to kiss her in that moment. Just like the day in the gym. And like that day, I couldn't make myself act. And even if I could have, the energy wafting off her told me I shouldn't.

A smirk pulled her lips to the side, and she shook her head while stepping back. She picked up her bowl, placed her hand on the knob of the door, and started to close it, but I stuck my hand out to stop her.

I took in a breath and forced myself not to flee like last time I'd been faced with this scenario. "What I want, Remi, is for you to give me half a chance." I released the door. "I'll go. Thank you for taking time out of your day to show me the place. And I hope your dad is okay." I quickly retreated to my car before I acted on an impulse that would surely backfire.

❧ 16 ❧

REMI

I PARKED MY '82 FIREBIRD NEXT TO THE DISABLED AUDI.
Axle hopped out of the car and trotted beside me as I headed
for my shop. It'd been two days since I'd had the run-in with
Irene. Two days since she'd basically cussed me out as she'd
stood on my porch because I wouldn't give her a pass on her
shitty comment. *A comment that reminded me of why I needed to
keep her at a distance.*

It had nothing to do with me holding a grudge and everything with me believing who she'd shown herself to be over
the years. However, her reaction...it'd been unexpected. She'd
been more than angry; she'd almost come across as upset. It'd
been the same sort of change when she'd stated she'd be
moving in alone. *Give her half a chance.*

I couldn't figure Irene out, and that unnerved me. Especially with the ill-conceived attraction, which was taking on a
life of its own. I knew how to deal with stuck-up Irene. But
the pseudo-flirty, wants to be friends, and compassionate
Irene? Her, I needed to be worried about.

Axle made a beeline for my office as I turned on lights
and fired up the computers for the day. As I went about

getting the rest of the stuff set up, my thoughts went to my father, who had asked when my "girlfriend" was stopping by again. I'd had to shut down the talk, especially with Aunt Ev. The absolute last thing I needed was for her to be talking to any of her friends and hinting at the wrong thing. Rumors flew too easily in this damn town as it was, and I'd already had my fair share of being at the center.

Once the guys arrived, we set about dealing with the appointments we had. New brakes for Pastor Jenkins' Cadillac. An oil change for MJ, new tires for the Hendersons, a new couple that moved to town a few months ago. The husband was starting up some sort of charter boat business.

"Hey, Boss, there's a guy out by the Audi," Devon said.

I stepped around the car I was working on to peer out the window. Sure enough, there was a light-skinned man standing out by Irene's car.

"You think she's finally having it picked up?" Tony asked.

I pulled the rag from my back pocket and wiped my hands. "She didn't call, but let me go check."

The stranger didn't look like a service tech, not dressed in the light blue button-down short-sleeve shirt paired with tan dress shorts and a pair of expensive-looking loafers on his feet.

"Can I help you?"

He paused his phone conversation to give me a dismissive once-over. "Go fetch your manager." He turned his back to me and started walking around the car. "Sometime today," he ordered when he noticed me again.

"I'm all you got. So, what can I do for you?"

He glared at me with light brown eyes, his shockingly well-manicured brows pulled into a deep V. "Let me call you back." He ended his call and the silver watch on his wrist caught the sun when he shoved the device into his pocket. "I'm sure you're adequate at whatever you do here, but I need to speak with your boss." He pointed at the Audi. "That car requires specialized care. Not something any old country mechanic can do. I need to see what has been done to my car to make sure you people didn't fuck it up. Then I'm taking it."

I stared up at the tall man who was trying to use his size as an intimidation tactic. He stood legs wide, and arms crossed with a scowl on his face. The man behind the rock on her finger. In the few minutes I interacted with him, I understood why she was moving alone. He was a pompous ass.

"Hey, Boss, all good? Devon yelled.

I kept my eyes on the dick in front of me when I answered, "All good. He was just leaving." Realization skirted across his face. "The building behind me bears my name. Now, you can get the hell off my property because the only person I'm releasing that car to is the one who dropped it off."

"Like hell. I'm the registered owner."

"My dude, I don't know you from Adam, so if you want that car, bring back the person who was driving it. Until then, leave before I call the sheriff to have you removed."

He stepped closer, the frown on his face deepening. "You can't do that."

I tilted my chin up and glared back at him. "Do you often go around telling people what they can and can't do just because you don't like what you hear?"

"Only when they're in the wrong. Which they frequently are," he scoffed.

I laughed quietly to myself and shook my head. The nerve of him. I would have almost said he and Irene were made for each other, but damn, I wouldn't wish this man on anyone. *You aren't the only one going through shit.* Irene's comment popped into my head along with every time her demeanor changed at the mention of her husband. If he talked to her like he was to me, I was glad she was moving.

What the hell? I didn't give myself time to process the meaning of the thought and turned my irritation on the man in front of me.

"I enjoy being the bearer of your bad news, but you're standing on private property, and I've told you to leave. So, regardless of what you think, you need to get back in your vehicle and go."

He looked past me to the garage, and I turned to see both Tony and Devon standing at the entrance, watching our interaction. He seemed to have some sort of internal debate before he stepped back and put his hands up.

A creepy smile stretched across his face, and he relaxed his posture. "We got off on the wrong foot. Let's try this again. Since you obviously know my wife, why don't you call her to come clear up this misunderstanding?"

It was too late for his fake with honey approach after he started out spitting vinegar. "How about you get in your car and leave. You and your wife can work out whatever you need to work out, and then you two come back once it's sorted."

Normally, I had no problem trying to be accommodating, especially to customers, but this man rubbed me the whole wrong way. He was an entitled dick and overall jackass, and I was not inclined to do any sort of compromise that didn't involve him leaving my property immediately.

He stared at me for a moment then looked over at the guys again before he pulled a pair of sunglasses from his shirt pocket and situated them onto his face. "Fine. I'll be back with Irene shortly."

"You do that."

I stood my ground, forcing him to walk around me to what I suspected was his rental car. I stayed there, watching until he backed out and drove off the lot.

"What was that all about?" Devon asked.

"I think that was Irene's husband."

"Oh, okay. Are you going to give her a call as a heads-up? Because that man didn't seem friendly."

I glanced back to the parking lot. No, he didn't seem friendly at all. I hadn't been around a lot of couples in the middle of a possible divorce, but it didn't take firsthand knowledge to know if he came here trying to take the car, I would put money on the fact she wasn't aware. Plenty of episodes of *Snapped* and *Law and Order* told me that.

She could do with a heads up because dealing with him in an almost ambush situation wasn't something she needed. *Why did I care?* The question gave me pause. But for as irritated as I was with Irene, I wouldn't wish that man on my worst enemy, even if she'd married him.

"Yeah, I think I left her card in my office. I'll go take care of that, and you two quit being gossip hags and get back to work."

Axle didn't even lift his head when I entered the room. I rounded the desk to retrieve her card from the top drawer. Scrawled in rather neat writing was the number I never imagined I'd ever dial.

❧ 17 ❧

IRENE

I CARRIED MY LATTE AND SCONE BACK TO MY TABLE. BEING
at the bakery was calming, and I didn't have to face my mother's all-knowing eye while I searched for rental options. They
hadn't questioned me too much on the divorce, though Mom
kept dropping hints that I might want to be sure I'd thought
things through. I had no idea why I continued to take the
heat as if the breakdown of the marriage rested solely on my
shoulders. But each time I asserted the decision wasn't made
lightly, and it was best for me to move on.

I clicked on the image of a cute bungalow near the beach.
It was homey, and I did love the sound of the ocean. But it
wasn't Remi's place. I sighed heavily, thinking about her. Sure,
I'd called her on her bullshit attitude, not that it'd done me
any favors. I couldn't figure out how not to fall into old habits
with her no matter what my intentions were. I covered my
face to muffle my groan.

She was so damn blunt and unmoving. Like she'd never
fucked up and said the wrong thing. "Of course, she doesn't
because she only calls it like she sees it," I muttered sarcasti-
cally to myself.

"Ooh, what's wrong wit' you? Over here frowning and talking to yourself." Mama Charles stood beside my chair, hands on hips and an expectant expression on her face.

My phone began vibrating before I could reply. I blinked twice, trying to figure out the number. It was local, but I didn't know whose.

"I'll let you get that," Mama Charles excused herself and I slid the green button over.

"Hello."

"Hey, Irene, it's Remi."

I tried to process the fact Remi had actually called me. The shock gave way to worry. Had something happened to my car? What other reason would make her call? It certainly wouldn't have been for a friendly chat. She'd made it perfectly clear her feelings on that. My mind raced with the possibilities.

"Are you there?"

"Yes, sorry. A little surprised. Is everything okay? Did someone back into my car or something?" There was a brief silence. "That wasn't an accusation. I'm just surprised you called and was trying to figure out why." I rushed to fill in.

"So you said. Your car is fine, but there was a man here trying to take it."

My heart rate spiked. It couldn't be him. Last time we'd talked he was still trying to deny the divorce was happening and telling me to come home. No way he flew to Georgia and didn't tell me. On top of that, he went to his car. How would he even find the damn thing?

"Did he say who he was?" I started packing up my stuff but maintained a sliver of hope that maybe just maybe he sent one of his assistants as an errand boy instead.

"Yep, said he was the registered owner."

The sliver dissipated. "Shit. Okay. Fuck, just what I need. I'm assuming you let him take it."

"Nope. First, it wasn't drivable when I towed it, and it still isn't now. Secondly, even if it were, I wouldn't have let him because his attitude pissed me off."

I paused as I digested her words. I could easily picture Derrick and how he undoubtedly spoke to her. Embarrassment bloomed at the thought of him insulting her in some way. "He's not a fan of not getting his way."

"I got that. But it was leave or be arrested for trespassing." There was a hint of humor in her tone. A smile formed as I thought about Remi going at it with Derrick. Her give-no-fucks attitude probably really pissed him off, and I would have given anything to see him be shot down.

Remi may not have been my biggest fan, but I wasn't sure what to read into her sort of being an ally against Derrick. Or if I could or should read anything into it.

"Anyway, I wanted to give you a heads-up."

"Thanks, Remi. And I mean it. Thank you."

"Don't mention it." She paused for a moment. "I hope everything's okay."

Her statement shocked me. "Thanks, Remi. And it will be."

We ended the call, and I carried my unconsumed items to the counter. My head swam and my stomach was in knots. "Hey, Regina. Can you make these to go?"

"Yeah. Sure. Everything okay? You just got here."

I shook my head and leaned in to whisper, "Not even close. Derrick is apparently in town."

She scrunched her face and pushed her lips into a frown. "For what?"

The insult of it all prickled my scalp and radiated beneath my skin like tiny shards of glass. "According to Remi, he wanted his car back."

She handed me the to-go cup and bagged up pastry. "Excuse me?"

"Uh, when I decided to do the road trip, I technically took his car." I made air quotes around the word. "We have two, but he gets all macho about the Audi, so I took it."

"Aye, I love a little petty." She high-fived me.

"Yeah, well, downside, he's here. And I assume he didn't tell me he was coming so he could sneak off with it or something, but Remi put a stop to that. However, there is only one place he'd go after that."

Her eyes went wide. "Oh. Oh, shit."

"What's happenin'? Why y'all looking like you both got caught with your hands in the cookie jar?" Mama Charles asked, resting a hip against the display case.

I laid a hand on her arm. "It's nothing. Derrick popped into town to surprise me." The excuse easily rolled off my tongue. Too easily. And I instantly got annoyed that even after everything I was willing to cover his ass.

"Hm-hm. I know surprises and I know sur-pris-es. And the two of you are acting like the latter. But I won't pry. You g'on and see your man." She gave me a quick embrace with a side dose of "you don't fool me."

On the drive to my parents' house, despite my annoyance earlier at making excuses and trying to save face with Mama Charles, I still flipped through my mental Rolodex of platitudes and plausible explanations. The latter would depend on what, if anything, he may have said to my parents. I couldn't believe he actually came here, and for that fucking car no less. He wanted to ignore I'd served him papers but was trying to snatch back his assets all the same. By the time I parked, I still hadn't donned the proper armor, but I was going to have to deal either way.

My heels echoed on the marble tiles. I squared my shoulders and headed first to the den. Empty. Next, on to Mom's favorite place, the veranda. There he was, laughing and easily shooting the breeze with my mother. Two against one, but I could do this. As if he sensed my presence, Derrick turned, and his smile faltered just enough that Mom noticed. He recovered quickly, and his snake oil salesman grin appeared on the face I once believed to be so handsome and distinguished.

"There's my lovely wife." He leaned in to kiss me when I got closer, but before I could think about my actions, I turned my head so he made contact with my cheek instead.

My mother cleared her throat. "Irene, dear, why didn't you tell us your husband was coming?"

I kept my attention on her and focused on making sure my tone remained even. "Because it seems he wanted to surprise me." I turned to face him. "Normally, he's too busy to get away, yet here he is. A most unexpected visit."

Mom stood and smoothed down the front of her dress. "I'll leave you two to discuss. Your father should be home shortly." She moved to walk past me but stopped and laid a gentle hand on my arm. "When you're done, let me know if we should set another place for dinner." With a subtle nod, she exited the room.

I stared after her retreating form. *If?* It was a little thing, but one that gave me pause all the same. Maybe she had been paying attention when I'd told her the divorce needed to happen for my sake and happiness. Was it actually possible my assertions hadn't been spoken into the void?

"What the hell was that?" he whispered harshly once she was out of earshot.

I scowled at him. "I don't know what you're talking about."

"Like hell. You wouldn't kiss me. Your mom's not-so-subtle rebuff."

"Nothing's changed, Derrick. I don't know where your lips have been, so they won't be on mine. As for my mother, I've told her we're getting divorced."

He threw his hands up and began pacing around the room. "You did what? Stop with the childish nonsense, Irene."

I sucked in a sharp breath as renewed anger burned hot and fast when he spoke that word. All thoughts of platitudes and niceties flew out the window. He wasn't even here for me; he flew in to take back his fucking car.

"Childish? Childish? You've been sticking your dick in any willing participant and you're calling me childish for not putting up with it any longer."

"Your mouth. I can tell you've been hanging around with those common friends of yours." The lip curl that accompanied his statement set my blood on fire.

He tolerated Regina and Cynthia, but to him there were never on "his level," not that I gave a shit. I wanted nothing more than to let loose a stream of expletives, but I had to remember where I was. Remember that these walls had ears even if they were out of sight.

I let out a breath, choosing to not be dragged into a sparring match with him. History had taught me it did nothing other than to fuel his belief I was dramatic and overly emotional over "nothing."

"Why are you fighting me? We ran our course, at least five years ago. There is nothing left between us. We haven't even shared the same room for two years."

He thrust a finger in my face. "That's on you."

Moving out of the bedroom had been my first major act of reclamation after I'd started therapy. Something else he'd been pissed about. Me "spreading our personal business" to a stranger. "Damn right. You couldn't keep your dick to yourself. I didn't want it anywhere near me."

He scrubbed his hands down his face. "You're throwing away the time, the investment over something as insignificant as sex. We're good together, Irene. We complement each other where it matters."

I pressed my fingertips to the corner of my eyes while taking a few deep breaths. I'd been a complacent bystander for far too long. But no more. Filing for divorce was the first step in standing my ground and reclaiming my sense of self. And he was making it easy to not want to go back, no matter how scary the thought of being on my own was. I thought about everything I'd worked on in therapy. How I wanted more. How I deserved more.

"An investment," I sighed. "Derrick, that statement alone tells me everything I need to know about the level of respect you have for me, or rather lack thereof. As if the cheating wasn't enough proof." I paused and willed the erratic beating of my heart to calm. "We weren't good together. I was good for your image. When was the last time you did anything that was important to me? When was the last time you put me and my wants and desires above your own? And to that end, when was the last time you even considered I had any?"

He started to speak, but I held up my hand to silence him. "None of it matters at this point. And for the record, sleeping with other women wasn't nothing. Getting one of them... getting one of them pregnant wasn't nothing." The last part I choked out past the emotion that threatened to clog my throat. I pressed my hand to my mouth and forced it back. "You all but celebrated when I got my diagnosis. And now... now you expect me to be okay playing stepmom to your... your love child."

A momentary softness blanketed his features before he went back to a glower. He crossed his arms and widened his stance. "I'll fight you. On everything."

I pulled out a chair and sat. Dealing with him was more exhausting than usual. And his lack of care was another knife. "You cheated. I have proof you cheated. The fidelity clause you didn't want but I held firm on means you're fighting your-self. But if you want to put your business out in the street trying to hold on to the inconsequential, by all means. I can go quietly into the night with what's owed to me. Or, I can really show you how dramatic, childish, overly emotional I can get. I will air every stitch of your dirty laundry. I have nothing to hide from anymore."

I stared at him and his odd game of chicken. We both knew he had more than money and property to lose. The image he cherished so much was also on the line. Any reply he was about to make was cut off by the clicking of my moth-er's heels and the voices of her and my father.

"Derrick, Viv said you were here." Dad greeted him with cautious regard.

His charmer smile quickly took over. "Yes. I had some time off and missed my wife."

The snort broke free before I could stop it, which drew curious stares from both men. I pushed to standing, emulating the same grace my mother put forth every day. I glanced at my father. "He missed his car. He only came to see me because Remi wouldn't let him take it." I turned my attention to Derrick. "Now, he's leaving because he has other *obligations* back in New York."

Tense silence filled the sunny room. The anxiousness clawed under my skin. Worry that he'd push the issue. That he'd say something that would further tarnish me in their eyes, because at the end of the day, I still wanted and needed the respect of my parents.

Mom walked over and placed her hand on his back, guiding Derrick toward the door. "Oh, that's too bad. But it was lovely to see you, and have a safe trip."

He stopped abruptly. "Irene?"

The bewildered and expectant expression on his face almost made me laugh. Derrick had been effectively dismissed earlier with Remi and now again with my mother. Treatment he wasn't used to being on the receiving end of, especially from women.

"There's nothing left to say, Derrick. I've made my wishes known. You've stated your opposition. Regardless, your inability to grasp the concept of fidelity is no longer my problem."

Dad stuck his hands into the pockets of his golf pants while moving closer to me. "Yes, well, as my wife said, have a safe trip."

I knew they'd want answers. Details. But I also knew they'd never get into it in front of Derrick. Image was still important to my parents. The questions would wait until we were alone. Even if they were disappointed in my failed marriage, for now we were a united front.

18

REMI

AXLE LIFTED HIS HEAD, AND HIS EARS PERKED UP. WHEN HE started barking, I peeked around the vintage Indian I was restoring to see what had him riled up. He hopped up from his spot in the garage and took off.

"What the hell?"

He was normally a good dog and not much got him excited. I set down the carburetor and picked up the rag from the floor before following after him. I rounded the corner of the detached garage to find my baby of a pit bull on his back getting belly rubs from Irene. So much for my quiet Sunday afternoon. Even if she'd been on my mind since yesterday. I'd been worried about her and that man. But here she was, seemingly unharmed, and looking as good as always.

My normal greeting sat on the tip of my tongue, but I held it back. *Not the only one going through shit.* "Good afternoon, Irene."

She stood and a small smile pulled her lips to the side. "Good afternoon, Remi." She nearly sang the words, and I suppressed an eye roll. "Sorry to drop by unannounced, but I don't have your number."

"Actually, you do."

Her perfectly groomed brows pulled together. "Oh, when you called me. I should save that." She beamed a full grin, and I kicked myself for saying anything. "But later. For today I brought you a thank-you gift. A genuine, I did it all on my own, olive branch." She held up the white grocery bag.

I took the offered package. Inside was two cartons of Rocky Road ice cream and a bag of mini marshmallows. "What's this for exactly?"

She shifted her weight. "When I was here last time, I noticed you were eating that. I would have gotten you wine or beer, but I don't know which you like."

"Neither. I don't drink."

She chewed the corner of her lip. "Huh. Well, good thing I went with the ice cream instead."

I walked past her toward my back door. "Yeah. But again why?" She followed me but stopped at the threshold. "You can come in, but I appreciate you waiting."

"Last time you didn't seem too keen on letting me inside." Irene jumped when Hemi meowed at her feet. "You have a cat, too?"

"I do. Meet Hemi. Though some days she has an identity crisis and believes she's a dog more than a cat," I answered while sticking the ice cream in the freezer then leaned against the counter.

Irene pulled a chair out, hung her purse on the back of it, and sat at my small kitchen table. Hemi weaved between her ankles, continuing to meow loudly.

"Is she okay?"

"Yeah, just a drama queen. She thinks everyone is supposed to grace her with undivided attention, but only when she wants it."

Irene tucked a strand of hair behind her ear. "So, there's hope."

"For what?"

"Me. Your cat is a drama queen. You think I'm a drama queen. But you like her, so...hope."

I shook my head and huffed a laugh. "You aren't going to drop the whole being friends thing, are you?"

She shrugged. "As you've said, I like to get my way."

And I apparently was keen to give in. I released a heavy exhale and rubbed the back of my neck. I had no idea what her deal was, and frankly, it hurt my head to try and figure out. She got up from the table to join me in the kitchen, shrinking the space with her presence. Her off-shoulder white sundress flowed with her movements which left a trail of enticing sweetness that was becoming a greater distraction the more I was around her.

Irene leaned against the counter opposite me. "But that's not why I'm here. I wanted to thank you for Derrick."

I waved her off. "Told you on the phone. He was a dick, and I wasn't inclined to be accomodatin'."

She rubbed at her left hand, and I noticed the rings were missing. "All the same, thank you. I have to fly back to work out my notice and pack. And still find a place to live." She paused to let that statement linger, and I held back a smile at her not-so-subtle nudge. "But I'll get the car moved soon."

The idea of her going back and being alone with her husband prickled under my skin. It had nothing to do with me and I shouldn't have been concerned, yet I was unsettled by the news all the same. "Is he still here?"

She shook her head. "No. I'm not sure if he flew back last night or this morning, but my mother politely kicked him out." I couldn't decipher if the sadness on her face was because he'd been kicked out or due to the status of their failing relationship.

Either way I could empathize with her situation. "Are you okay?"

Her eyes shot up to lock with mine. She pulled in a deep breath and released it slow. "Yeah. I will be."

I did a slow nod and pushed off the counter, crossing over to the sink. Irene didn't move, not even when I brushed against her to wash my hands. "Personal space. You ever hear of it?"

She did a slight side-step. "Technically, I was here first." She inched closer again. "Does being near me bother you?"

She smelled good enough to eat, and the answer to her question would have been yes, being near her bothered me more than I wanted to admit. And for all the wrong reasons.

I yanked two paper towels from the roll. "Are you trying to bother me?"

"Not presently."

"But that's an admission, at times it is your goal to bother me."

She lifted one shoulder, and the haughty smirk I knew all too well formed on her lips. I pressed my palms to my eyes.

"I'm not getting rid of you, am I?"

"You're friends with my friends."

"By default. I'm closer friends with your friends' other halves."

She tilted her head. "That's always the case with you, isn't it? Having more male friends. Is that a lesbian stud thing?"

I opened my mouth to speak but closed it again. I didn't know how to respond so all I could do was laugh. When she joined in, I paused for a moment. The sound carefree and rhythmic. I'd never heard her laugh before, and I sure as hell never expected to be sharing in the activity with her standing in my kitchen. Twilight zone indeed.

"Guess I find them less judgmental," I finally answered.

"Tell that to my soon-to-be ex," she snorted.

"There's an exception to everything."

She turned so we stood face to face. She really did have a

thing with invading my personal space. But her sweet aroma
was becoming oddly familiar. My attention went to her collarbone. Not a feature I'd normally find enticing, yet with
Irene...

She tilted her head as she walked her fingers back and
forth along the granite countertop. "How's your dad?"

The change of topic was much appreciated to keep my
mind from veering down paths it had no business going. I ran
my tongue along the front of my teeth and crossed my arms.
"Do you really care?"

She matched my stance. "Would I ask if I didn't?"

"Possibly. You are all about image and niceties."

"And you're all about bluntness and truth absolute?" She
arched a brow as if challenging me.

"You say that like it's a bad thing. I find it much easier to
say what I mean."

"I know you do. And I know your dad is...you're sensitive,
protective about him." She laid her hand on my arm, and the
contact sent electrodes of awareness zapping through me.
"Therefore, yes, I am being sincere in asking about your
father. I've been thinking about you and him and how you're
handling it all." Her tone was soft, and she stared at me with
gentle eyes.

It was the same genuine expression she'd had the day
she'd learned about Pop's condition. Friendly Irene was
enough to try and figure out. Caring Irene went against everything I'd believed to be true about the woman standing in
front of me. Maybe the breakup of her marriage was some
sort of humbling experience, or maybe I was subconsciously
more susceptible because her question tapped into my secret
desire of wanting someone to understand and care. Just never
thought that person would be Irene. But it was too much, and
I needed to trust my instincts.

I stepped away and opened the fridge. "Would you like

something to drink?" Her eyes went wide, and a large grin graced her face. "Chill. It's an offer of water or Coke. Or sweet tea."

She swayed from side to side. "But you are offering, which is inviting me to say longer, which is progress."

I stifled a sigh and chose not to say anything else. Pulling out two bottles, I popped the top on hers before handing it to her, then took a seat on my couch. Hemi waited until Irene got situated next to me before she planted herself in my guest's lap, purring.

"Does she do this to everyone?"

I took a swig of my soda and shook my head. "She seems to like you. She must recognize a fellow drama queen."

Irene ran her hand down my cat's fluffy fur, which only made her purr more. "Guess we have to stick together since the world judges us so harshly."

I regarded her for a moment but kept quiet and took another pull from my bottle.

She did the same, then patted her chest. "Woah, these are stronger than out of a can."

"Yup, which is why I like them. And my dad is fine. Had lunch with him earlier."

"A good day then?"

I shifted to the side to get a better look at her. "What do you want, Irene?"

"Why do you keep asking me that?"

"Because I feel like you're after something. You've never been this interested in spending time getting to know anything about me. Now you want to be friends and live near me. We've interacted more in the last two weeks than we have ever."

She took another drink. "I know. Or rather, I don't know. I've left my husband. Put in notice at my job. I'm trying to figure stuff...figure *me* out."

"And I'm part of this because?"

She held my gaze and I waited for her to find the right words to answer my question. Irene ran her fingers through her hair and the strands feathered down around her shoulders one by one. "I've been interested in you. Admired you for being absolutely and unapologetically you." She inched closer until our knees touched. "I'm a moth to your flame, desperately hoping for some of that freedom to live my life, my truth without hesitation or second-guessing. Like you've always done."

I massaged my temples. She gave one hell of an unexpected answer. I couldn't detect a hint of smugness. I searched her deep-brown eyes for insincerity and came up empty. *Holy shit.* Words for me were only part of the equation, but hers still landed harder than I'd ever imagined.

Life changes were hard. Breakups could be even harder. *"Give a little grace."* Something Aunt Ev was good about saying anytime I was ready to write people off. Which was the similar statement when Irene had gotten pissed when I'd shown her the apartment. I could be unmoving, didn't give people too many chances. She wasn't perfect. I sure as hell wasn't, as she'd so eloquently pointed out. There was another side to Irene Johnson, and I needed to give her a little grace to figure herself out and hope I didn't get burned in the end. *Fuck. I was really going to do this?*

"Fourteen-hundred a month."

"What?"

"That's how much the rent is for the apartment."

A radiant grin spread across her face. "You're going to rent to me?"

"You asked for half a chance. I'm giving you one. Don't make me regret it."

She squealed and threw her arms around me. The action startled both me and Hemi. "Thank you."

The passing touches we'd exchanged did little to prepare me for being embraced by her. Irene was the embodiment of all things feminine, soft and beautiful. I struggled to not breathe in too deeply for fear I'd be lost in her alluring scent.

I tightened my hand around my bottle and waited for her to let go. I *needed* her to let go before I gave in to the overwhelming and inappropriate urge to kiss her neck and find out if she tasted as sweet as I imagined. "You people sure love to hug." My voice sounded scratchy in my ears.

She let go, but didn't move. Her closeness continued to taunt me. "What's wrong with hugs?"

I slid away, creating the distance she had no interest in providing. Not that it helped as the phantom feel of her lingered on my skin. "Nothing. I'm just not use to receiving them as frequently as the group of y'all hand them out."

She moistened her lips, before drawing the corner in between her teeth. "Now that we're going to be roommates, I'll have to break you in."

"I'm sorry, what?"

"Daily hugs. So you get used to them. I feel it's only fair."

I frowned at her. "You're planning to force yourself on me daily?"

She took a drink from her bottle and lifted a shoulder. "It's only forcing if you don't want it."

I stared at her for a moment before laughter took over. "There is so much wrong with that sentence."

"Yeah, that sounded bad. What I meant—"

I held up my hand to stop her. "I get it."

"Then it's a deal?"

"I didn't say that."

"You didn't say no, either."

❧ 19 ❧

IRENE

IT WAS MY LAST NIGHT IN MADISON. TOMORROW afternoon I would be flying back to New York, to faceoff with Derrick. We hadn't spoken since his impromptu trip here to try and get his damn car back, but I suspected he was up to something. I knew he was just biding his time to come up with a way to hurt me or persuade me not to stick with my course of action.

But I'd worry about him later and not let him bring me down. I'd made progress with Remi that I could be proud about. We'd actually spent time together without me saying or doing anything to annoy her. That fact had me riding high. A sendoff with my girls would be a good way to further boost my confidence and send me on my way as a whole new woman.

I knocked twice before opening the door and popped my head in. "Hey, hey, I'm here."

"Come on in, we're in the kitchen," Regina called out.

I made my way through the living room to find my friends hanging out in Cynthia's kitchen. I went over to Marcel first to give him a quick hug. "Hey, how you doing?"

"Nothing to complain about." He smiled in Cynthia's direction. Simply being in the same room as the two of them allowed you to feel the love in the air. Touching wasn't a requirement for their displays of affection, and the little spark of envy jolted.

"Oh, I wanted to ask, when I get back do you think you can come by where I'm going to be staying and give me an idea of how much it's going to be to have a closet system put in?"

He nodded. "Sure, I can swing by and check it out. Shouldn't be too difficult."

"Thanks."

"Don't mention it. You ladies have fun. I have some wood that's calling my name outside." He placed a kiss on his wife's cheek, then exited out the side door toward his woodshop in the back.

"What's he making this time?" I asked Cynthia.

She pulled down three plates from the cabinet. "A new bench for the ice cream shop."

It didn't surprise me. Marcel was the end all be all on the island for anything relating to construction, and for good reason. The work he'd done at Cynthia's B&B and on the rebuild of Regina's bakery was a small but extraordinary example of his work. Add to that he was a total sweetheart, and it made me even more thrilled that he and Cynthia reconnected after so many years apart. Both of my friends' relationships gave me hope that my happiness was on the horizon.

"You really doing it, huh? Moving in with Remi," Regina asked, pulling me from my thoughts.

"I'm not moving in with her. She's simply going to be my landlord for a while."

"But of all the places in town you could have possibly

lived, you went to Remi," Regina pressed as she started fixing her plate.

I shook my head. "I know. I know. But when I toured it, I kinda fell in love. It's smaller, but a hell of a lot different from my norm, and that's what I want right now."

They both seemed to accept that answer. And I was being honest. I loved my material possessions, but the whole ordeal with the divorce and the years wasted had made it abundantly clear there was more I wanted out of life. Pairing down and living simply—to a degree—would help me achieve my goals.

We settled at the table, and I admired my food. Cynthia had made baked chicken, mashed potatoes, and a cold snap pea and beet salad with buttery yeast rolls. I couldn't wait to dig in then get my hands on the German chocolate cupcakes I'd spied on the counter. My favorite and something else I hadn't indulged in having for far too long.

"Damn, Cynthia, this looks delicious. I hate that Marcel is missing out."

She laughed. "Please. That man already had seconds before y'all even got here. He ain't missed nothin'."

"Oh, good. I don't feel as bad then for taking up more of your time. Both your men will be ready for me to be gone."

"Nonsense. They know better," Regina stated. "Togetherness is great, but you know absence making the heart grow fonder and all that shit."

She tried to have a blasé attitude, but both Cynthia and I knew the deal. Taking a bite into the crispy and juicy chicken was a flavor explosion on my tastebuds. Both of them were excellent cooks, while I could wield a takeout menu with precision.

After a few bites, Regina wiped her mouth and started up the conversation again. "You sure going back to New York is the right thing to do?"

I speared my fork into the vegetables on my plate and

nodded while chewing. "I don't really have a choice. I need to work out my notice at the office and pack. Well, rather, hire people to pack and ship my stuff.

"And what about Derrick?" Cynthia asked.

"What about him? It's a couple of weeks. We've been living as roommates the last few years anyway. I don't see what needs to change about that."

"You aren't worried he'll try some dumb shit?" The concern was clear in Regina's voice.

I shook my head. "Nothing physical if that's what you're worried about. He's sneaky, manipulative, like when he came down to try and whisk his car away."

"Understood," Cynthia said.

"So, if anything, he might try to make staying at the penthouse as unpleasant as possible when we have to see each other by being an absolute dick about any and everything. But I'm ready for that and nothing will persuade me to change my mind. The divorce will happen."

Silence followed after that statement. The clink of silverware against the plates. Sounds of the buzz in the distance from Marcel's saws. It gave me time to think about what Derrick might do. How he'd try and make the divorce as tedious as possible even with the prenup in place. He'd already warned me he'd not make it easy.

Regina took a long drink of her Cabernet. "Alright, Irene, it's time."

"Time for what?"

They both looked at each other briefly before she spoke again. "For us to find out what the hell's going on."

"What do you mean? I've told you everything."

"No, ma'am, you have not. I mean you did, but the heart-to-heart was hella delayed. So, we need to know what the fuck was up with that?"

I took a long drink from my wineglass and my heart began

to race. They'd told me the reckoning was coming, and I knew it would. I just didn't imagine it'd be on my last night, though I had to give them credit for waiting out so long before holding my feet to the fire. And while I knew their love and support would be unconditional, it was also unfair to them. I'd been unfair for way too long. And they knew the same and wanted to know why.

I settled back in my chair, staring at the faces of the two women I loved with all my heart. "What do you want to know?"

"The truth. You've gone through some pretty major stuff and stayed mum. For years. Make it make sense, Irene," Cynthia said.

"I just...I don't know. I don't know what to tell you."

The looks on both their faces were a mixture of shock and frustration.

"How do you not know what to say?" Regina challenged. "Tell us why you had no trust or faith in us. Because I said it before and I'll say it again, that shit hurts to know after all these years you didn't think you could, or maybe it's that you didn't want to open up to us."

Cynthia nodded in agreement. "We're just trying to understand."

Her comment cut me deep. I never imagined they'd take my silence as me not trusting them. "What? No...it's not that...I trust both of you with my life."

"But not with your trials and tribulations?" Regina countered.

A basic statement, but it knocked the wind out of me. "I'm sorry. Honestly I am." My eyes burned. "I was only trying to be who y'all expected me to be."

"I don't even know what that means," Cynthia said. "The only thing we've ever expected is for you to be you."

"I know you think that, but it's more complicated."

"How so?"

I refilled my wine, took another long drink, and searched for the words that would help them understand. "Take our family situations. Cynthia, you had the dysfunctional home life. I don't mean to say that as a put-down or anything, it's just that your folks were...are..." I let the comment hang. I may have had an almost business-like relationship with my mother, but I also knew she loved me and never regretted having me. Cynthia wasn't so lucky.

"Okay. My parents are shitty. That is no big secret." The air around us got tenser by the moment.

"I know. And in comparison, Regina, your parents were everybody's favorite. They are fun, and warm, and welcoming."

"Okay, and? What does any of this have to do with why you said jack shit all these years?"

"Because," I snapped. "By default, what was left was the well-to-do perfect family. The ones who went on trips and had the nicest cars and clothes. That's where I fit in with the two of you."

Silence stretched as they looked at each other. Both had deep frowns on their faces, and neither looked convinced by my explanation.

Regina sighed loudly and slowly tilted her head. "What in the entire hell are you talking about?"

The night was barreling downhill like a bike with no brakes. "Neither of you can understand the pressure I've been under trying to keep up with everyone's expectations of me."

"You keep saying what people expected, but what does that mean?" Cynthia asked.

I rolled my eyes and drained the last of my wine. "Exactly what I said. We all have our role to play. I was the good daughter, followed in my father's footsteps, the perfect socialite wife, y'all's constant and supportive friend. I played my roles," I yelled, the frustration finally reaching a breaking point for me. I'd just wanted to have a relaxing night with them, not get into the specifics of my chaotic and fraudulent life.

"No one is playin' any role, Irene," Regina shot back.

"Oh really? When was I going to have time for my issues when the two of you had your stuff going on? I couldn't exactly come around complaining about my shitty husband after you'd lost yours. That would have been tacky and insensitive." I whipped around to look at Cynthia. "And would you really care about me going through menopause at thirty, unable to have kids when you..."

"Irene!" Regina snapped.

A tense silence fell over the room as I stared at my friends. I tried to suck in a breath, but my chest was tight. What the hell was wrong with me? They both held a look of disbelief and hurt...and I'd done that.

"Cynthia... I didn't..."

She held up her hand and shook her head. "Uh-huh. Nope. I get you're going through a tough time, and I feel for you, but this martyr shit, that's on you. I made my choices in life. Thirty years, Irene, and the only thing we...I expected from you... Nope, never mind. You were so busy living in your head, thinking, guessing, assuming, when all you had to do was open your damn mouth. I may not have wanted children but...but that doesn't mean if that was the path you wanted and you were hit with the knowledge you couldn't, you seriously think I wouldn't have, I don't give a damn?"

"Cynthia...no, that's not what I meant."

"Really? Because that's sure as hell how it sounded. My choices were my choices. But that'd be like me trying to look at Regina sideways for having Darnell. So, what the fuck are you on with this nonsense?"

I looked to Regina for some sort of help but found none.

"Cynthia's right, we only expected you. Yes, I lost Lawrence, but that doesn't mean I would have been unsympathetic to your struggles. Situations may have been different, but one hurt doesn't outweigh the other. What's tacky and insensitive is you thinking that it would even be a question in the first place."

She didn't yell, or even sound remotely angry, unlike Cynthia, who wouldn't even look at me. I'd been wrong for what I'd said to her, and to Regina. I slid from the bar stool and grabbed my purse. "I should probably go."

The fact neither of them attempted to talk me out of it— didn't try to stop me—was proof enough I'd fucked up in a major way. I climbed into my car and squeezed the steering wheel while pulling in a few calming breaths. I glanced at the front door, hoping in vain that one of them would come to try and continue the conversation. To lead me down a path where I could apologize for all of it. Instead, I cranked up the engine and slowly backed out of Cynthia's driveway. I'd fucked up a lot of things, but I never imagined my friendships would be on the line because of my actions.

❧ 20 ❧

REMI

I DROPPED MY HEAD BACK ONTO THE SOFA AND SIGHED heavily at the sound of my doorbell. Who the hell would be stopping by without calling ahead first? When I yanked open the door, I blinked once then twice at the sight of Irene standing on my porch.

She thrust a wine bottle she held toward me. "I need an opener."

"I don't drink, remember. I can't help you."

In near slow motion she pulled in a breath then broke down in tears. *What the fuck?* "Um, Irene. It's not that serious. You can drink it tomorrow."

"They hate me," she whined.

Her comment was a switch I wasn't prepared for, but it was clear sending her away wasn't an option in her state. I stepped to the side and let her enter. Axle perked his head up to watch her crying form briefly before he readjusted on his dog bed. She plopped down onto my sofa, and I stared at her from my doorway. Why would she come here of all places to deal with whatever emotional crisis she seemed to be in the middle of? Not that it mattered. I'd let her in, so I was stuck with her for now.

"Should I call Cynthia or Regina?" I asked on my way to the kitchen to get her a paper towel.

"No. They don't want to see me because I fucked up."

Well that explained why she'd show up here. Partially. I handed her the paper towel as I sat beside her. "And how did you manage that?"

She wiped her eyes and took a few stuttered breaths. "I said some things, but they didn't come out right. I was just trying to explain why I didn't open up to them before. That it wasn't personal. That I was simply fulfilling my role in our friendship." New tears rolled down her cheeks.

"I...I don't know what that means."

She sighed. "You sound like them. People have expectations. Ideas of what I'm supposed to do. They don't understand. I tried to explain it to them. They just don't get it."

"Understand what?"

"How hard it is to be everything to everybody all the time."

"Why do you have to do that?"

"What do you mean why? That's what I was supposed to do."

"Says who?"

"Everyone sees a version of me. That's what they expected, and that's what they got."

I ran my hand over my head, trying to process what she was saying. When she'd talked about living her truth I'd thought she'd meant simplifying her life. The living up to expectations, it made no sense to me and sounded like a lot of extra hassle for no reason. "This is how you all operate?"

She played with the tissue in her hand and shook her head. "It's how I operated. They were both as appalled as you seem to be."

"Well, how did you expect them to react when they find out their long-time friend has been living a lie this whole time."

She straightened up and drew her brows together. "It's not been a lie."

"Sounds like a lie to me."

"You aren't very good at the comforting thing, are you?"

I tilted my head. "Is that why you came here?"

She shrugged then shot up from the couch and started pacing in circles. Her sudden movements made Axle sit up, and he watched her with as much confusion as I did.

I could tell she was troubled by the whole ordeal, she had to be to come here, but what she was saying didn't fully make sense. "Again, why all the cloak and dagger? It seems exhausting."

She stopped and turned to face me. "It is. But what was I supposed to do?"

"Be honest."

She glared at me, putting her hands on her slender hips. "It's not always that easy, Remi."

"Why not, Irene? I mean, what are we even discussing right now?"

If this was how she had talked with Cynthia and Regina, I could see why they'd gotten annoyed with her. She was talking in circles. On the bright side, her getting frustrated at my lack of understanding had stopped the tears. I'd never been a crier, and other people's tears tended to make me uncomfortable.

Sadness blanketed her features again. "It's all so embar-rassing. They are so together and sure of themselves. And here I was living with a man who couldn't keep his dick to himself. Who showed a lack of respect for me time after fucking time. The high life was all an illusion." She plopped back onto the sofa, sitting closer to me than before. "I pretend to be strong like Cynthia and Regina." She paused. "But inside I'm uncertain. Unsure. Both of them have dealt with so many obstacles and come out stronger on the other side. I don't know if I'm that person."

A blessed bit of clarity. "Do you want to be?"

"Yes. That's why...that's why I came home. It's why I filed for divorce from my cheating husband." She sighed and pulled the corner of her bottom lip between her teeth. "He's having a baby with his mistress. He's cheated on me for years, but even after finding out I didn't file right away because the unknown scares me. For years I took it...but the baby." New tears fell from her eyes as she spoke. "He acted like it was no big deal. And he wasn't going to tell me. I found out..."

—she let out a long breath— "I found out because she came to my office as a new patient and told me as I was verifying her preliminary health questions prior to her exam. But my years of putting on masks served me well in that moment. On the outside I held it together and made it through the entire appointment. But on the inside...on the inside she'd hit the jugular." She covered her face and started sobbing.

I sat speechless as her heart broke, and I was unable to offer up any words to make it better for her. Being cheated on, that was a pain I hadn't experienced, but as I listened to her cry, I hurt for her. I was angry for her. I didn't care what my history was with Irene, she didn't deserve the agony she was letting out. Not knowing what else to do, I slid over and put my arms around her shoulders. She latched on the minute I made contact, gripping my shirt and hanging on for dear life. I sat, continuing to hold her, running my fingers up and down the soft skin of her arms while she got it out of her system.

After a few minutes, her hard tears turned to stuttered shudders, and intermittent sniffles. "You're the first person

I've told that to," she said quietly. "I mean, they know he cheated, but not the other stuff."

She glanced up at me, her long lashes damp, eyes glazed in sadness and something inside of me constricted at the sight. Vulnerable Irene. No pretenses. No judgement. Raw and honest in her pain and I wanted to take it away.

I ran my thumb across her cheek, wiping an errant tear away. "Well, I've never been one to gossip, so they won't hear it from me."

She was quiet for a moment, and seemingly in no hurry to remove herself from my arms. And I couldn't say I was in a rush to let her go.

"I don't know who I am without filling a part. For so long, I've been the good daughter, the supportive friend, the dutiful wife." She paused and a ghost of a smile formed on her lips. "And the snobby rich girl. But I don't know if all, none, or some of those people are me. No. Correction, I do know the supportive friend is one hundred percent real. Though after tonight they may not believe it since I've held back so much from them." New tears fell, and she wiped them away.

"Regina and Cynthia are amazing women and I'm sure they will forgive your lack of vulnerability with them."

She kept a grip on my shirt. "My fear of being seen as weak, at being judged, it clouded so much."

"I'm fairly certain that's part of human nature."

"You don't seem to suffer from that infliction. I want to be like that. Like you."

I huffed a laugh. "Not to make you feel worse, but being like others, isn't that what got you here, literally crying on my shoulder. Of all people."

She nuzzled her head closer to my neck. "I like your shoulders." She slid her arm along my midsection. "And how you feel."

When her lips made contact with my skin, I jumped away.

"Okay. I think you're moving into creepy line crossing territory."

She wiped her eyes. "Why? I'm being honest." She held my gaze with her big brown eyes as she ran her tongue over her bottom lip.

I'd been getting an energy from her before that I'd worked to ignore. I'd wanted to play it off at her overzealousness at attempting a friendship, but with the way she was staring at me, I would not go there. Could not go there. I'd had my own struggles with conflicting and inappropriate thoughts so I wouldn't fault her too much. Plus, she was emotional and not thinking clearly, but none of what was in her head was even remotely a good idea.

"Look, I'm going to stop you now before you end up saying more things this evening you don't want to."

She lowered her gaze to the paper towel in her hand, twisting it tighter and tighter. "You're right. I've done enough of that." She looked up at me. "I'm not the woman you think I am."

"That's all well and good, but...whatever line of conversation you're thinking about heading down, I suggest you don't."

"How do you know what I'm about to say?"

I took slow, controlled breaths and worked to ignore the longing in her eyes. "Because it's a road I've been down before. Life changes, curiosities, whatever it is... I'm not the one. Look, we can end this now, okay. No harm, no foul. You had a fight with your friends, you're emotional over your personal life falling apart. I'm glad you seem to feel better now, and I won't hold any of this...whatever against you."

She bit the corner of her lip while nodding slowly. "You're right. I am going through a life change. I'm getting divorced and learning to be honest with myself and others...completely honest, for the first time." She leaned closer. "However, the only curiosity I have is what it would be like to kiss you. Like I said, I'm not the woman you think I am."

I let my eyes drop to her lips briefly, then slowly lifted my gaze up to her face. "That may be true, but I know the kind of woman I am."

"Which is?"

I pinched the bridge of my nose and wondered why I continued to humor her with the conversation. With agreeing to rent to her. To dealing with her at all. But instead of turning her away, I'd let her talk through her issues, and my kindness was being repaid in her come-on attempts.

But if she wanted to do this; I could do this. "I'm a woman who won't be the rebound for a person going through all those changes. You admitted it yourself, you don't know who you are, Irene. How in the hell do you expect to enter into any sort of a relationship while you are figuring that out?" I leaned forward so our faces were inches apart. "Let alone one with a *woman* who you've not even liked most of your life."

I expected her to retreat, to back off, but she didn't. We sat, staring at each other, neither apparently wanting to be the first one to blink.

Then she smiled. Slow and easy. "You make valid points. I am figuring my shit out. However, you're wrong. I've always liked you, Remi."

21

REMI

I SLID AWAY FROM HER, PUTTING MORE SPACE BETWEEN US. My ears burned hot as my heart rate increased in speed. "You could have fooled me."

She shrugged. "I fooled everybody. It's what I'm good at." She licked her lips. "It's a terrible analogy, but you know the bullshit about why boys would pull a girl's pigtails."

"You're joking right?" This was not...she was not.

"I need to apologize to you, Remi. Honestly, and sincerely apologize." She got up to walk around again. "I think I've always been trying to find my way. And with you I was jealous."

That was the last thing I expected to come out of her mouth. Irene Johnson jealous of me? That was a bigger shock than her misguided belief she had interest in me. But, like before, I had some sort of morbid curiosity on where she was going with things. "Why?"

"You were you. Despite the rumors. Or attitudes. Or the dumbasses who refused to change in front of you in gym. You were you and it made me jealous."

I stared at her, the hairs on the back of my neck prickled. She just kept going, and I needed her to stop. Whatever she was going through that had dropped her on my doorstep had completely thrown off my evening and I just wanted it over. But her comment about gym brought up memories. The snide comments. Some of the girls being over-dramatic about covering up when I'd walk in. And then there'd been Irene. She'd always seem to be deliberately there. I pushed off the couch and walked around the back of it to avoid her.

"Are you going to say anything?"

I yanked open my freezer and pulled out my tub of ice cream. Ironically, it was one she'd bought me. I stayed quiet and hoped she'd go away. Like when she'd practically run from the locker room the day I'd finally gotten tired of her always being there. Lurking.

"I'm opening up to you and you're making ice cream?"

I stopped scooping and whipped around to face her. "You're stressing me the fuck out. So, yes, ice cream. You wanted wine. I need sweets." I went back to my task, then added the marshmallows and finished it off with some chocolate sauce for good measure.

"Can I have some?"

I let my head hang for a moment then blew out a breath as I pulled down a second bowl. She entered my small galley kitchen, making the space even tighter given the circumstances. She quietly thanked me when I handed her the bowl but didn't move when I went to rinse off the scooper. My arm brushed against hers, and it could have been my imagination, but she seemed to lean closer.

"I'm sorry."

"For what this time?"

"Stressing you."

I scowled at her as I dried my hands. "Are you?"

Irene didn't reply but followed me when I returned to the couch. Axle stood, gave his body a good shake, then sniffed the air.

"No," I said in his direction. "You've already had your treat."

He plopped back down, sitting and staring at me with his sad puppy eyes.

"How do you resist that face?"

"Easy, because he's spoiled rotten, and I know his eyes are a trick." I looked directly at her when I said the last part.

She diverted her attention to dig into her ice cream. The long moan she released after her bite made me tighten the grip on my bowl. I did my best to ignore her, but it was made harder to do when she slowly licked the remaining chocolate from her spoon.

"This is delicious. I don't usually eat this flavor, but I might be a convert.

In more ways than one, but I kept that thought to myself.

"I am, you know," she said after a beat.

I sighed. "You are what, Irene?"

"Sorry for stressing you. But..."

"There usually shouldn't be a 'but' after an apology."

She rolled her eyes and continued. "But I'm not sorry for finally being honest with you. And I was...*am* being honest, Remi."

I shoved another bite into my mouth, but the cold treat did nothing to cool my heated irritation. I set my bowl down and slid to the end of the cushion. "Irene, I'm going to say this as slowly as possible. You didn't come here tonight because you had some sort of epiphany about some mystical crush you think you had or have on me. You came here because you had a fight with your friends and had nowhere else to go. And interjecting yourself into my life seems to be your favorite pastime. Then and now."

She stabbed her spoon into her ice cream. "Don't do that."

"Do what? Lay out the facts?" I answered with as much frustration as she was giving off.

"Tell me what I do or don't think. Been there done that. No repeats. If you're not into me, that's one thing. But don't sit there and act like you know me. Or you know how I feel."

"You're right, Irene. I haven't the foggiest idea who you are or how you feel. And in your own damn words, neither do you. Your ass is here, right fucking now, because you came out to your friends as some sort of emotional chameleon, and they got pissed. And fucking rightly so. On top of that, let's not forget that for what, twenty fucking years you've been a pebble in my shoe with nary a nice fucking thing to say."

There weren't many people who could make me lose my cool. Most folks weren't worth the effort or energy. But the woman sitting on my couch, interrupting my night with her emotional dumping, had always managed to push my buttons. But I was usually better at hiding it.

I glared at her. My breathing was exaggerated, and unease coursed through my veins making me damn near jittery. "The only lesson you'll get from me on how the other half lives will be in regard to the side of town." I pressed my fists to my thighs in an attempt to calm myself. I'd been down that road before and wasn't looking to travel it again.

She lowered her eyes and quietly finished her treat then went to the sink to rinse out her bowl. She remained there, gripping the lip of the counter. I'd been harsh, probably harsher than I needed to be, but she needed to hear it. She was dealing with a lot, I understood, I could empathize, but I had my own feelings to consider.

Finally, she straightened and crossed her arms. "Again, I don't deny anything you've said. Could your delivery have been softer? Sure. But you don't sugar coat. At least not with me; you never have. You mean what you say and say what you mean. And I appreciate that."

I knew better than to get my hopes up that the whole ordeal was coming to an end. She was making no move to leave and had a look of absolute determination on her face. On one hand, I was flattered. I couldn't remember the last time someone pursued me so hard. On the other, my history with her and in general told me my skepticism was more than valid.

"Can I ask you a question?"

I sighed. "I don't think I could stop you."

She strolled toward me, slow and deliberate. Her dark brown eyes focused on my face, a slight smile on her lips. "Are you attracted to me?"

"What does that matter?"

"Humor me."

"That's all I've been doing since you arrived in Madison." There was a truth to that statement that shocked me. I had been giving her a lot more leeway for some reason. Maybe it was the soft spot I now had for Cynthia and Regina, or maybe it was because she did show moments of sadness which let me know there was more going on that she was trying to hide. Whatever it was, I kept inviting her in regardless of how much I protested about her.

"Remi, if you want me to leave, the best way is to be direct. Should be easy for you, right?"

"Or I could call your friends to come drag you away."

"But you won't. And the fact you refuse to answer is confirmation enough."

"I don't think it works that way."

She sat beside me. Once again too close. She reached out to touch me but stopped and instead shoved her hands between her thighs. "I did come here because I was upset. I am emotional. I am going through life changes. I am trying to find my way. But I came here. To you. Because contrary to what you believe, I actually like being around you. Always have. Even if I've admittedly had a shitty way of showing it."

She inched closer until our knees touched. The skin-to-skin contact sent a jolt through me. "There are a lot of things I'm figuring out. The fact I have the hots for you, however, is not one of them."

She didn't turn away or mix her words. Irene Johnson was fully committed to her confession of attraction. I sat back and stretched my arm along the top of my couch. "You are persistent. I give you that."

"Are you surprised? You say I like to get what I want."

My irritation crept back up. It had to be about her, always was that way. What she wanted. What she thought. I sat up, moving close 'til I was right in her face and narrowed my eyes. "And what did you imagine would happen, Irene? You'd come here, lay out this story in some sort of outburst, and I was supposed to what? Take you to bed? Fuck you senseless? What was I supposed to do with this information?"

She forced out an exacerbated sigh. "I don't know, Remi. I didn't think. None of this was planned. I just...acted." She held my gaze, refusing to back down. "Do you remember the day in the locker room? You did this. Got right up in my face."

I remembered that day. She'd been there, lurking about. Pretending not to watch me. "What about it?"

"I'd wanted something that day, but the way you'd stared at me... You'd asked me then, 'What do you want, Irene?' And I chickened out. I couldn't form the words. And I've always wondered what would have happened if I'd answered. If I'd told you then that what I'd wanted was to kiss you."

The memory of that day better formed. She'd stood there,

lips parted, chest rising and falling. And staring at me, not in her normal haughty way. She'd looked at me much like she was currently. Waiting. Wanting.

"And it's all I've thought about for so long." Her tongue darted out to moisten her lips and she released a small sigh. "I know how the other half lives, Remi." She paused and maintained eye contact with me. "It's not about that. It's about you. And only you. What would you have done if I'd said something all those years ago? Or even last week when I stood on your porch with you once again in my face, asking me what I wanted."

My hands were on her face and my lips on hers before I had time to process what I was doing. She squealed a small surprise but gripped my shoulders, pulling me closer. I kissed her hard, holding her head in place with one hand at the nape of her neck as I shoved my tongue forward into her warm and welcoming mouth.

She moaned, low and deep, which made me hungrier. Her lips were soft, and she felt good—too good against me. Irene leaned into me, chasing for a deeper contact. The delicious scent of her invaded my senses making me lightheaded, near delirious. She tasted of chocolate and hope. Of promises for wishes fulfilled. My body hummed, alive with anticipation for the first time in a long time, and the thrum of arousal pulsated between my legs.

I lost myself in her, drinking her in, but not getting enough. More, I searched for more. All that I could get. I pulled back, gasping for air. "That," I spoke in heavy pants. "And now you should go." My heart raced and alarm bells went off in my ears.

Her eyes went wide. I tried to ignore the hardened buds poking through her shirt. "Wha...Remi."

"Irene, this is me, asking you nicely, to go."

She covered her mouth with her hand, lowered her gaze, and nodded. She stood, shaky, and walked toward the door. She paused, started to speak, but turned and left.

22

IRENE

THE WEEKS SPENT IN NEW YORK WERE STRESSFUL. THE only upside to being worried about how I could repair my friendship was that my preoccupation meant I had little to no patience in dealing with Derrick. A fact that annoyed him.

I had no capacity to care about his complaints or the demands he attempted to make on me and my time. It felt amazing to give him back a modicum of the treatment I'd experienced from him. Me no longer giving a damn was a freedom like no other.

When my girls weren't on my mind, Remi was. The damn kiss. I'd built up the what-ifs in my head for so long. Imagined what would have happened if I'd acted the day in the locker room. The reality was lightyears better. Just the memory of it heated me to my core. Right up until she'd kicked me out. I'd been trying to figure out what I'd done wrong.

If ever there'd been a time I needed my girls, it was now. But with us still on the outs, I couldn't even confide in them. Not until I made things right. *An emotional chameleon.* The term Remi had called me was spot on. But with the way she'd acted last time we were together, maybe I wasn't the only one. There was an attraction between us, and it wasn't just my wishful thinking.

I parked next to my still-disabled Audi. Derrick would have had an absolute fit to see how his precious car currently looked under a heavy layer of pollen. I flipped down the visor to check my hair and makeup. After a day of travel, I was beat, but determined. I needed to make amends sooner rather than later.

Instead of entering the lobby, I followed the sounds of voices and clinking of tools to the bay area. They were all busy working but joking about. The younger one was first to notice me. He held up a finger then knocked on the hood of a car. Remi popped her head up, he spoke, and she glanced around to see me. No smile, but also no grimace. Neutral indifference. The pang of that set my nerves on edge more than they already were. But seeing her again...I'd missed her.

I waited, watching as she slowly strolled toward me. My stomach did somersaults and my mouth went dry. Three weeks since I'd seen her. Three weeks since she'd kissed me senseless. I ran my fingers along my lips, recalling the pressure of hers. Recalling the warmth of her hand tangled in my hair and the weight of her body pressed against mine. Then the ice bucket of her sending me away.

"You just love interrupting my day."

"Sorry. I didn't think about that. I just wanted to check and see if I still had a place to live or not. Considering how we left things."

She rolled her tongue along her bottom lip and did a subtle shake of her head, pulling in a long breath. "When did you want to move in?"

I worked to suppress my smile over the small victory. "My belongings are due to arrive next week."

"Next week it is then."

She turned to leave when I called out to stop her. "Remi."

MEKA JAMES

"What?"

Her clipped tone kept the question I wanted to ask her locked in my throat. "Thanks."

She nodded and continued on her way back to work. I'd hoped the time I'd been gone would have helped, but it appeared she remained as annoyed with me as she had been that night. Maybe I shouldn't have dumped all my feelings onto her. Should have chosen a better way to tell her everything. Sadly, I couldn't change it now, but since she'd still agreed to rent to me, maybe all wasn't lost.

I wouldn't have a chance to speak with Regina and Cynthia until later, and I knew that would be an even harder conversation. While I'd spoken to both women, it'd felt different. They asked questions, shared concerns, but they'd also seemed to hold back. Or it could have been in my head. The moment of truth would be seeing them in person.

Until then, I headed to my dad's office. Medicine had been his dream for at least one of his children, and I'd jumped in to fulfill when my brother decided it wasn't for him. I'd spent years questioning if medicine was truly my calling since I'd never considered anything else. However, the fact my knowledge and expertise could be possibly put to use in a more personal way, I was thinking maybe I'd taken the right path after all.

I waved to the receptionist on my way to Dad's office. The room hadn't changed much over the years. The pictures on his desk were swapped out with new ones every so often. Currently, he displayed the smiling images of my niece and nephews. I picked up the one from my niece's sixth birthday party. A party I'd missed. Being back in Madison also meant I'd be closer to them.

"There's my baby girl. Ready to get started today?" Dad's jovial voice made me jump.

"Not just yet," I laughed, putting the picture back. "Wanted to pop in and talk to you if you had a minute."

His face turned serious. "Everything okay?"

I nodded. "Yeah. It will be. Just need to get my bearings a little."

He closed his office door and pointed to the chair on the opposite side of his desk. "I have a couple of minutes before my next patient."

I'd debated on whether or not to bring this to him, but he'd been the main doctor in Madison for years. Had seen and taken care of probably every resident at some point, so I doubted I was spilling a great secret. But the guilt lingered in the back of my mind all the same.

"Is Randal Martin one of our patients?"

Dad folded his hands together on top of his desk. "He was for a while, but his daughter had his records transferred to a specialist. Why do you ask?"

"I was just curious. She's a friend, and I wanted to find a way to help her, if I could. It was just a thought."

He leaned back in his chair, rocking a bit. "I have thought about him from time to time. I don't see him around town like I used to."

That was no surprise. Between how bad Mr. Martin's tremors had been and his difficulty walking, coupled with Remi's fierce need to keep her situation private, I figured he spent a majority of his time in the house.

There was a knock on his door before his nurse, Gloria, popped her head in. "Doc, Mr. Hudson is waiting. Afternoon, Irene." She ducked out as quickly as she'd come.

Gloria had brought the practice into the twenty-first century when she was hired on. Converted all of his patient records to digital, which was something he'd fought tooth and nail. He still wasn't the biggest fan and had taken to handwriting his notes which she had to input at the end of the day. Not efficient, but a compromise they'd seemed to work out.

"Welp, sweet pea, I gotta run or Gloria will be back in here fussin' at me. I got her here, your mom at home. They keep this old guy in line."

I stood as he did. "I don't want to throw off your schedule." I leaned in to kiss his cheek.

He held onto my hand. "If you want to get more information, once you're official you can take a look at his records. Until then, you can do some research on different treatment options, therapies. However, the best way to help is ask her what she needs. I suspect the poor girl is in charge of his care, and that can be a hardship."

He left me standing in his office, and I thought about what he said. Ask Remi what she needed, knowing her she'd say nothing. She'd seemed pretty adamant on handling everything herself. I knew she held a slight distrust where I was concerned, and I couldn't fully blame her. But I wanted to change that perception.

※

I HAD SPENT my time keeping busy by doing what Dad suggested. I looked up medications, holistic therapy options. Dug into the different stages of the disease. It kept my mind off the dinner with Cynthia and Regina.

"The gang's all here," Alec greeted when he opened the door. He pulled me into a bear hug, a wide smile on his handsome face. "I'm looking forward to some girl time. Wine, ice cream, and wings. Y'all have all the fun." He led me into the kitchen where they both waited.

I tried to keep a game face on, at least in front of Alec, but inside the butterflies in my stomach were going ten rounds.

Regina planted her hands on her hips and rolled her eyes. "Don't listen to him. He was supposed to have been gone already." She tried to come across as annoyed, but a slight smile tugged at her lips.

He leaned and planted a kiss on her before pulling her into an embrace.

"I don't know why I invited his foolish self into my life."

His smile widened and he winked. "Oh, you know why."

She laughed and shook her head. "Like I said, foolishness."

"And you love every minute of it," Cynthia laughed.

Regina reached up to cup Alec's face. "I guess that's true."

He stole another quick kiss. "Alright, I'll leave you ladies to it."

"Don't go on my account. I didn't mean to get you kicked out."

"Nah, it's all good. Got plans to head over to The Shack. Meeting up with Marcel and some of the guys from the station to watch the game." He said his goodbyes, leaving us ladies behind. I gnawed on my lower lip, waiting to see who'd speak first.

Cynthia quickly hugged me. "How was your trip?"

I set the bag containing two bottles of wine on the island. I was certain Regina had plenty, but tonight I needed to just completely let go. "Good, but tiring. Thank you both for agreeing to see me."

Regina frowned. "Girl, why you say that like we cut you out or something"

I settled into one of the barstools. "'Cus we left things on such bad terms. And I know I've apologized, but I've still not felt right."

They both looked at each other, then Cynthia spoke. "You were on some bullshit, Irene." She leaned against the island, crossing her arms and twisting her lips to the side.

"I know."

"And I can't wrap my head around it fully. I mean, we all do shit. Look at my history with Marcel. I just thought we—" she gestured to herself and Regina, "—were different. Immune, I guess, to that expectation role filling you say you do."

Guilt once again had a vise grip on me. "Can I get a glass of that?" I pointed to the wine bottle.

Cynthia poured me a drink before she continued. "But I went twenty-five years actively avoiding my man so I wouldn't have to confront my feelings."

"Yup. She did," Regina agreed, which got an eye roll from Cynthia. "And I spent sixteen dipping and dodging all things that resembled a commitment."

"Glass houses and all," Cynthia said. "But that doesn't mean the hurt has gone away, because you... It'll take time."

"I know, and I'm sorry. I can't say that enough. But believe, it was never about y'all. It was always my hang up. Caring too damn much about what people thought about me. That I'd disappoint. That I'd be judged." That last part held more truth than I cared to admit.

Regina and Cynthia looked at each other, and Cyn settled onto the stool beside me. Something more was coming.

She turned to face me. "We'll move forward, heal, forgive, all that jazz. But you have to answer me one thing."

"Anything."

"Your comment. Have you been sitting in judgment all these years?" She maintained eye contact. Staring directly at me as she spoke.

I drew in a sharp breath and grabbed her hand. "Oh god no, Cynthia. Never. Not a single day. I lashed out because I went on the defense. It was wrong and a fucked-up thing to do and say. I should have never implied..." I paused. Sorry had been said, but it was more, and I couldn't find the right words to express myself.

She squeezed my hand. "Okay."

A simple word, but it was exactly the one I needed to hear.

"And Regina."

She held her hand up. "We're good. But keep your head out of your ass from now on. You hear me?"

I grinned and nodded. The anvil in my stomach disappeared, and my world seemed to right itself. Those two women meant the world to me, and I couldn't imagine a life that didn't include them. I knew I was lucky for their understanding and forgiveness, and I wouldn't make the same mistakes again.

"I want you both to know how much I appreciate you and love you. And y'all may not have known, but still, without your friendship, I wouldn't have gotten through it."

Tears burned in the back of my eyes. There'd been plenty of times their collective strength had been a source of support, and I was pissed at myself when I thought about how much better it could have been if they'd known. But the past couldn't be changed. I could only learn and grow moving forward.

Regina clapped her hands. "Okay, now that we've cleared the air, let's eat."

I loaded up with wings and refilled my glass. We settled at her table, and my world felt right again. I moaned the moment I sank my teeth into the spicy meat. It'd been a long time since I'd dined on hot wings, and I was set on enjoying each messy bite.

"Gurl, you over there sounding like you getting more than just nourishment out of those," Regina joked.

I licked the sauce from my fingers. "Don't judge me. Your girl is stressed, okay?"

"The trip to New York that bad?" Cynthia asked.

After wiping my hands, I picked up my Pinot. "Nothing more than I expected. He kept trying to plead his case, but honestly, I was so worried over y'all and Remi, I didn't have time to care about him. It was kinda freeing actually, to know that I was done, done, you know?" I inhaled deep and let it out slow. "I...um...I stayed too long. That's all that replays in my head."

Regina wrapped her hand around mine. "We all make the choices we need to at the time. There's no use in beating yourself up over it."

"Exactly. You made the decision when it was the right time for you." Cynthia gestured between herself and Regina. "We've both been there. And honestly," she huffed a small laugh, "it took something drastic to set it in motion. I lost my job. Regina...Regina had the fire. But we came out on the other side, and so will you."

Her confident words coiled around me, seeping into my heart. She spoke the truth, I knew that, but they'd also lived their lives how they'd seen fit in the years leading up to the events. They had a sense of self that I was trying to find.

"You're right. And maybe I'll be lucky like you two and find my new sexy partner."

Regina squealed. "Or a few," she said, raising her glass to clink against mine.

Cynthia cackled.

"I'm just sayin', you've had the same wandering dick for twenty years, time to go forth and sample."

I drained my glass and refilled it nearly to the brim. "Seventeen. I haven't had sex with anything not electronic in three years."

They both hollered. "Damn, you really do need to go forth and sample like Regina said."

Derrick's comment about my "common friends" popped

into my head and I guzzled more of my drink. He was wrong. They were amazing people. And genuine, unlike the crowd we'd socialized with in New York. "I love y'all."

"We love you, too," Regina replied.

Cynthia settled back against her chair with her refilled glass. "Question for you, Irene."

"Shoot." I let the word out easily, no longer worried about keeping things from them.

"What's up with you and Remi?"

My thoughts went back to my last night in Madison. I took another big gulp of wine. I briefly considered downplaying, but I dismissed it as quickly as the thought had come. I was putting it all out to them. "A lot."

Again, they exchanged looks, and Regina leaned forward. "Spill it."

"Well, after we got into it, I was upset, couldn't go home, and ended up knocking on her door."

Cynthia's eyes went wide. "You...you went to Remi?"

I nodded. "You two were rightly pissed at me, and I needed to talk. Long story short, I continued the tradition of sticking both my feet in my mouth, and then we kissed."

They collectively gasped, and Regina squeezed my hand while doing a little shimmy. "That was an unexpected development. But yas...good for you."

"Don't get too excited. She promptly kicked me out afterwards." The sting of rejection hit again.

I knew we had our issues, but I'd honestly thought progress and some sort of understanding had been made.

"What do you mean she kicked you out?" Cynthia pushed.

"Just that. We had what I thought was an amazing connection. She broke away, looking somewhat horrified, and asked me to leave."

"You know," Regina chimed in, "you two are like magnets. How when you push them together, they have an initial resistance. That's you and Remi, that current that keeps the magnets from clicking right away."

"So that explains it," Cynthia said, her voice filled with excitement.

"Explains what?"

"Yeah, what?" Regina also asked.

"I could never understand why you always gave her a hard time, but...but it makes sense now."

Cynthia and Regina exchanged a look before Regina screamed out, scaring us both. "You don't want to go ride new dick; you want to ride Remi's face."

I chewed the inside of my cheek while they both looked on, waiting for an answer. Finally, I shrugged. They screamed again, and all I could do was laugh. It was good to at least get that part out.

"Well, you have your work cut out for you," Regina said. "Remi is gonna be one tough nut to crack. Especially if you keep being a pain in her ass."

"I'm not..." I didn't finish the statement when they both gave me looks. "I'm trying, but damn if I keep just...I don't even know. I went there, and while my intention wasn't to say all the stuff I said about how I felt, it came out. And then she kissed me. Totally blew my mind, then sent me packing."

"I mean, I love you, Irene, but can you blame her?" Cynthia stated.

She wasn't wrong. I knew we had a history, and despite my best efforts, despite her declaration of taking people as they were when they were, Remi had a hard time letting me out of the box I'd placed myself in.

"What do I do?"

They looked at each other again. Regina finished off her wine, then pinned me with a hard stare. "Irene, like Cyn said, we love you, but have you thought about what you want? With her, I mean? Because you're my girl, but, Remi, she doesn't let people in easily. Hell, at times I feel like I barely know her, and that's with us interacting more. Sometimes I think she only really deals with me because I buy her affections with sugar." She stopped and laughed quietly to herself. "Look, you wanna sow your oats or whatever, you know I'm in support of that, you know I am. I'll get you set up on the best sites and shit for that. But Remi, she's not the one."

I sat back and let her words sink in. My friends, my ride or die bitches, were issuing a warning for Remi. They were standing up for her. Not really picking a side, but putting me on notice all the same. They were closer to her than I'd imagined. But then, maybe not, when thinking about what Regina, and hell, even Remi had said. Remi admitted to being closer to the men in my friends' lives. Males were less judgmental, in her opinion.

A thought formed in my head. Remi and I were more alike than she probably wanted to admit. She showed people what she wanted them to see, same as I did. Though not to appease them, but more to keep them at a distance. Like she'd done to me. It wasn't a rejection, her sending me away. She'd been in self-preservation mode. Something I knew a lot about.

"How do I win her over?"

❦ 23 ❦

REMI

WHEN I STEPPED ONTO THE PORCH OF MY FATHER'S HOUSE, the sound of laughter—*her* laughter—stopped me in my tracks. What the hell? Why was she here, uninvited, at my father's house? Slow breath in. Slow breath out. Going in annoyed wouldn't be good because I didn't want to explain to Pop or my aunt the why.

I opened the door, and there she was, sitting on the couch talking with them both as if she belonged. The woman seemingly determined to throw my laid-back life into chaos. Our eyes locked, and she sank her teeth into her bottom lip before diverting her attention. Wasn't it enough I'd still let her move in? Though, to her credit, she'd not bothered me other than the lease signing.

"How was your day, Remi?" Aunt Ev asked.

I tore my gaze away from Irene to kiss Aunt Ev's cheek. "It was good. How was yours?"

"Can't complain."

"Hey, Pop. How are you?"

"Great since my pretty new doctor stopped in to see me."

"She's not your doctor, Pop. You have one, in Savannah, who we'll be seeing tomorrow."

He frowned and grumbled. "Don't know why, when she makes house calls."

I turned my attention to Irene. "Can I speak with you?"

She had the nerve to pat my father's arm and tell him she'd be right back as if she belonged here. Or more, was really his caregiver. She stood, smoothed down the front of her tan linen pants, then followed me down the hall. Once inside, the bathroom seemed to shrink in size after the door was shut.

I'd locked myself in with her enticing scent, hypnotic eyes, and tempting lips I now had knowledge of. I pushed the distracting thoughts away while taking a step back to put as much space between us as I could.

"What are you doing here?" I kept my voice low.

"I wanted to see how your dad was doing."

I narrowed my eyes at her. "Why? I told you whatever issues you have with me, he's not part of it."

A deep frown marred her beautiful features. "And I told you I would never do that. I am genuinely concerned about your father. And you. I know how hard it can be to be in charge of caring for a loved one. I'm not his doctor, but I am a doctor. I can help. I *want* to help."

She crossed her arms, standing her ground. Irene was confusing and frustrating, and I didn't like the conflicting thoughts she inspired. I tried not to live in the past, but history kept me on the side of cautious. For a lot of things.

I stepped closer and stared up at her. "And when the novelty wears off? Once you've gotten your life in order. When you aren't living in this state of transition, then what?"

She softened her stance, the frown disappeared, and she sucked in a low but audible breath. Irene started to answer when my aunt called out, "Y'all okay back there?"

I kept my eyes on Irene. "You're overstepping," I whispered before answering my aunt. "Yeah, all good."

I started to exit, but she grabbed my wrist. "For the record, I tried to leave before you got here like I've done the other days. They kept asking me to stay a bit longer."

There was a lot to process in that statement, mainly the part about this not being the first time. No wonder Pop had been in unusually high spirits over the last week. And neither of those old folks had said a word. Nor had Irene. All of them in cahoots.

"You and your girlfriend got a house down the street to do all that," Dad grumbled when we rejoined them.

"Leave them be, you old fart," Aunt Ev scolded.

I scrubbed my hands down my face. "Conversation, Pop. That's it. And what's with the girlfriend business? You ain't cared about my dating life before."

He waved at the air and turned his lips down into a deep scowl. "Wasn't no reason. You only brought that one 'round, and she—" He stopped talking and shook his head, a forlorn look shadowing his features. "I know...I was sure you would've stuck my ass in a home first chance you got. But you didn't. You came back, gave up your life in the city to take care of me."

I glanced around the room at my father, then to my aunt, and ending on a quick look at Irene, who I wished more than ever wasn't around to hear my father's out-of-the-blue declaration. He was a man of few words, and next to none of them ever came close to anything remotely emotional. A fact that set off warning bells.

I walked over and took a seat on the couch. "Pop, what's wrong."

"Nothin'. I'm just tryin' to tell ya everybody needs somebody, Remi."

My gaze went to Irene again, who stared right back at me. What had she been filling their heads with?

Aunt Ev squeezed my hand. "I've been sayin' it can't all be on you."

"What has gotten into both of y'all? I got it handled."

My aunt held her hand out toward Irene, who tentatively stepped forward. Auntie put Irene's hand in mine and squeezed them between her two. "I know you do, but quit tryin' to do it alone." With a final tap, she slid to the front of the couch and hoisted herself to standing. "And now I need to be on my way. Irene, baby, walk me out."

Irene glanced at me, seemingly reluctant to release my hand before obediently doing as my aunt had asked.

"Guess that leaves you to fix me a plate," Pop said, eyes trained on the news as if the last few minutes hadn't happened.

As I went about my task, I took deep relaxing breaths in hopes of uncoiling the tension squeezing me like an anaconda. The oppressive weight of trying to juggle so much all the damn time bore down on me. A fact complicated by the heart-to-heart both the elders in my life had laid on me. I gave Pop his meal and Irene reentered the house just as I carried out the other two plates.

"Is this your way of inviting me to dinner?"

"I figured you invited yourself. Or he did."

"Would it be so hard for you to admit you enjoy my company?"

Pop snorted a laugh. "Good luck with that, Doc. That one frowns more than she smiles."

I glared at him. "And I wonder where I learned it."

It was strange having dinner with Irene and my father. She was relaxed. I could tell how at ease he was with her and her with him. He talked about the upcoming Formula 1 races, of which Irene had no idea but got a quick education. To my surprise, she seemed genuinely interested, asked questions, and completely engaged with him as he talked stats and favorites.

Easy smiles graced her face and I found myself being lured in by her. It was an insight, like when she'd shown up at my door upset. Was this the real woman behind the façade? After we finished our meal, she started gathering the empty plates. "What are you doing?"

"Cleaning up."

I couldn't keep the shock out of my voice. "You do dishes?"

A slow smile spread across her lips. "There are plenty of things I do."

I blinked a few times as she sashayed her ass into the kitchen.

Pop settled back in his recliner, rested his hands on his stomach, and closed his eyes. "Does she cook?"

"Who?"

"Doc."

"I don't know, Pop."

"Well, one of ya need to."

"I've been feeding myself for a long time. I'm good."

"Did the best I could."

I let out a sigh. My comment had nothing to do with my childhood and everything to do with his insistence about the relationship with Irene. But today, he seemed to be more sentimental than I ever recalled. "I know you did, Pop."

After my mom had walked out, he never spoke about her again. He'd acted as if she had never existed. We'd picked up and moved to Madison where no one knew us or her, and we'd started over. He'd been gruff, not affectionate, and wanted to know absolutely nothing about any aspects of me being female and the changes that came along with it, but he'd been there. He'd stayed. And, for the first time, I was realizing that her leaving had affected him more than he'd wanted to let on. He'd never really dated that I could recall. He'd worked and taken care of me.

I pushed to standing. "You good for the night?"

"Yeah. G'on and leave me in peace."

"Night, Mr. Martin," Irene said.

"Told you to call me Red."

"Goodnight, Red."

"See ya later, Doc."

Once outside, I stood at the bottom of the steps and let out a slow exhale.

"Are you okay?"

"Yup." I started for home with her on my heels. "You've been checking in on my father?"

"I stopped in to say hello one day, and your aunt was sweet. We got to talking, they asked me to come back, so... But I can stop, if you'd like me to."

I didn't respond. What I wanted, needed, was quiet alone time to process the new revelation, but that was the one thing I didn't see myself getting with Irene keeping in step with me all the way to my house.

"Don't you have somewhere to be?"

"Not presently."

I didn't fight it when she entered behind me. "My lucky day."

"Are you mad?"

"Nope."

She stepped in front of me, making me stop short. "You're lying."

"Excuse me?"

"I know the tone of a 'nope' like that. You're mad about me checking on your dad."

I walked around her and continued to my pantry. "Not mad." I yanked a package of cookies free. "Slightly annoyed that all three of you have been keeping stuff from me." I pulled the milk from the fridge and poured a generous glass.

Again, she parked herself in my line of sight, invading my space the same way she seemed intent to invade my life. My thoughts...

"I'm sorry. I wasn't trying to keep it from you. Honestly, I figured one of them would have told you."

I dunked my cookie, then took a big bite. "They didn't," I mumbled around it. "And why didn't you ask me before you just took it upon yourself to show up."

She moved closer. "Okay, I admit that was an overstep. But from the moment I learned about your dad and all that you're doing, I felt like I needed to make it better somehow. To be useful. Helpful. I want to make it better for you. I've been doing research, trying to find ways to help that won't interfere with his medical care. Like the walks, and dancing. Less exciting is the knowledge he shares about cars, but—"

"I'm not your charity project while you're finding yourself." I knew how to deal with the old Irene. The one that made an art of belittling. Of only seeming to care about the labels in her clothes. Caring, genuine Irene was a whole new beast attacking my lonely heart.

"Damn it, Remi. Why is it so hard to believe I care?"

I glared up at her. "What do you want, Irene? Really, what are you hoping to get out of all of this?"

"If the situation was reversed, what would you do? Would you find a way to help alleviate the strain if you could?"

"Yes."

"And you'd do so without any ulterior motives. You'd do it simply because you wanted to. Because you cared." She softened her voice on the last word.

I didn't want to answer her question. Somehow, Irene of all fucking people, had tapped into my secret wants in life. Each day it got a little harder to breathe under the weight of it all, but I handled it. She was offering up something I was scared to rely on.

She sighed and pinched the bridge of her nose. "I realized something."

"And that would be?"

She put her hand over mine. I tried to ignore her proximity. To ignore how an innocent touch set off fireworks that zapped through me hard and fast. To ignore her familiarity with me. She rubbed her warm thumb across my knuckles. "We're more alike than you want to believe. You wear a mask of your own, Remi."

"Not true."

She tightened her grip on my hand. "Bullshit. You had so much to say about me and how I acted around my friends, when you're a fucking hypocrite."

I snatched my hand free. "We are not the same. You've been friends with those women for years and lied to them."

"And what do you call what you're doing?"

"I'm not lying to anyone."

"So, Regina and Cynthia, women you also call friends, know about your father and all you do?"

I shook my head. "No. They don't ask. I don't volunteer. It's not the same. My father retired. They know that. They ask how he's doing. I say as well as can be. Not a lie spoken."

Her lips moved in a "wow" before she actually spoke the word. "Splitting hairs much. But okay. Since you don't lie, I'm asking direct. What happened with your ex?"

Great. Of all the days for my pop to locate his emotional side, it had to be when Irene was present. "What the hell does that have to do with anything?"

She crossed her arms and leaned against the counter. "I'm starting to figure you out. Whenever I don't want to answer, or would like the subject changed, I deflect. Typically, I have a bit more finesse when I do it, unlike you. But it's something else we have in common." Her signature smug grin lifted the corner of her mouth.

"I moved back to Madison to care for Pop, she didn't want to. The end." I finished off one of my cookies and grabbed for another.

"And?"

"And what?"

She inched closer. "Is it just me, or do you put up this blockade with everyone?"

I dunked another cookie. "There is no blockade, Irene. You asked. I answered."

Axle came in through his doggy door and trotted directly over to us. He sat in the space between Irene and me, glancing back and forth, waiting on one of us to pet him. She obliged first, and I was thankful for his timing. I didn't want to think about my ex or how maintaining the relationship long distance hadn't even been a consideration for her. Five years together, and she was able to quickly cut ties the moment I mentioned I'd possibly have to move back.

I massaged my neck, attempting to work out the tension growing there. Irene moved so she stood behind me. I jumped when her hands made contact with my skin. They were soft and warm and felt way too good. She applied just enough pressure to work out the kinks but not to be painful. My first instinct was to tell her to stop, but I found myself relaxing into her actions.

"Why do your father and aunt believe you're going to end up alone?" She spoke softly, and like the day at the shop, her voice was soothing. Concern laced her words and lulled me into a sense of comfort that was dangerous around her.

I leaned against the counter and released a low sigh as she continued her treatment. I didn't have the energy or desire left to attempt to deflect her prying questions. "Because I don't trust easily. At least not when it comes to relying on people." The words tumbled free with her hypnotic actions.

"Why didn't she want to move with you?"

"Who?"

"Your ex."

I reached up to grab her hand, which stopped her massage, then turned to face her. "Why do you need to know?"

Irene tilted her head. "Curiosity. You know all about my shitty ex. You're a good person, Remi. Caring, and you want to do for others. Look at what you do for your dad. How you helped Regina. Hell, even with you dealing with me. I don't understand how she could have walked away."

I stared into her beautiful brown eyes that gazed upon me expectantly. "She didn't want to move to Madison. She didn't want to have her life upset by the stresses of being a caretaker, even though I would be the one doing it. Because being with me meant the responsibility would also be part of who we were as a couple. She was quick and decisive in her decision, so we parted ways."

Irene's face registered shock, or maybe disbelief. I couldn't tell which.

"How long were you together?"

"Five years, lived together for four."

She regarded me for a moment then wrapped her arms around me.

"What are you doing?"

"It's called a hug."

"I know that, but why?"

She squeezed tighter. "Because I promised you daily hugs so you get used to them. And, more importantly, you need one. I'm sorry she hurt you, Remi."

My heart constricted. I'd never registered breaking up with Melissa as her hurting me. She'd wanted what she'd wanted, though I had been a little stunned that she hadn't even needed to think about options, I had to respect she didn't lie or pretend to be okay with the change and we slowly crumbled apart.

Irene tightened her hold on me. Like with the massage, her actions pulled me in deeper. I wrapped my arms around her and pulled our bodies closer. I briefly gave in to the longing, to the desire. I enjoyed the feel of her, her warmth, her scent. *Her.*

But Irene remained an enigma. She said all the right things, but by her own admission she'd lived her life as a chameleon of sorts. And I needed more than the physical attraction. I stepped out of her arms, trying to create some distance, but she wasn't prepared to let me go and held onto my hands.

"You ask me what I want, and the answer is simple. I want you."

"Irene."

"I meant every word I said the night you kissed me. Because that's what happened. You. Kissed. Me. Therefore I suspect some part of you wants me, too. And as long as you aren't completely shutting me down, I'm going to have hope that the lady doth protest too much."

I had kissed her and had wanted to do more, but the logical part of my brain could not fully reconcile with her unexpected declaration. And it still couldn't. Again, she looked at me with longing, with want dancing in her eyes.

"I've thought about you. And that kiss you laid on me, and wondered what I needed to do for it to happen again."

I'd been thinking about it, too. Wanted a repeat but couldn't. Whatever change was taking place between us was too new. Too risky. And I wasn't prepared to trust it. "I think it's time for you to go."

"Why are you always kicking me out?"

"Because you keep showing up." *And because it's getting harder to keep you at a distance. Because the small part of me that wants to explore what you seem to be offering grows just a bit bigger with each interaction.*

I rolled my shoulders and forced myself to ignore the disappointment clearly in her eyes. "I meant what I said that night as well, Irene. I won't be the rebound. We can be friends without the everything else."

"But what if I want the everything else?"

"Then I'd ask you why. Why now? And why me?"

I was probably making too much of everything. Over-thinking and doing what I did best by taking the cautious approach. Part of me wanted to be carefree, but I'd been burned too many times in the past.

She moved around me and headed for the door, but stopped. "Do you want me to stop checking in with your father? Because me doing that for him, is separate from what I want with you."

Again, her words were tapping into my longing. She'd taken it upon herself to check in on him. To help. And she'd done so without expectation of anything in return.

"No," I sighed. "He likes you. He'd been in a better mood because of you. So, I'll concede on that."

A pleased expression colored her features. "I do keep showing up, but you...*you* keep letting me in. And that tells me everything I need to know"

She blew me an air kiss then walked out, smirk on her face and head in the air. Irene needing to get her way, get what she wanted was something I'd witnessed plenty of. I'd been in her crosshairs before, but never like this. And never did I imagine I'd want to be.

24

IRENE

"You have entirely too much shit," Cynthia commented as she tried to shove another sundress on the rack of the closet system. Marcel had finally found time to install it last week, though I was sure my friend had made sure he'd found that time.

"I know, and this isn't even all of it." I sat in a sea of boxes. Most were unpacked and broken down, but others remained full. In theory, renting this place was a good idea, but where was I supposed to really put all my stuff? I scrubbed my hands down my face. "I'll have to ask my parents if I can store some of the overflow at their house." I paused and thought about that statement. "Never mind, I'll look into getting a storage unit. Vivian Johnson doesn't like clutter, and her own overflow wardrobe is probably filling all the excess closet space."

Cynthia laughed. "I mean, you get it honestly."

My parents wanted to see where I was staying, but I couldn't let them—especially not my mother—see it in the current condition. Old habits died hard, and in the case of putting on airs to please my mother, that one was holding strong.

Cynthia eased down beside me, groaning as she did. "Whew. We've made a dent."

"My furniture is supposed to arrive tomorrow, which is good. I'm tired of sitting on folding chairs and sleeping on a blow-up mattress."

"I bet. But you know you could have stayed with me or Gina while you waited."

I reached over to squeeze her hand. "I know, but it's kind of nice to have my own place. I haven't lived alone ever." I'd gone from my parents, to a roommate in the dorms, to living with Derrick.

"I get that. The first time I got my own place I was in heaven."

The loud rumble stole my attention and made me get up from my sea of boxes and go to the window. Pulling into the back drive was my landlord on her motorcycle. There was something sort of bad-girl sexy about that. I leaned against the window and watched as she climbed off the bike. She pulled off the helmet then ran her hand over her hair before hanging the safety device on the handlebars. I sank my teeth into my lip as she unzipped the black leather jacket, revealing the white tank top beneath.

My thoughts went back to the first time I'd seen her in that get-up. I'd been working hard to keep my eyes from tracking her every movement. She had to know how much sexy confidence she oozed. She didn't try, she just was, and it was hot.

I waited to see if she'd look up. I wanted her to. She didn't. Instead, I heard the low hum of the garage door opening, a few moments later she reappeared with her jacket over her shoulder and headed toward her house. Turning away, I meant my friend's curious stare.

"How's that going?"

I groaned on my way to the kitchen. "Like I'm chipping away at a mountain with a doll-sized chisel and hammer." I handed Cynthia a bottle of water and used my hip to close the fridge as I cracked my own open.

"That good, huh? Regina told you Remi would be a tough one."

"I know. I know. We're friendly at least. She thinks I'm using her as a rebound and I don't know how to prove I'm not. I don't know how to get her to let her guard down."

"Are you sure she hasn't? Because Remi is pretty much the definition of understated."

As soon as Cynthia asked the question, I slapped my palm against my forehead. I'd said as much before. She kept letting me in. She'd opened up about her ex. Dinner with her and her father was becoming a regular occurrence. I knew her willingly letting me help with Red had been a huge step. The door was opening. Without much fanfare or pizazz, but that's how she was.

I wouldn't lie; I desperately wanted the sex. Craved for the physical connection not just with another person, but with her. And she'd not shut down the possibility, but for all the attraction that sizzled between us when we were together, she held back. That was what I needed to figure out.

After Cynthia left, I carefully stepped around my chaos and headed into the bathroom. I looked like a hot mess. Hair in a haphazard bun on top of my head, no makeup, and my outfit... My mother would not be pleased. Floral-print sports bra and my cashmere joggers. My at-home, bedroom chill attire, and not an outfit suitable for leaving the house in. Hell, Derrick had never seen me this dressed down.

The doorbell rang, making me jump. "Hey, did you forget something?" I called out on my way down the stairs then yanked open the door. "Shit, Remi," I gasped before slamming it shut again.

My heart pounded as I yanked my hair free and frantically combed my fingers through it. She couldn't see me like this. Why was she here? All I could hear in my head was my mother, who'd never be caught out like I was currently.

Two knocks. "Irene?"

I had no time to change, to make myself look more presentable. I gripped the handle and fought the urge to run upstairs to find something, anything different to put on. She knocked again.

Swallowing past the lump in my throat, I cracked the door, doing my best to keep my body hidden. "Hey, what... what's going on?"

She narrowed her eyes, and scrunched her brows together. "Uh...is everything okay?"

I nodded quickly. "Yeah. Everything's fine. What brings you by?"

"Are you going to open the door?"

"I'm not really decent right now."

Remi maintained her look of confusion. "Oh-kay. I'll go then."

She turned to leave when I called out, "Wait. Why did you come over?" Two weeks I'd been here and not once had she knocked on my door, and the one day she does I look terrible.

"To see if you wanted to have dinner with me, just pizza, but it doesn't sound like a good time, so..."

My mind worked to process her statement. In all our interactions, I'd been the initiator. But she was inviting me... she wanted to voluntarily and purposefully spend time with me. "I like pizza."

"You seem to be in the middle of something. We can call it a raincheck."

I bit the inside of my cheek, took a big inhale, and opened the door more. "I look terrible. I'm sorry. I was unpacking and everything with Cynthia, and I didn't want you to see me like this." I gestured up and down my body to push home the point.

Her eyes roamed the length of my body before she looked at me directly. "You don't look terrible." A smile formed on her lips as she gave me another once over. "Far from it in fact. What do you like on your pizza?"

Her quick change in statement was like whiplash. "I'm good with whatever."

"Okay. Come over in an hour. I need to go check on Pop."

Wait, this wasn't another family dinner in front of the TV at her dad's? "To your place?"

She nodded slowly. "Yes."

I bit down on my bottom lip to keep myself in check. She turned and walked off and I quietly closed the door, then bolted upstairs to shower and change.

Axle was sunning himself on the small patch of grass that separated the main house from the garage apartment. On my approach, he hopped up, shook, then trotted over to catch up with me. He ducked inside via the doggie door, and I smoothed down the front of my lavender halter top, ruffled mini-dress. To me it said casual, but flirty, a good choice for a night in. Hair tamed with loose curls tumbling around my shoulders, a bit of sparkling eye shadow and my favorite lip gloss and I felt more me. I took one more calming breath before I knocked.

When she opened the door, her eyes traveled the length of my body. "You changed."

I couldn't tell if she thought it was a good thing or not. "Of course, I did. I couldn't go on our first date looking so unkempt."

She stepped to the side to allow me in. "This isn't a date. When I take you on one, you'll know."

It wasn't missed on me that she'd said when and not if. In comparison to how I'd changed, she wore the same light blue shorts and basic white T-shirt. She pulled off relaxed effortlessly. My thoughts wandered to poker night, when I'd nearly drooled at the sight of her, and I couldn't help but wonder how lethal she'd look when she was dressed up for a night out. Maybe I'd find out on that date she promised.

"Here you go," she said, holding out a wineglass.

I blinked a few times as I took it. "You bought wine? For me?"

The half-grin that I enjoyed seeing so much graced her face. "Not quite. You brought the wine the night you came over all upset. I bought an opener and a set of glasses."

With all that took place that night, I'd forgotten about the Syrah I'd brought along. "I would have been fine with your too-strong soda."

She carried two plates over to her small dinette table. "I know."

It was a little thing, but her answer blanketed me in warmth. She didn't drink, but she'd made accommodations for the fact I did. I took a sip of the bold red, letting the dark cherry notes coat my tongue. *Definition of understated.* Cynthia's accurate description rang true. Actions. Remi was a woman of few words, but her actions had meaning.

"Those are for you, though."

In the center of the table was a bouquet of roses in a glass vase. My heart did a flip. "You bought me flowers?"

"I thought you might like them."

I leaned down to sniff the gorgeous bulbs. "They're beautiful. Thank you. The last time I had flowers I bought them myself."

She frowned. "You shouldn't have to do that."

The corkscrew, flowers, and now her temporary displeasure over the fact I bought myself flowers. My earlier lamenting about her not having thawed was wrong. "Are you volunteering to buy them for me?"

She bit into her pizza, then nodded as she wiped her mouth. "I can make that happen."

I couldn't keep the smile off my face as I finally paid attention to the food before me. "Pepperoni?"

She lifted a shoulder. "I asked, you said whatever. I only like pepperoni." She took another bite but kept her eyes on me as she chewed. "You weren't unkempt."

"What?"

"Earlier. I didn't think you were unkempt. It was nice to meet Casual Irene."

I took a sip of wine and tried not to squirm in my chair. "This is a casual outfit."

"Okay. Then maybe Bummy Irene."

I ran my hand across my lap, then tucked my hair behind my ear. "I like looking my best. I wanted to look my best. For you."

She finished off her slice. "I always think you look your best."

Each of her subtle compliments and assurances were hitting me in the heart. No grand gestures, just simple truths. And coming from her, I knew they were truths. After dinner, she settled on the couch and picked up the remote.

"What do you want to watch?"

I slipped off my ballet flats and curled up on a cushion. "Dinner, flowers, and a movie. This is starting to feel more like a date."

She cut her eyes over at me. "For a woman getting out of a marriage, you're really quick to jump back into the dating game."

"Is that why you're being hesitant?"

"It's a valid concern. What is the status of your impending divorce?"

I rolled my neck, trying to work out the instantaneous tension at the mere mention. I didn't want talk of him ruining my mood, but she was concerned and deserved to know the deal. "At a standstill. He calls saying he won't sign until he gets his car back. Meanwhile, as much as I want it over, I'm hanging on to the damn thing out of pure spite."

"So, you want out, know how to make it happen, but..."

Every time he mentioned the car, I thought about getting it fixed, but never followed through. I didn't care about it, but it'd irked my soul he'd tried to be backhanded and take it.

"It's not that simple. I've always given into his ultimatums, and I don't want to do that any longer. You may not understand it, but the demand with the car is just that. With him, it's always been if I wanted something, he needed to bargain for something to benefit him. It was always a game."

"But aren't you staying in the game by doing this tug of war thing with him?"

I sighed. "Probably, but I know it won't stop with the car. Once I cave on that, I know he'll attack parts of the prenup, doing whatever he can to dwindle down what he owes me. So, the fucking Audi is my line in the sand with him."

She leaned back against the couch. "Is that the only hold up? You standing your ground to come out on top so to speak?"

I inched closer to her, draping my legs across her lap. "Yes. That's the only reason. I've been detached from that relationship for years." I grabbed her hands. I needed my words, the conviction of them to somehow seep through my skin into her so she'd understand.

She remained skeptical. I could tell by the look on her face. And I'm sure it didn't make sense from the outside looking in, but I had to do this. I had to make him see I was done with his bull, and he couldn't push me around anymore.

"The only thing I'm second-guessing are my past choices. Do you know my biggest what-if?"

"No, but I have a feeling you're about to tell me."

"You are. What if I'd been brave enough to say how I felt back then, how would my...our lives be different today?"

"Can't change the past."

"I know. But we can see what the future holds. You'd asked me why now and why you. I've harbored a thing for you, and I'm finally brave enough to act on it."

I waited on bated breath for her. To react. To say something. With the boundary she'd set, I needed her to make the first move. To let me know it was okay, that she was okay with the physical. She cupped my face, staring at me with her intense eyes, then her lips were on mine. Slow at first, almost like a tease with soft pecks and tentative movements.

I leaned into her, chasing as she retreated. I felt her smile before she slipped her tongue into my mouth. With one hand, I squeezed her bicep, with the other I wrapped my fingers around her wrist to anchor myself because I worried I'd float away with her tender care.

The tango of tongues, the simple airy scent with a small hint of spice that was her. The pressure of her lips against mine, her warm palm on the back of my neck, holding me secure as she took her time exploring my mouth. She was everything and everywhere. The world stopped and my universe became all things Remi Martin. My nipples hardened and arousal pulsed between my legs.

She trailed her fingers up my outer thigh, leaving goosebumps in her wake. My body was alive and on edge. I rocked my hips in vain, attempting to alleviate the mounting pressure. Remi pressed forward as she grabbed my ass, then pulled away.

My heart raced, my nipples ached, and my pussy begged for relief. She ran her thumb across my lips. The memory of the last time we'd kissed rushed forward.

"Are you going to ask me to leave?" I whispered.

She didn't reply. Instead, she picked up the remote and handed it to me, then adjusted so she laid her head on my chest. My breathing remained shallow, and she had to hear the erratic beating of my heart. There was no way she was unaffected, though her demeanor said otherwise. As I lazily flipped through the options, I worked to process the last few minutes. My lips still tingled, my body was heated, and my nerve endings zapped with awareness.

Remi leisurely ran her fingers up and down my leg. "I do like this dress." Her voice was low, almost sleepy like. "It shows off your very sexy legs."

"If I hadn't changed, you wouldn't be enjoying them right now."

"Hm-hm," she murmured, keeping the pattern of up, a small circle, then down again.

With her head nestled against my breasts and the weight of her body on me, coupled with her gentle touch, focusing on finding a movie was the last thing on my mind.

I rested my chin on her head and started playing with her curls, wrapping a strand around my finger then watching it bounce back into place. "You're a tease."

She laughed quietly but didn't deny the statement. "How many more Irenes do I get to meet?"

"What?"

"I've met Snobby Irene, Bitchy Irene, Emotional Irene, Caring Irene..." she let the list drop off. I hadn't realized she had labels for the many faces of me.

Eventually, her movements slowed, and her breathing evened out. She'd fallen asleep. I shut off the TV and gingerly maneuvered so I was in a more comfortable position. Hemi waited until I settled before she jumped up and curled up on the back of the couch. If I stayed, I'd look terrible in the morning, but I couldn't make myself get up and leave.

❧ 25 ❧

REMI

HEMI'S SOFT MEOWING BROKE THROUGH MY SLEEP STUPOR. I started to sit up and paused when I realized I was in my living room, and I wasn't alone. Easing up slowly, I found Irene, hair a mess, mouth open, and her chest rising and falling with easy breaths.

I'd fallen asleep on her.

It'd been a long day, but damn, the fact I went to sleep while she was still here...and she'd stayed. She'd probably be mortified, but I loved seeing her knocked out, softly snoring. I tried to make as little noise as possible as I got ready for work.

By the time I'd gotten dressed and reentered the living room, she'd changed positions to curl up with her face smooshed against the couch. I pulled a blanket from the closet and gently covered her and pressed a soft kiss to her disheveled hair, filled food bowls, then left her a note before quietly exiting my house.

The guys were already waiting for me when I arrived at the shop. "Sorry, sorry. I overslept." It drove home the fact I probably should have given one of them a key for just-in-case situations, especially with Pop's condition.

"Everything okay, Boss?" Devon asked.

"Yeah, yeah. My alarm didn't go off."

They looked at each other like they didn't believe me, but with one glare, I dared them to question any further. Once we opened, I did my best to keep busy and not think about Irene.

But she was getting harder to resist. A smile pulled at my lips at being called a tease. That wasn't my intention. I wanted her, but my reservations remained, though her words, her attempts at assurances that whatever she was after with me wasn't part of her life transition, had at least partially hit their target. I was holding out for absolutes that in the best of circumstances couldn't be guaranteed.

After lunch, we had a lull in the day, and I headed outside to the car I'd been sneaking peeks at all day. I walked around the pollen- and dirt-covered Audi. When the thing had been dropped off, she'd been so damned concerned about it being outside. But since the day her husband showed up, she'd stopped checking on it. However, it hurt my heart to see such a fine piece of machinery be neglected, despite my initial attitude toward its owner. Jacking up the front of the car, I lifted it enough to get on the dolly and slide beneath for a better look.

Irene.

The definition of irony was every interaction I'd had with the woman whose mere presence once was enough to annoy the hell out of me. But during time spent with her and getting to know the caring and sometimes funny woman behind the designer clothes and meticulous makeup, she'd wormed her way past my defenses.

She was determined and persistent in her attempts to pursue something with me. And I had to admit, being wanted was a nice feeling, and one I'd not experienced in a long time. I rolled out, squeezing my eyes shut against the bright light. When I opened them again a pair of killer legs filled my vision. Her legs. Legs that caused my fingers to tingle as I recalled stroking them as we watched whatever movie she'd put on.

As my gaze traveled upward, standing above me in a white trench coat and a smile wide on her bright-red lips was the very woman I'd been thinking about.

I stood and pulled the rag from my back pocket to wipe my hands. "What can I do for you, Carmen Sandiego?"

"Who?" She paused and laughed. "Because of the coat?"

I nodded. "Yeah, a little warm for that, don't you think?"

She shrugged and jutted her chin toward the Audi. "Are you going to fix it?"

"You didn't want me to, remember."

"Can you fix it? And that's not a knock on your abilities, but I don't know what I broke, and specialized needs and all that jazz for luxury cars, or so I was repeatedly told." She rolled her eyes on the last part, and I could only guess it had something to do with the man she was divorcing.

"I was simply doing a cursory examination. I'd need to get it up on the lift and really check before I know exactly what's wrong. But, yes, I can fix it."

"Okay. Well, if I were keeping it, I'd say do it, but I want out."

My eyes went wide at her statement. "You're letting him have it?"

She nodded. "I'm not saying that'll speed things along, but I no longer want to do the tug of war."

I blew out a breath. I didn't understand the dynamics fully, and while I thought the best way out was to just leave and be done, from what she'd explained I wasn't sure I wanted her caving to that bastard. "Is that what you really want? Because..."

"It is." She stepped closer. "Can we go to your office?"

"Why?"

"Please?"

"Sure thing."

Her shoes tapped on the linoleum as she trailed behind me, and I ignored the curious looks from Devon and Tony. I waited for her to enter then closed the door. "I'm sorry for falling asleep last night and for running out on you this morning."

"It's fine. I guess it says a lot that you were comfortable enough with me, to do both."

"You could say that. Though I figured if you stole anything I'd charge it back in your rent."

She laughed. A soft, musical sound. "I enjoyed sleeping with you." There was a playful glint in her eyes when she made that statement. "And I spent last night and most of today thinking about what you said."

"Is that why you caved on the car?"

She started untying the belt, then moved on to the buttons. "You're more important than a car." When the fabric parted, she revealed her toned body in nothing more than a delicate and intricately designed lingerie set.

"You get another Irene today."

I opened my mouth then closed it again. Dark nipples that were begging to be sucked poked out behind fabric that almost appeared to be not there. The demi cup bra lifted her small breasts, enhancing her cleavage, and the light color stood out against her smooth ebony skin. The abstract floral design around the top of the cups was mimicked at the leg of the panties.

Fuck she was exquisite.

My gaze lingered on the apex of her legs as the sheerness left nothing to the imagination. "Where are your clothes?"

She pulled her perfectly arched brows into a deep V. "That's the first thing you have to say about this?" She gestured up and down her body.

I managed to tear my eyes away and focus my attention on her face. "Sorry. My bad. I just...wasn't expecting... What do you mean another Irene?"

She moved forward in red fuck-me heels that matched the color on her lips. "Last night as you used my boobs for pillows, you asked me how many more Irenes you'd get to meet."

I nodded as fragments started coming back to me "So, this is walk out of the house with no clothes on Irene?"

She slipped the coat off and tossed it onto the chair. "Yes, but in simpler terms, meet Sexy Irene." She stopped in front of me and slowly turned, giving me a three-sixty view.

The back was as sheer as the front, and I flexed my fingers on instinct, remembering the feel of her ass in my hand. I didn't move as she unzipped my coveralls, or when she slipped her hands along my waist. She didn't move up or down, simply held me close, letting her intoxicating scent invade my senses and weaken my knees.

Irene placed a small kiss to the side of my neck. "Are you impressed?" she asked between feather-light kisses.

"Very." I forced out the word, struggling to maintain my composure.

She slowly eased the hem of my tank top up, opening and closing her fingers on my waist. "I like impressing you." She nipped at my earlobe.

I grabbed her ass, pulling her closer as she continued her downy-soft kisses along my jawline until she lightly captured my bottom lip between her teeth. She was testing every ounce of my willpower, but the first time with her would not be a quickie situation.

I sucked in a breath and tightened my grip on her butt as she journeyed a hand south. "Irene." There was a hint of warning in my tone.

She licked the spot she'd gently bitten. "Yes?"

She lightly skimmed her fingers across my pussy that was heavy with need. "You've kissed me twice now," she whispered, trailing her lips down the side of my neck. "Left me in a state of horny need." She pressed her lips to mine. Easily slipping her tongue into my mouth and wrapped a leg around mine. I held onto her ass, pressing her body against me as much as I could. The little whimper she released was a direct jolt to my pussy and I was losing the battle fast.

She stepped back. "I decided it was time to return the favor."

I stood slightly dumbfounded as she picked up her coat and resecured it.

"I'll get out of your hair. Enjoy the rest of your day." Before I could say anything, she turned on her spindly heels and strolled out of my office with an exaggerated swing of her hips.

❧ 2 6 ❧

IRENE

I HAD TO GIVE IT TO REMI, SHE HAD ONE HELL OF A POKER face. Or will power, or both. It'd been days since I'd braved her shop in nothing but my underwear and confidence and still nothing. Not even a damn kiss. She was driving me slowly batty, but at the same time I enjoyed the chase. I'd never been on that side of the pursuit, and it was fun.

But with all the flirty games aside, I felt like there was still a barrier. Some hesitation on her part even after my decision about the car. When I'd mentioned the situation to Dr. Adams, that Remi seemed to have more trust issues considering I was the one coming out of a less-than-stellar relationship, she reminded me that while I was forging ahead with this idea in my head, I didn't actually know what had gone on in Remi's life. She'd told me some, and what I'd learned was enough to give anyone pause. For all her stoic-ness, at the end of the day she kept her heart guarded. Though she had sent me flowers for my first day at work which was an amazing surprise. When the beautiful bouquet had been delivered my day had been made.

I'd thought her comment was something in passing, but I

should have known better coming from Remi. She'd said she'd give me flowers and that's what she'd done. Of course having them sent to the office meant I'd gotten quite a few questions from Dad which in turn had gotten me questions from Mom.

Which had led me to my grand plan to show her I was serious.

The familiar ding of the bell as I entered Regina's bakery always acted like a welcome home. The place where we'd spent much of our youth had always been a comfort. I inhaled deep—coffee and caramel. There were some familiar faces sitting around, and some new ones.

"Hey, Ms. Irene," Tricia, Regina's niece, greeted from behind the counter.

"Afternoon. How are you today?"

"Not bad, you need me to get Auntie?"

"If she's not busy."

She stepped to the metal swinging door and hollered for Regina. A few minutes later, my friend came out, all smiles. "Ms. Lady."

I was engulfed in her tight embrace. "Hey, I won't keep you long. I need a favor."

She tilted her head and planted her hands on her hips. "What?"

"Why you look like that? It's not a bad thing."

"Huh-uh. I'll be the judge of that."

"How hard is it for you to make Remi's cookie sandwiches?"

"Oh, you getting a sweet tooth now?"

"No, they're for her."

Her frown deepened. "What are you makin' nice for this time?"

"Nothing. I swear. This is simply a gesture of thanks. She's put up with me. Let me move into her place. I'm making friends." I smiled, but Regina's continued narrowed eyes and pursed lips told me she didn't one hundred percent believe me.

"Right. Okay. Give me a few. I think I still have the filling. How many are you buying her affections with?"

"Why do you have to say it like that?"

"Because you ain't slick, woman. You up to something and using me and my cookies to do it. Now, how many?"

"The fact that you are willing to be a co-conspirator means you approve of my choices. And six should do the trick if you can make that many."

She huffed a loud sigh. "Let me see." With a parting eye roll, she headed to the back, and I took a seat by the large picture window to wait.

I'd racked my brain trying to figure out the best way to show Remi I was serious, and my plan was the most logical. But it wouldn't hurt to have some back-up bribery just in case. With my contraband secured and another stern but loving warning, I headed to my apartment to get changed and prepare.

Remi was nothing if not a creature of habit. I made my way to her front porch and was there to greet her when she pulled into her driveway at six fifteen with Axle sitting at my side. If the cookies didn't do the trick, I hoped the mid-thigh shorts would help. She liked my legs, and I was more than happy to show them off to her.

She looked at the box in my hand and frowned. "What did you break?"

"Ouch. Why would you ask that?"

"Because you are standing on my porch with sweets in hand." She rubbed Axle on the head as she entered her house.

"I could simply be wanting to do something nice for you."

She sat on the bench by the door and pulled off her heavy work boots. "You said 'could' not am." I didn't miss the way her eyes traveled the length of my body.

"Why are you so cranky?"

"I'm not. It's just too easy to give you a hard time." The wink that followed her statement was combined with her signature grin and the embers of lust sparked to life. "How was Pop today?" she asked on the way to her bedroom.

Hemi meowed at my feet, weaving between my legs, rubbing her soft fur against me. I lingered in the foyer, tempted to walk farther in to catch a glimpse. She left the door open almost as if it were an invitation. But no. I resisted the urge. "Bad tremor day, which made him a bit moody."

"Shit. Why didn't either of you call?" She'd pulled on a T-shirt and shorts.

"I didn't want to bother you."

"He's my dad. I would rather know."

I bit the inside of my cheek. "Sorry."

She stopped in front of me. "No. It's fine. Because if anyone could handle it, it'd be you, Dr. Johnson." She smiled and held out her hand, and I realized I was still holding the box.

Something sparked in me with the use of that moniker coming from her. There was no malice or condescension in her tone.

"I appreciate the vote of confidence."

"I speak the truth. Having you around...my aunt can't always deal with him, I want you to know how much I do appreciate you for helping out."

I'd been serious about helping with her father and had set my schedule at work to allow me time to check in with him a few hours a day. We'd go on short walks; getting out of the house seemed to lift his spirits. And his change in attitude had an effect on her, so to hear her voice her gratitude. It made me excited. What I was doing mattered. And it didn't go unnoticed.

She opened the box. "Are you sure you're not trying to butter me up?"

"Okay. Maybe a little. I may or may not have told my mother I was bringing a guest for dinner tomorrow night."

She glanced at the cookie sandwiches and back up at me. "You're joking, right?"

I shook my head. She pulled one of the treats from the box and bit into it, scowl firmly on her face as she chewed.

"*Asking* me would have been nice. Because the way you said that makes me think you've already made these plans."

I winced and squeaked out, "Possibly."

She carried the box to the table, pulling another one free as she sat. "Tomorrow is Friday. I usually play poker on Friday."

Shit. I'd forgotten about that even though I'd had to turn Regina and Cynthia down for girls' night. Since everything with Derrick, Mom had been trying to make more of an effort, and I was trying to live Remi's motto of taking people as they were instead of how I thought they were. "I'm sorry. I...it slipped my mind. I'll just tell her something came up and that I'd double-booked your schedule."

My grand plan was going downhill fast. I should have asked Remi instead of springing it on her. And I should have remembered about her poker nights.

"Did you tell your mother who you were bringing to dinner?"

"Of course. Mother doesn't do surprise guests."

"And your mother. Vivian Johnson, self-proclaimed first lady of Madison Island, is okay with *me* coming to dinner?"

"She's not that...okay she's getting better. Or trying. And, yes, she's delighted to meet you."

"Yeah...somehow I doubt that."

She wasn't far off. Both Dad and I had to remind her who Remi was. And her attitude had made me cringe thinking I'd once acted the same dismissive way toward Remi. Again, I understood her hesitation. But I had told both my parents Remi was important to me and reiterated how I was living a happier life on my terms.

Remi pushed from the table, closed the box, then placed it in the fridge. "What time?"

Her question stunned me. After years of dealing with a man who couldn't be bothered even when given advanced notice, blooms of happiness unfolded in my chest. "I thought you had poker."

"I do. But I'll have to let the guys know I won't be making it. At least I'm not hosting this week."

"You'll actually come?"

"For a woman who just ambushed me into dinner with her parents, why are you sounding so shocked?"

"Because I ambushed you. And you already have plans."

She stepped closer, peering at me. "Do you want me to go?"

Why did this woman staring at me always turn me into a puddle? I shifted my weight and nodded. "Yes."

"Then what time?"

"Seven."

"Okay." She headed toward the front door to go visit with her dad, then stopped holding her hand out toward me. "You comin'?"

I hurried to catch up, still slightly shocked she wasn't as pissed as I'd imagined about me making plans for her to meet my parents. And that she'd agreed to accommodate said plans even though it meant rearranging something she already had scheduled.

I linked my fingers with hers. *The little things.*

❧ 27 ❧

REMI

"How come neither of you talked me out of this?" Neither of my furry companions bothered to acknowledge I'd spoken as they both slept on my bed.

Dinner with the Johnsons. Was I so easily swayed by a nice pair of legs, pleading brown eyes, and full lips that came bearing gifts? As I double-checked to make sure the knot in my tie was straight, I knew the answer was a hard yes. I should have asked about the dress code, but given how Irene presented herself on a daily basis and the few times I'd seen her mother, I figured it wouldn't be a T-shirt and jeans affair.

Hopefully, the plaid ankle length dress pants with matching dark blue vest and crisp white dress shirt would pass muster in the Johnson household. With one final check of my reflection, I turned off the light in my bathroom and snatched up my keys and bouquet of flowers.

"No wild parties while I'm gone," I called out over my shoulder as I exited out the back door to retrieve Irene.

She was coming out of her apartment as I crossed the small yard. I stopped short as I took in her outfit. She was a vision in white. The one-shoulder dress hugged her curves.

The large ruffle down the center started at her left breast and stopped just below her knees like an arrow pointing to the toned exposed skin beneath. *Sexy legs indeed.*

Her hair was up, showing off her delicate neck, accented with a simple gold chain that disappeared into her cleavage, and she wore matching gold teardrop earrings. To finish off the look, she wore a pair of gold heels that had to be at least six inches high. Irene Johnson was an absolutely beautiful and sophisticated woman who was used to the finer things in life and deserved them all. And I found myself wanting to give her everything she desired.

I started to speak, but she cut me off. "Wow, Remi. You look...wow." She closed the distance between us. "I've tried to imagine what dressed-up Remi would wear. And this...this is better than anything I could have come up with."

"I figured your family was more business than casual, so I broke out my Sunday best."

"You know how to make a woman drool, that's for sure." She gave me another appreciative once-over, and while I'd never cared before about her opinions on how I dressed, I was glad my choice of outfit pleased her.

Impressing people was never high on my list of priorities, but that sort of thing mattered to Irene, and I had a feeling there was more to the dinner with her parents than she was letting on. But even if it was a simple meal, I wanted at least for the night to somewhat fit into her world.

I took her hand and directed her to do a little spin. "You're one to talk. You're wearing the hell out of that dress."

Her face broke out into a large grin. "Thank you. I wasn't sure if it was too much but I'm glad you approve."

"It's perfect for you." Like the day she'd blown back into town, I took extra liberty in checking out her ass in the fitted dress. "You always look good, but damn."

"You certainly know how to make a girl feel good about herself. Are those for me?" She pointed at the flowers.

"Not this time. I picked them up for your mom. I wasn't sure what to bring."

"She'll love them."

I held my hand out. "Ready?"

"We can take my car. Well, my parents' car since it's right here." She handed me the keys. "But you drive because I don't want to scuff my shoes."

I preferred my Firebird to the Lexus SUV she'd been using, but I led us to it all the same and opened the door for her to climb in. The closer we got to the other side of town, the more my unease for the night ahead grew. Doc Johnson was nice, friendly enough, though our conversations had always been limited. However, Irene's mother was a different story.

On the super rare occasions, I'd happen to be in the same space as the older woman, I don't think we'd ever spoken. Dinner with them was going to be an experience. When I parked, Irene placed her hand over mine.

"Thank you again for coming tonight."

I kissed the inside of her wrist. "You're welcome."

The closer we got to the door, she linked her fingers with mine and squeezed lightly. I thought it was a quick moment of silent encouragement, but she didn't let go when she rang the bell.

"Ms. Irene, you're looking as stunning as ever," an older woman in a pair of simple gray slacks and light blue striped button-down greeted.

"Thank you, Patrice. And I'd like to introduce my friend, Remi."

Patrice nodded her head in my direction. "A pleasure to meet you, Ms. Remi."

"Just Remi's fine."

The woman smiled politely as she quietly shut the door. "Your parents are waiting in the parlor, I've prepared some hors d'oeuvres." She held her hand out for the flowers. "These are beautiful. I'll take them and put them in a vase."

"Patrice is our house manager," Irene whispered as the woman disappeared down the hall.

A house manager? Irene's heels clicked on what I was certain were marble floors as she led us deeper into the house. We entered a room that reminded me of something I'd seen only in movies. The dark wood paneled walls. Leather tufted couch flanked by glass topped side tables, and over-sized club chairs angled toward it. Complete with a fireplace surrounded by an ornate mantel.

The conversation between her parents stopped when they laid eyes on us, and there was a three-second moment of silence where their focus seemed to be on the fact Irene was still holding my hand. In the momentary stoppage of time, I recognized the situation for what it was, and what I should have picked up on when she'd invited me. This wasn't dinner with her parents, it was dinner to *meet* her parents. Which was an entirely different ballgame. *Fuck!*

It was Mrs. Johnson who spoke first. "Irene, darling. Right on time. How are you this evening?" She leaned in to give Irene that strange cheek air kiss, and it was then that Irene released her hold on me.

Then the older woman set her sights on me. She and Irene bore a striking resemblance, almost as if Irene could have been her mother's clone. "Remi. I don't believe we've ever formally met." She held her hand out. "I'm glad you could join us this evening." Her smile was polite, but she looked at me with damn near X-ray vision.

I curled my fingers around hers for a quick shake. "Uh, thanks for the invite."

"Remi, can I get you a drink?" Doc Johnson asked, handing Irene a glass of white wine.

"Remi doesn't drink," Irene rushed to answer before I could.

"Tea or Coke will be fine," I replied, dragging my confused gaze from Irene back to her father.

"I'll see what I can wrestle up," he said before exiting the room.

"Any particular reason you don't drink, Remi?" Mrs. Johnson asked.

It was a simple question; one I'd fielded plenty of times. However, coming from Irene's mom, coupled with the way she kept her focus solely on me, there was definitely more to it.

"I don't like the taste of alcohol."

Mrs. Johnson arched a single brow and cut her eyes over to Irene before indicating toward the buffet cabinet against the far wall. "Please, help yourself while we wait for dinner to be ready."

Silver platters filled with finger foods set next to what were probably fine china saucers. This was how they did a simple family meal?

"Have you had caviar before, Remi?"

"I can't say that I have, Mrs. Johnson."

She kept her hands clasped in front of her body, and her expression maintained a pleasant neutrality. "Well, I do hope you will enjoy your first taste."

Irene handed me one of the mini plates with one of each of the four options offered. Her father returned with my tea in one of those stemmed glasses fancy restaurants served water in. We settled on the couch with Irene beside me, so close that our knees touched, and she laid her hand on my thigh.

Ms. Johnson sat at the edge of her chair, back straight and

legs crossed at the ankle. Irene was certainly her mother's child with the posture they both possessed. "Remi, let us get to know you."

"Mom, I told you already. Remi is one of Madison's esteemed business owners. And she has a few investment properties."

Esteemed business owner? And investment *properties?* I took slow, steady controlled breaths as I listened to Irene "sell" me to her mother. I couldn't figure out if she was nervous, defensive or a combination of the two. Either way, I curled my fingers around hers and gently squeezed. "Relax."

She nodded and took a sip of her wine.

"Remi, how is your father?" Doc Johnson asked.

I set my plate on the table and shifted a quick glance to Mrs. Johnson. Another simple question, and one I should have expected considering. "He's doing well most days. Irene has been a great help."

Irene's mother shifted her attention to her daughter. "How so?"

Irene sat even straighter as she faced off with the matri-arch of the family. This was a new Irene. A more self-conscience one under the eye of her mother. The whole ordeal was strange, and unbelievably formal.

"Nothing major. I mostly sit with him. Occasionally charm him into taking his meds when he's being moody and wanting to refuse."

I placed my hand on her back, rubbing small strokes with my thumb. "Don't downplay. My father has Parkinson's, Mrs. Johnson, and Irene has stepped in, which has been a relief." I glanced over at her. "She's been a wonderful help with the stress of it all."

A full, beautiful smile stretched across Irene's face, and I had to stop myself from leaning in to kiss her. I wasn't one for public displays of affection, but the energy radiating from her was beckoning me to rethink that stance.

"That's kind of you to say."

"I only say what I mean."

Her parents exchanged a look, her father seemingly amused and her mother a bit shocked. Maybe. The woman had one hell of a poker face, so she was harder to read.

Patrice returned to inform us dinner was ready. Doc Johnson grunted to standing then held his hand out for his wife, who, in contrast, rose with quiet grace. She was an elegant piece of work. As if there were some sort of succession protocol, Irene stood but waited until her parents passed first.

The rest of the night was interesting. We sat at a large dining room table, and I had to stop myself from laughing as I'd pictured the scene from *Batman* with Michael Keaton and Kim Basinger. The meal, however, was delicious, though I'd never had a three course "family" dinner. Regardless of how stiff the whole thing felt, it was enlightening to witness Irene with her parents.

How she almost seemed to look to her mother every time she said something positive about herself. And how she held her breath each time they, more specifically her mother, asked me a direct question. By the time we got to after dinner coffee I was over it and ready to go and was grateful when Irene called it a night.

Her parents walked us to the door and Ms. Johnson stopped in front of me and smiled. "Remi, thank you for joining us tonight."

"Thank you for inviting me, Mrs. Johnson."

She pulled in a breath and rolled her shoulders back. A move I knew all too well from Irene. "You may call me Vivian. Mrs. Johnson seems rather formal if you're going to be dating my daughter."

Irene squeezed my hand. I guess that was the stamp of approval she'd been hoping for all night.

"I think that went well," she commented as I drove us home.

"I'll take your word for it. But are dinners with your family always so...formal?"

"What are you talking about?"

I glanced at her briefly. "It was just different. You've had meals with my family. The contrast is stark."

"Mostly. She doesn't always do the hors d'oeuvres and before dinner drinks. That was in your honor. But to see more relaxed, you'll have to come when my brother is around with his kids."

I couldn't imagine children running around that house, but it was a whole different world than what I was used to. "So, I'm an esteemed business owner? You made mechanic sound really ideal."

"But it's true, regardless of how I phrased it. You *do* own the business." She slumped back against the plush leather seat. "I wanted them to like you."

"And I wanted them to see what an amazing daughter they have. Even if she couldn't keep her hands to herself." I cast a quick smile at her. Even after the initial show, Irene found ways to constantly have some physical connection.

A hand on my arm or thigh. Leaning closer than necessary as she informed me what fork was for what course.

"That was your fault really."

"How so?"

"Looking as sexy as you do in general, but tonight, all decked out.... I needed to touch you. To remind myself it was real. You were real. Did you mind?"

Again, her complimentary words spoke directly to the part of me that wanted connection and commitment. "Not really."

She slid to the edge of her seat, leaning close, and placed her palm on my upper thigh. "Then the night wasn't a total bust. And hopefully, you believe me now."

"About?"

"I wouldn't subject you to my mother if I wasn't serious about what I wanted." She placed a quick kiss on my cheek before settling back in her seat. "I'm not hiding, dodging, or pretending, Remi."

She spoke the truth. Since her return from New York, she'd been nothing more than pure and genuine Irene. She'd shown me a side...no she'd shown me her true self and it was a beautiful sight.

I glanced over at her again and gazing into her eyes, I knew without a doubt all was lost. "I believe you."

Reaching across, I laced my fingers with hers and we rode the rest of the way in a comfortable silence. Neither of us made a move to get out of the car after I pulled into the back drive. I killed the engine then handed her the keys.

She twisted in her seat to face me. "Do you want to come up?"

"I have work tomorrow."

She leaned closer. "Have I kept you out past your bedtime?"

"If I come up, yes."

Still, we remained. Everything in me screamed to take her up on the offer. Her intoxicating scent teased me once more. I reached up and slid my hand around to the nape of her neck. "You always smell good enough to eat."

She ran her tongue along her bottom lip. "I don't mind being dessert."

I laughed quietly at her retort. We sat there, foreheads touching, gazing into each other's eyes. She was beautiful. Sexy. And so much more than I ever imagined. My nipples ached. My body screamed with want. But if I kissed her, I wouldn't be able to stop.

"Good to know," I finally whispered. "Good night, Irene."

I exited the car before I had a chance to second guess myself.

28

IRENE

THE SOUND OF MY DOORBELL MADE ME CLOSE THE LID OF my laptop and set down my wineglass. I'd turned down Cynthia's dinner invite, opting for a quiet evening in. After the night with my parents, and then Remi leaving me more sexually frustrated than I could ever remember, I'd needed time to myself.

"Remi."

She took in my outfit. Black capri leggings and an oversized tank top. "Are you going to slam the door in my face again?"

I shook my head. "I know how I looked when I woke up on your couch. That ship has sailed."

She smiled. "You busy?"

"No, was just scrolling online for a little retail therapy." Hunting for new vibrators because I was wearing mine out thanks to her. Though I kept that comment to myself.

I moved to the side to let her in. A soft smile stretched across her teasing lips as she adjusted the strap of her bookbag when she eased by me. I stared at her ascending backside, following her up the stairs.

"Looks really nice. You transformed the place."

I glanced around. It was a far cry from my norm, but I'd never been more at peace. Felt more at home. Marcel had loaned me a painter who'd made quick work of putting a soothing light green on the walls. Both Cynthia and Regina had helped me hang pictures and I had pops of color with the furnishings and accent pieces. "Thank you. Would you like something to drink? I have water, tea, and Coke in the bottle."

She slipped the bag onto my deep-green velvet sofa. "I've made you a convert."

"You could say that." My mind raced with reasons for her visit, and she seemed to be in no hurry to explain.

Remi offered a quiet "thank you" when I handed her the bottle, letting her fingertips brush against mine. Ever so slightly, but enough to make me shiver. I settled beside her, tucking my feet under my ass and willing the flutters in my stomach to calm.

"I like your outfit," she said before taking a long drink of her soda.

I picked up my wine and ran my hands over the soft fabric of my leggings. "Thank you. You finally get to see Bummy Irene in all her glory. If you'd called first, I probably would have changed."

"I like Bummy Irene." She leaned a little closer and lowered her voice. "And Sexy Irene. To think you called me a tease." A delicious smirk lifted the corner of her mouth. A mouth I recalled vividly. A mouth I'd wanted to explore again last night. And for longer. For so much longer.

It'd been a week since I gave into one of my biggest fantasies. I'd never had the nerve to actually go through with it for Derrick, and truth be told I wasn't sure he'd have appreciated the effort. Then again, I wasn't sure Remi had, either. With her willpower and the way she could just walk away, I'd been at a loss. But a wave of triumph rolled through me. Twice, she'd kissed me and then left me a horny mess. Turning the tables on her had been fun, and her reaction had let me know without a doubt the attraction wasn't one-sided. "All's fair in love and war, right?"

Remi nodded while rolling the bottle between her palms. "What do you want, Irene?"

Her question confused me. "Um, you came to me."

She set her drink on the table and slid closer to me. "What do you want, Irene?" She spoke the question slow, deliberate.

Fire alarms went off in my head. My breath caught as I stared into her deep brown eyes. My heart rate spiked, and I focused hard on not spilling my wine when I put the glass down. Pulling in a slow inhale, I moved until our faces were inches apart. "To get absolutely Black girl wasted on you, Remi Martin."

She shook her head and laughed low. "That can be arranged."

Before I could respond, our mouths connected. One hand on the back of my neck the way I was starting to love, the other on my waist, Remi pulled me to her with gentle pressure. When she slipped her tongue into my mouth I moaned, grateful for the connection. Electric currents of eager anticipation zapped under my skin.

I pushed forward, deepening the kiss I'd been wanting to relive as I straddled her. I wanted more. Needed more. And tonight, I prayed for a different outcome. Remi trailed her hands down my sides until she grabbed my ass, squeezing hard. I groaned, pressing against her more, rocking my hips.

Her warm hands roamed beneath my shirt, leaving a trail of goosebumps each time her fingers stroked my skin. I held her face in my palms, our tongues swirled, soft moans danced in my ears. Finally, I pulled back, breathing heavy, nipples hard, and pussy tingling with the promise of things to come. My head swam, and I was sure if I moved too fast I'd be light-headed. Once again kissed senseless.

Remi kept her eyes on me as she moved her hands around, inching them up until her thumbs grazed the under-side of my breasts. I craved her touch. The need to have the full weight of my breasts in her hands, to have her taunt and tease my nipples until I was about to come, that desire burned through me with desperation.

"What do you want, Irene?" Her voice was a husky whis-per. Heavy with the same lust running rampant through me.

I eased off her lap but kept my attention on her beautiful face when I shimmied out of my pants. "I thought my first answer was pretty clear." I pulled off my shirt.

Standing before her in nothing but my panties gave me a surge of confidence. Remi gazed at me with open apprecia-tion. Desire. Want. It was a look, a feeling I'd not experi-enced in years and damn I'd missed it.

I held my hand out to her. "What do you want, Remi?"

She slipped her palm into mine with a lazy grin on her face. "To leave you with one hell of a hangover."

My lower half clenched at her words. As I started to lead us to my room, she grabbed her backpack.

"What's with the bag?"

Her grin widened. "Supplies."

"Huh?"

"Water, snacks, and other fun stuff." She winked on the last part.

"I have food here, you know."

She tugged me closer, then kissed me again soft and slow. "Trust me, you will appreciate that I came prepared."

The simple statement held the mystery of a promise I was ready to uncover. But Remi...she was the bigger mystery I wanted to unwrap. A basic black T-shirt and light blue joggers stood in my way. I walked us backward until her legs hit the foot of my bed. Running my hands beneath the hem of her top, I sighed at the contact. Inching upward. Remi lifted her arms, allowing me to remove the fabric. Hardened nipples prominent behind a basic black sports bra that blocked my view but didn't stop me from exploring her now exposed skin.

I trailed my fingers across her soft abdomen and placed gentle kisses along the side of her neck. Inhaling deeply, I pulled in the light and simplistically clean scent that was Remi. Easy, fresh, with a hint of spice. Remi gently opened and closed her fingers long my sides while craning her neck to allow more access.

She didn't rush my exploration, and her soft moans let me know she enjoyed the sensual touches. I ran my thumbs over her hard nipples, thankful the utilitarian choice of a bra was front closure. The quiet whisper as the zipper released was like the heavens opening. Her breasts were beautiful and full, with dark areolas. Her oversized clothes hid a treasure I was grateful to discover.

My heart rate hadn't slowed since I opened the door, and with her partially nude form on display, I was sure it'd beat right out of my chest. She shrugged out of the fabric, letting it join her shirt on the floor. Remi tugged my wrist and we tumbled onto my bed. Skin to skin. Face to face.

Again, her lips claimed mine, gentle yet determined as she straddled me, pinning my arms above my head. "You smell so sweet," she whispered, running her nose along my jaw. "Tantalizing, tempting me each time you were near." She licked the column of my neck.

Each time she moved, her nipples brushed against mine in a kiss of their own. I flexed my fingers beneath her gentle hold. As she moved down my body, kissing and licking my heated skin, my hands were freed, but I kept them in place.

When she finally palmed my breast, I released a shuddered breath.

A long groan poured from me when she closed her lips around one of my tight buds. She flicked her tongue across the taut peak before closing her teeth gently around my sensitive flesh, all the while tormenting the other side, pinching it between her fingers. I fisted my hands around the comforter and arched my back, a deep moan rumbled in the back of my throat.

Remi wedged her thigh between my legs while she continued her teasing assault. Each flick of her tongue and scrape of her teeth had me whimpering and wiggling beneath her. A low ringing in my ears as my senses slipped further and further away. I rocked my hips, the dampness of my panties evident as I pressed against her thigh, the friction created added to the over-stimulation of my body.

I'd forgotten how good it could be. To not only be with a lover, but be with one that had your pleasure in the forefront of their mind. And with Remi, her every touch, lick, and kiss was with my satisfaction in mind. She took her time, alternating her attention on my chest, leaving no inch of my skin untouched. I writhed against her, the wetness of my panties increasing as my arousal climbed higher and higher.

"Yes," I cried out as my release ripped through me, sending me into a spiral of bliss.

I pulled in heavy gulps of air, breathing through the tiny aftershocks as Remi kissed her way down my stomach until she curled her fingers around the waistband of my panties. I found the strength to lift my hips to aid in their removal. My legs drooped open, and the throbbing in my pussy intensified as Remi trailed small kisses along the inside of my thigh.

As she got closer, my mouth went dry. I managed to prop myself up onto my elbows. Remi glanced up at me through hooded eyes, a look that stole my breath. First contact of her tongue had me gasping. The second pass made me flop back onto the bed. A long lick, with a quick flick against my sensitive clit before she closed her lips around it. She hummed while giving gentle suction, a move I was certain made my heart temporarily stop.

I propped my feet up onto the bed, opening myself to her wide and without shame. Remi ate my pussy with practiced ease. The alternation between languid passes of her tongue through my slit to slow, tortured attention on my clit had my body on edge, ready and willing to freefall into euphoric happiness a second time. I ran my hand through her curls, their softness a gentle caress against my palm as I gyrated my hips to match her movements.

Our mutual moans mingled in the air. "Oh," is all I managed to gasp in breathy pants. My thighs began to quiver, a gentle tremor that gradually spread throughout me. A strangled cry got trapped in my throat as she worked feverishly with her magical mouth alone. The tight grip of her fingers on my legs kept me splayed open for her enjoyment.

Ears ringing. Mouth dry. Breathing constricted. I no longer had control over my body. I'd handed it over to the woman between my legs as she pushed me over the precipice repeatedly. Senses obliterated, leaving me unable to even beg for mercy. All I could do was hang onto the comforter for dear life until she'd had her fill.

29

REMI

IRENE'S GARBLED MOANS AND INCOHERENT WORDS DROVE me wild. Her body shook, and she thrashed her head from side to side, all while giving me more to dine on. She was decadence. My own pussy ached for attention. My nipples were painfully hard. But it was worth it to have Irene falling apart at my doing. Finally taking pity on her, I gave one final pass with my tongue before kissing my way up her sweat-covered body.

The glimmer of soft sheen coating her skin brought a smile to my lips. She stared up at the ceiling, chest rising and falling in exaggerated movements. Strands of hair clung to her damp forehead, and her normally straight locks had a bit of wave to them. Walking away from her after dinner had been damn hard and I'd laid awake for hours, talking myself out of knocking on her door. I'd known I would need to take my time with her, to learn every part of her intimately. To give her everything she'd wanted and more. And I wasn't done yet. Far from it.

Reaching over the side of the bed, I grabbed my backpack and pulled out two bottles of water. I propped up onto my elbow and placed the still-cool bottle in the center of her chest. The contrast in temperature made her squeak, and it rolled off onto the bed.

I kept my attention on her as I cracked mine open and drank a long gulp while using my other hand to trace circles around her erect nipple. Her sweet scent lingered under my nose, and the taste of her was now burned into my memory. She blinked rapidly and flexed her fingers as she seemed to come down from her high. She felt around for the water; I reached across her to pick it up.

A lazy grin spread across her face as she sat up to drink. "Thanks." Her voice was hoarse, scratchy, like when you first wake in the morning. And it was the sexiest sound next to the moans and whimpers she'd made minutes earlier.

"Told you you'd appreciate me being prepared," I replied with a wink before finishing off my bottle.

She dabbed her mouth with the back of her hand while nodding. "I needed this. I didn't think the room would stop spinning."

The fact she still sounded a bit breathless sent a surge of pride and amusement through me. "You wanted drunk, and I'm just getting started."

She choke-coughed on the sip she'd taken. My body screamed out for a release, my own arousal heightened the more she'd come. Keeping her eyes on me, she capped her bottle, brushing against me as she set it on the small table beside her bed.

With slow movements, she straddled me, holding my face between her hands. "When they said it's the quiet ones you have to watch out for, I'm certain they meant you."

I had no chance to respond as she kissed me. I wrapped my arms around her waist. Her wet hairs tickled my stomach, a reminder of where I'd been, what'd I'd done to her, and my eagerness to return. She moved her hands down until she palmed my breasts, squeezing and pinching my nipples. I thrust my tongue forward and she suckled it. The action was like a tether to my neglected libido, teasing it with promises of a release on the horizon.

Using her body weight, she forced me back, the tables turned on our earlier positions. She lazily traced a finger down my chest as she loomed above me. Trailing it around one breast. "That sports bra works magic."

I tilted my head. "Say what?"

She cupped both breasts in her hands, pushing them together and circling her thumbs across my erect nipples. "I had no idea you were hiding such glorious secrets." She spoke the words softly, with a slight smile on her face as she continued her actions.

"I didn't take you for a boob lady," I answered with a quiet laugh.

She leaned forward and rolled her tongue around one of my nipples. The action drawing a small moan from my lips. "Haven't you learned by now?" She teased the other side. "I'm full of surprises." She drew the tight bud into her mouth.

"That you are," I groaned.

Irene sat up, smiling at me before she stretched over to the side table and retrieved a small plastic box from the drawer. "And I have more in store. Are you okay with toys?"

I nodded as I ran my hands up her thighs until my thumbs met at her center. My digits easily glided through her wetness. I gazed at her, slowly stroking up and down, and she began rocking her hips against my touch.

"I'm supposed to be..."

"Hm...you're supposed to be what?" I crooned.

Each movement she made slickened my stomach with her arousal, the scent of her mingling into the air around us. She managed to set the box beside me, and I noticed a pink silicon device shaped like a butterfly on her finger.

"I'm supposed to be finding out what you sound like when you come." She spoke the words through slight tremors and heavy pants. Irene flattened her palm between my breasts to ride out the orgasm.

I sucked one of my thumbs clean. "I like hearing you."

Irene placed a soft kiss on my lips. "I can tell, but you can't have all the fun."

"I don't know, it sounded like you had plenty of fun yourself."

She kissed me again. "I did." She held up a finger and clicked a hidden button. No sound could be heard, but the gentle flutters of the wings were noticeable. "This is one of my favorites. It's like tiny kisses and feather light touches." She licked her lips as she worked to free me from my remaining clothes.

Settling beside me, Irene captured my mouth again. "I like the way I taste on you," she whispered. She draped her leg over mine, wedging one of my hands between our bodies.

I cupped her cheek with the other and thrust my tongue forward while working my wrist so my knuckles rubbed against her clit.

She pressed forward taking control of the connection. "You can't help yourself, huh?" The humor in her voice had me smiling against her lips.

Instead of trying to stop me, she pushed closer and slid her hand down my stomach, the soft nodules along with the tiny flutters of the toy against my skin revved up the anticipation of what was to come. When she reached her destination, my entire body shivered.

"I want to make you feel good," she murmured.

A languid up and down of her finger along my clit. The slow motion worked well with the gentle vibrations and the tickling sensations created by the wings. Lower she ventured, teasing at my opening, then up again. An exquisitely torturous pattern, all while she continued to kiss me. Suckling my tongue and nipping at my lips.

I rocked my hips and gripped her thigh as the build started. Closer and closer, but frustratingly out of reach.

She licked the column of my neck. "Tell me what you need."

"Faster," I panted.

Without hesitation, she worked her hand faster, moving her finger in quick circles. The vibrations of the toy increased as she maneuvered to suck one of my tight nipples into her mouth. A perfect combination of her tongue and hand working in concert to get me where I desperately needed to go. My body tensed and shuddered as the orgasm burst free, bathing me in waves of pleasure.

It was as if thousands of tiny firecrackers were being set off under my skin as my nerve endings zinged with life. I barely registered Irene's movements as a sight I never imagined was playing out before me. Her head between my legs.

She lapped her tongue up and down my slit, eagerly drinking in the release she'd unleashed. I grabbed the short strands of my hair, arched my back, and let loose a deep, guttural grunt as I was bathed in pleasure.

Slowly, Irene kissed and licked a path up my body. She cupped my tits, flicking her tongue against one nipple then the other. The action made me shudder with aftershocks. Eventually, she settled her body atop mine and pulled the toy from her finger. Every part of me was hyperaware of every part of her. The dampness of her skin. Her pebbled nipples pressed against me. The tickle of her hairs on my thigh.

I smoothed her hair back from her face. "That's a fun little gadget."

"Thanks. It gets the job done."

I linked my fingers together at her lower back. "Clearly."

Slowly, she traced her fingertips along my collarbone, then

followed the path with her mouth. I inched my hands down and held onto the firm globes of her behind, her soft affections once again stoking the embers of my desire.

The movement started easy, an unhurried back and forth of her hips. Chaste touches of her lips to my neck as her hand explored south.

"Ready for more?" I asked between kisses to her shoulder.

Her answer came in the form of a nod while she rolled my nipple between her thumb and forefinger. I lifted my leg, pressing it against her more and pushed down on her ass to maximize the contact.

The smell of sex lingered in the air. Tangy and erotic.

"Kiss me," I breathed low.

Without hesitation, Irene complied with my request while snaking her hand south until she cupped my attention-greedy pussy. We moaned in unison. Her hard buds scraped against me as she slid along my thigh, gyrating in deliberate circles.

Our mouths worked in unison, our tastes mingling while our bodies moved at a frenzied pace. She pressed her palm against my sensitive center and stroked my inner walls with two fingers. The come-hither motion a call, bringing forth my next release.

Faster, she moved, fucking my leg until we both cried out in breaths, grunts, and groans. My fingers dug into her soft flesh, holding her to me while I enjoyed the feel of her body shaking against me as my own twitched with satisfaction.

30

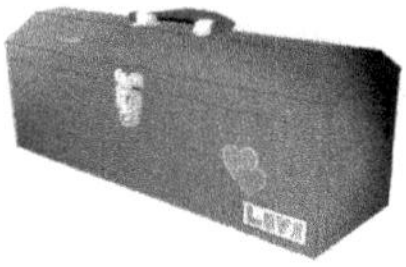

IRENE

I ROLLED OFF REMI, PLACING MY HAND TO MY CHEST IN hopes of slowing my breathing. I'd lost count of how many times she'd commanded pleasure from my body. I'd been frustrated by the lack of physical, and how slowly things seemed to progress but damn, she'd been worth the wait.

"You got more water in your magic bag? Not sure my legs will work right now." I sounded breathless, as if I'd been running a marathon.

Remi let out a soft "oof" when she rolled to the side to retrieve her backpack. She unceremoniously plopped it onto the bed and rummaged around with her eyes closed but produced a bottle for me along with a travel-sized trail mix and wet wipes. She really was prepared.

I managed to drag my body into a sitting position and quickly cleaned my hands before digging into the snacks offered. For a woman who hid her body behind oversized clothes, I marveled at how relaxed she was lounging on my bed fully nude. I let my eyes take in the sight of her, slightly jealous of her nice rack. They were full and sat up high, capped with large areolas and nipples that fit perfectly in my mouth.

It'd been a long time since I'd been with a woman, and I was surprised my nerves hadn't gotten the better of me. But I'd fed off her energy and my desperate desire to please and take care of her.

She shifted, propping the pillows behind her as she sat up. "You're staring at me."

"I am. It's a magnificent sight."

"Is that so?"

I nodded. She widened her legs and opened her arms. I crawled over and settled into the V created, my back to her front. She closed me in her embrace. My gaze traveled to the spot on her leg, now drying with the residue from my arousal. The immediate recall made me clench and I pushed my ass back. Her resulting moan made me do it again. Heat radiated from her center.

Remi moved my hair to the side and nipped at my neck while sliding a hand up to cup my breast. I arched into her touch and whimpered when she pinched my taut nipple.

She ran her nose up and down my heated flesh. "You always smelled good enough to eat." Her other hand journeyed down my stomach until she coated her fingers in my wetness.

I rocked with the slow in and out, a gentle penetration that ended all too soon. I had no time to complain as my mouth went dry when she stuck those same fingers between her lips and moaned. A rush of wanton desire pooled between my legs.

"Let's see what else you have," she whispered.

"Wha'?" My question was answered when she reached for my container of toys without breaking contact with the nipple she continued to play with. Each pinch, twist, and light tug had my pussy pulsing with need.

She pulled free my bright pink wand vibrator and turned it on. "Oh, this'll do nicely." She spoke with her lips close to my ear; her warm breath made me shiver. "Lube."

With shaky hands, I managed to flip the cap on the bottle to lightly coat the bulbous vibrating head.

"Legs wider. Either side of mine."

Gripping onto her thighs, pressed back against her, feeling the wetness dripping from her as I complied with her quiet demand. She opened hers wider, pushing mine out so I was properly splayed open for her enjoyment.

"Fuck!" I cried out at the first touch.

She chuckled low, moving the toy down. The pressure enough that my nether lips opened to the intrusion. Up again as she clicked the button to intensify the speed and pattern. I dug my fingers into her thighs, panting. There was no retreat. She wrapped her arm around my waist, holding me secure.

"I wish there was a mirror on that wall," she breathed. "So, you could see how fucking sexy you are."

I sucked in a sharp gasp at her lust-filled words. She rocked her hips against my ass, hardened nipples poked my back, and her low whispers of pleasure danced in my head.

I closed my eyes when she went down, holding the toy at my opening, moving it in slow circles before going back to torturing my clit. My legs began to shake. I pushed down on her thighs, arched my back, and a scream ripped free as the orgasm tore through me. She held the toy to my overly stimulated bundle of nerves while my body convulsed. It wasn't until I folded into near fetal position, clamping my wobbly legs shut, did she stop, and I became aware of her jittery movements along with the low muttering of cuss words.

I laid on my side and waited for the world to stop spinning. Remi laid behind me, her breathing almost as labored as mine. She draped her arm around me and moved closer, an innocent move, but with every fiber of my being alert and sensitive, I sucked in a sharp breath and shivered.

"Oh god, woman. I have never..." My words came out in forced breaths. I was covered in sweat, and I didn't even want to think about how my hair might look.

She peppered kisses along my upper back, and I could feel her deep inhales and exhales. "Are you okay?" Her voice was low and lust laden wrapped in care. The slightly gravelly tone stoked at the inferno of my need, making me want even more. I had no idea how that was possible, but having knowledge of her, after being with her, I was addicted.

I flipped so that we faced each other, slipping my arm under hers, grabbing onto her firm ass. I studied her features up close and personal. Full lips slightly pouty from all the kissing. Dark eyes half closed. And her cheekbones more prominent with the way we were laying. "You're beautiful. I've always thought so."

Her signature half-grin lifted the corner of her mouth, and I leaned forward to kiss the spot. It was meant to be a quick moment, but she ran her knuckles along my cheek before deepening the connection. Remi moved her lips atop mine tenderly, alternating between tiny pecks to a more drawn-out action, softly sweeping her tongue through and back again.

Each pass tugged at my heart, refilling the depleted well of affection. Reminding me I was important. That I was enough. That I was wanted. Emotion splintered through me with the thought. Remi showing up at my door was about more than sex. She'd had her own reservations over being hurt, that I'd hurt her, but she was here. With me. She'd come to me.

I broke from the kiss and ran my tongue along my lips. "I understand what all this means, and I won't squander what you've given me."

REMI

I RESTED MY FOREHEAD ON IRENE'S, CLOSED MY EYES, AND released a slow breath. "And what have I given you?"

She wiggled closer. "You trust me." She spoke low, her voice a soothing balm of truth. "You had your fears. Your doubts. With anyone else, this would have been just mind-blowing exceptional sex."

I couldn't help but to laugh at her description.

"But with you...you've given more than just your body tonight. And I appreciate that. Truly. Honestly. From the bottom of my heart."

Emotion clogged my throat. I never expected her to have that sort of perception into my actions. Never expected her to understand without being told that casual wasn't how I operated. I'd tried it in the past, but for me it never worked out, and I inevitably ended up hurt. It was why I'd written off love as an option. *Love.* She was still married and trying to adjust to her new life.

I detangled from our embrace. My course of action was foolish, but the heart wants what it wants, and somehow it'd decided Irene was the who. "Do you need anything?" I asked, grabbing for my bag.

She laid a hand on my arm. "Are you okay? Because I thought we were having a moment, and now..."

"We were, are having a moment. Your understanding just sorta got to me in an unexpected way." I unwrapped a chocolate bar and took a bite.

A slow smile stretched across her face, and she inched closer. "You're having feelings." She lifted my hand to her mouth and bit into the candy. "And you're stress eating them." She spoke the teasing words around her mouthful.

Her playful tone put me somewhat at ease. "Something like that."

"Imagine that. Blunt, tell it like it is Remi doesn't like talking about her emotions."

"I do. In vague, non-specific ways."

She walked her fingers back and forth along my arm. "I don't want to do vague, Remi. I've lived that life. And you don't have to say the words. I'm understanding how you work, which is why I said what I said."

"And that is a bit uncanny, honestly."

"Why? Because I figured out the meaning behind your actions?"

I nodded and offered up the last bit of the bar to her. When she declined, I finished it off and grabbed another.

"What all do you have in there?"

I handed her the backpack. She started laughing as she pulled out a handful of travel-sized trail mix packages, various candy bars, and peanut butter crackers. She dumped the stuff back in, and I stopped chewing as she pulled out my container of toys. Her eyes lit up when she lifted the lid to find my strap-on on top.

"This for me or you?"

"I wear, you receive. I'm a fingers-only gal."

"Really? So, you've never..."

I shook my head.

"It has balls," she giggled. "Pink balls."

I lifted a shoulder. "That was the only color it came in." I glanced at the two we'd used from her stash. "Pretty sure it seems like you're partial to pink anyway."

"True." She freed the small remote from the harness, letting out a squeak when the vibrator moved. "I think I'm going to like this." Irene turned it off and waited until I was done eating then moved into my lap, straddling me.

She held my face between her hands. "I've lived twenty years with a man who was king of saying one thing, of being one way in public, but whose actions were the exact opposite of that. Empty words. I've been that way myself, covering up and projecting to display the person I thought people wanted to see." She paused and took a breath. "I've said it before, and I'll say it again. You have always been you. I know when you say, or better yet, when you do something it has meaning."

"You're awful insightful."

"You can thank my therapist for that. She's helped me see a lot. Plus, Regina and Cynthia, who, by the way, are very much Team Remi."

"What?"

I suspected they talked about relationships and things of that nature among themselves. I, however, never pictured Irene opening up to either of them about anything to do with me. Let alone them being Team Remi, whatever the hell that meant.

"When they realized I had a thing for you, they went into protective mode. They warned me against using you just for sex. You're a friend to them, and whether you believe it or not, they do care about you. And you should let them in more."

I knew that last part had to do with my father and not

allowing others in to help where he was concerned. I wasn't sure I'd be ready for that just yet, but I heard her all the same.

I squeezed her ass. "Are you?"

"Am I what?"

"Using me for sex?"

She slowly shook her head. "Nope. I'm in this, Remi." A lazy smile spread across her beautiful face. "But you are free to use me for sex."

I laughed. "Is that so?"

"Oh yeah."

I flipped us so she was pinned beneath me and rested my head against hers. "My sweet, sweet, Irene, when I fall, I fall hard."

Her eyes crinkled at the side from the force of her smile. "I like the sound of that," she purred.

I claimed her mouth again. Her lips tasted of chocolate and sex, an intoxicating combination. "Mussed-up Irene might be my favorite." I suckled at the tender flesh on her neck.

She raked her nails down my back. "You're the first to meet her."

I couldn't have heard her correctly. "What? How is that possible?"

She shrugged. "I always stopped before things got too heated to tie down my hair." As she spoke, she tried to smooth down some of the flyaways.

I wrapped my fingers around her wrist and brought it to my lips. "Nope. I've earned this look."

She felt around until she found what she was after. "Mussed-up Irene is all yours."

She watched me intently as I stepped into the harness then slid to the edge of the bed, the bottle of lube in her hands. The silicone dick was at her eye level, and she bit the corner of her lip as she reached out to stroke it, letting her

MEKA JAMES

fingers glide across the realistic head then down to the balls she'd laughed about.

Attention on me, she opened the bottle and squirted a dime-sized amount into her palm then stroked the toy again, coating all sides. I leaned to capture her lips, forcing her backward. She laid back, legs open. I ran my fingers through her slickness, pumping them in and out, reveling in how aroused she was again.

Settling my body over hers, I outlined her lips. She darted her tongue out to follow the path I'd taken, licking off the traces of her I'd left behind. I swallowed hard when she grabbed my hand and sucked my fingers clean. She moaned around them as I pushed my hips forward. Out then in again, slow to allow her time to get used to the intrusion.

"Let me know when you're okay," I whispered into her ear.

She pulled in a slow breath. "I'm ready."

I rolled us so she was on top and handed her the remote. She wiggled into a better position then jumped a little when she turned it on, placing a palm on my stomach.

"Woah." She took a few rounds of breaths.

The weight of her body intensified the vibrations against me. I needed the time as well to work through the initial reactions. Irene began circling her hips in a sensual rotation. I held her waist, groaned as each tiny motion increased the friction for me.

Dropping the remote onto the pillow, she grabbed for my hands, interlinking our fingers as she leaned forward, pinning my arms beside my head. The ride began. Irene's grip was tight as she slowly lifted herself up and down along the dildo. Once again, we went for every connection possible. Fresh taste of her coated her lips. Tango of tongues. A mix of moans, the subtle wet slapping noise as she rode harder.

My stomach muscles tensed as the shocks of pleasure

234

rolled through. I arched my neck as I surrendered. Irene sat up, bracing her hands behind her on my legs. I watched her through heavy eyes. Mouth open, nipples hard, pussy glistening. I licked my fingertips then pressed them to her clit.

She continued to rock back and forth. Soft, mewling noises bubbled free. The pinch of her nails into my flesh, and the continued vibrations coupled with her movements took my hyper-aroused body to its second freefall as hers shuddered atop me. She was beautiful in the throes of passion.

Irene collapsed forward, tiny shivers still in control of her limbs. I was near spent, but not ready for the night to end. Wrapping my arms around her, I got her beneath me. We shared lazy kisses and gentle touches while I pumped my hips ever so slightly with her moving in sync.

"Remi...dear god, Remi," she moaned, picking up the pace of her movements.

"Hmmm, yes," I murmured against her damp skin, the saltiness a welcome flavor.

She slipped her arms under mine, holding me close. I trailed my fingers down the outside of her thigh, gripping it as I began to increase my tempo to match hers.

"Remi, Remi, Remi..."

The breathless repeat of my name, the way she dug in, the way our slick bodies moved against one another. Body already sensitive and stimulated. The vibrator giving off continuous pulses. And the tale-tell sign of her body going into gentle spasms beneath me sent me spiraling one more time.

❧ 32 ❧

IRENE

I STRETCHED AND REACHED OVER TO FIND THE BED EMPTY.

"Remi?"

My call was met with silence. I tossed the covers back and had to balance myself when I moved too fast. Hangover indeed. A lazy grin tugged the corners of my mouth. It was almost noon; I couldn't remember the last time I'd slept in so late. Yeah, that had been totally worth the wait. On my way out of my room, I grabbed the throw at the foot of my bed to wrap it around myself.

This was the second time she'd managed to leave without waking me. She had some serious ninja skills. As I turned back, I took in the space, scanning to see if she'd left a note or anything. My eyes landed on her pack of goodies propped up neatly in the corner and flutters started in my stomach.

After showering and taming my wild hair, I made my way to her back door. My knock was answered by Axle barking twice before deciding no more effort was needed. A twist of the knob found the door unlocked. "Remi?" More silence.

Her car was still in the driveway. The shop was closed on Sundays, so I headed to the last place I figured she'd be, only my knocks there went unanswered as well. Panic set in. She was nowhere to be found, and her father wasn't here. By the time I got back to my apartment, Cynthia and Regina were piling out of Regina's SUV.

"There you are. We've been calling."

"My phone is...I don't know. What's up?" I asked as I climbed the stairs in search of the device.

"We were going to ask you. Jennifer called Marcel saying Remi was in the ER."

My heart stopped. "Is she okay?"

"Not her. Jennifer couldn't say much other than she saw Remi when she went on shift at County, but it's her dad."

"Oh no." I tossed the cushions off the couch and finally located my phone. Missed calls and texts from my friends, and one lone voicemail. I grabbed my keys from the island, then turned in circles looking for my purse.

Cynthia grabbed my shoulders. "Regina will drive."

I nodded and let them lead me out while I listened to the message. My heart sank when I heard her voice. I franticly dialed her number, but her phone rang then went to voicemail. Over and over the same thing. Why wouldn't she answer? She probably thought I was ignoring her. Bile rose up my throat at that idea. When she needed me, reached out, I wasn't there.

The drive seemed to take forever and I got more and more impatient as the minutes ticked by and I was still unable to reach Remi. After such an amazing night, how could I have let her down in such a way? Regina had barely put the car in park before I was jumping out. They hadn't asked me any questions, but I knew they could feel my anxiety.

The doors opened with a soft swish, and Cynthia took charge. "Let me find Jennifer."

The perk of her sister-in-law being charge nurse, she could

get me answers quicker and with less run-around. Regina squeezed my hand while rubbing my arm.

Cynthia returned a few minutes later. "Let's go."

We followed her down the hall and onto the elevator to the third floor: Imaging. The doors opened and there Remi sat. Alone. Wringing her hands and knee bouncing a mile a minute.

"Remi."

She looked up at the sound of her name. The moment I got close I engulfed her in a hug, and she wrapped her arms around me, holding tight.

"He had a stroke," she spoke with her face buried in my shoulder. "One minute we were talking and the next..."

So many thoughts swirled through my head, how scared she'd looked. The stress she had to be under. The loudest being concern for Red, and hoping he pulled through. She pulled back, and even though I didn't want to let her go, I loosened my grip on her but kept a hold of her arm.

"Oh. Everyone's here," she said after noticing Regina and Cynthia behind me. "How did y'all...?"

"Jennifer saw you when she got here, called Marcel because you were alone, and well, we came to be with you," Cynthia answered, moving in to hug her. Regina did the same.

"Thank you." She glanced at me. "All of you for coming."

A ping of guilt hit me for missing her call and not getting to her sooner. We settled back into the uncomfortable plastic chairs, with her keeping her fingers intertwined with mine. "Do I need to call your aunt?"

She shook her head. "She's here. She just went to get some coffee."

No sooner than she answered, Ms. Ev came walking around the corner. She stopped when she saw us all, but a relieved smile graced her lips.

Remi filled Regina and Cynthia in on her father, and

Cynthia was extra sympathetic to the situation. We all stayed with her until tests were run and it was determined he'd be kept overnight for observation. He had slight paralysis on his right side. They were hopeful the medication he'd been given would work, but if not, they'd need to do surgery to clear the blockage in his heart. She held on to my hand the entire time, and I offered my opinion when she asked. The reality of the situation was that her father couldn't be on his own anymore. It was a fact I was sure she was also realizing, but it would be something we'd discuss later.

"Thank you," she whispered as we sat in Regina's back seat. "For coming, staying, just being here." She rested her head on my shoulder, and I turned and placed a soft kiss to her forehead.

"I'm sorry I wasn't there right away," I whispered.

She tightened her grip on my fingers and brought our joined hands to her lips, placing a soft kiss to my hand. "But you came, and that's what matters."

A tidal wave of relief hit me. I'd been silently battling anxious jitters, worried I'd somehow let her down after she'd opened up so much. I was supposed to be comforting her, but the soft strokes of her thumb put me at ease.

When we got back, Regina and Cynthia hung around for a little while. After they left, I made two bowls of ice cream, remembering the extra marshmallows and chocolate sauce.

"You're a keeper," she said with a sad smile as she took the bowl.

"I'm going to hold you to that."

She set her bowl on the table the turned to face me, cupping my cheek. "I wouldn't say it if I didn't mean it."

I wrapped my fingers around her wrist. "I know."

She pressed her lips to mine. Soft, gentle, and full of the appreciation she'd already verbalized. Then she picked up her bowl, rested her head on my breasts, and started eating her ice cream. She'd done the same thing last night, snuggling me close with her head laying on my chest.

"Are my boobs comfortable?"

"Mm-hm. Nature's perfect pillows." To sell her comment, she wiggled her head, nuzzling closer to me.

"If that's the case, shouldn't I lay on yours? You do have more cushion."

She tilted her head back to look up at me, broad smile on her face. "If you'd like." She started to sit up, but I stopped her.

"I like being your pillow." I kissed the top of her head as she readjusted.

"You left the house as Bummy Irene."

I hadn't thought about the camel joggers and off-shoulder oversized T-shirt I'd thrown on. I had only planned on seeing Remi, and after the night we'd shared, getting completely dressed up hadn't been a priority for once. "Getting to you was more important than what I was wearing."

We continued to eat our ice cream in silence. Hemi slept perched on the back of the sofa. Axle stood, stretched, then exited out the doggie door. It was almost like a quiet, normal afternoon.

"I don't know what I'm gonna do. I don't want to put him in a home," she said after a few minutes.

"We'll figure it out."

She sat up, took the bowl from me, and carried them both to the sink. When she returned, she held her hand out to me and led me to her room. We curled up on her bed, and she again nestled her head between my breasts as I held her.

"If anyone had told me three months ago I would have fallen for you, I would have thought they were off their rocker, but I have. The relief and happiness I felt when you showed up today..." She tightened her arms around me. "Seeing you made it better, manageable."

I pushed my body as close to hers as possible, throwing my leg over hers to hold and surround her with as much of me as I could.

"Either your phone is ringing, or you're really excited to be close to me right now," she joked as someone decided now was the time to call. Remi fished the device free from my pocket before I could, and her face changed when she looked at the display.

I grabbed her arm as she rolled away. "Where are you going?"

"Bathroom while you talk to him."

"I don't want or need to talk to him." My phone stopped ringing only to start again.

"Seems like he really has something to say to you."

My heart twisted. He had unbelievably horrid timing. And he was a reminder that for all the progress Remi and I had made, I wasn't a hundred percent free, and that fact remained a sore spot. And today of all fucking days.

"I told him he could have the car and I just wanted it to be over. But as predicted telling him he could have the car hadn't been enough, especially since he was pissed he'd have to come pick it up and get it repaired."

My phone stopped vibrating and the ding of a new voice-mail popped up.

She leaned and kissed me softly. "Nothing I just said has changed. I can't help you with the divorce. I wish I could. I wish there was some way I could make it all go away for you. But I can't." She reached up to caress my cheek. "What I can do is support your choices and how you handle it, and I'm here to do that. When this is all said and done, I want to know that you feel good about the outcome. And if that means you have to fight him for stuff, then fight him for stuff. But I do have to pee."

I kissed her again. "Fine, but hurry back."

There wasn't anything else I needed to say to Derrick. I'd call my attorney in the morning and find out the best way to expedite the divorce. We had a pre-nup that afforded me a certain payout regardless of what he wanted. I didn't care about the penthouse or the damn car. The outcome that would make me feel the best would be my freedom and peace. And being with the woman in the next room.

33

REMI

THE WEEKS FOLLOWING POP'S STROKE WERE PROBABLY SOME of the hardest ones I'd had to handle, but Irene was with me every step. She demystified the medical speak. His paralysis had gotten better, but his range of motion had been severely limited, which meant he couldn't be on his own. Irene helped me decide between a home or an in-home nurse, but in the end, Pop had asked for a facility.

I was having a harder time adjusting to not seeing him every day than he was. Part of me held out hope he'd be able to return home, but I also had to be realistic about the situation. Plus, he was happy at the place we'd found. The setup was more like apartment living rather than nursing home, and that was better for my peace of mind as well as his mental health.

It'd been weird to have so much attention on me during the transition. Cynthia and Regina had gone into "take care" mode, Irene had explained. They cooked, they called or texted, constant questions of did I need anything, especially from Cynthia. She'd been the primary care giver for her aunt after her cancer diagnosis, so she understood the pressure and struggle to handle it all. Aunt Ev had been thrilled at the rally. She had it in her mind I was going to end up some sort of spinster hermit, but I also knew her exaggerations were out of love.

After a quick shower, I headed up to Irene. Some days she'd be at my house waiting, but others she'd be in the apartment enjoying the retreat she'd created. I understood. I enjoyed my alone time as well, though we both agreed we rather sleep together.

"Honey, I'm home," I called when I got to the top of the stairs. I dropped my bookbag on the floor.

Her eyes went there as she unfolded from the couch to greet me with a quick kiss, but I wrapped my arm around her waist and held her for longer. She held my face, moaning against my lips. I cupped her ass as I slipped my tongue into her mouth. Kissing her was one of my favorite pastimes. The feel of her in my arms, the taste of her, and her deliciously intoxicating smell.

"Somebody missed me," she whispered breathless, cutting her eyes over at the bag again and a large grin spreading across her face.

"Don't I always?" I stepped back and took in her outfit. "Um, can you put on pants and pack?"

"Yes. Are you going to tell me why?"

"I owe you a ride."

Her face lit up.

"Not that kind. At least not now."

She pouted but headed to the bedroom all the same. "One day I'm going to learn how you do it."

I flopped onto the bed to watch her change. I was not disappointed when her ass was revealed in a pair of sexy, cheeky panties. "How I do what?"

"Kiss me into a state of horniness then switch subjects on a dime."

"Is that what I do?"

"Yes," she answered, wiggling into a pair of jeans. "Oh. I have the perfect shoes." She ran over to the other room and came back with a box. "I bought these like a year or two ago. Retail therapy in between real therapy. But haven't had a chance to wear them. What do you think?"

I sat up and took the black leather ankle boot from her. They were a simple design with a block heel and two straps, one across the toe and the other at the top, which doubled as the buckle. They were adorned with pyramid gold spikes. An interesting choice for sure. "You bought a pair of boots with no purpose behind them?"

"They had a purpose at the time, which was to make me feel better. And now they can be my Remi shoes." She whipped her shirt off and replaced it with a plain white T-shirt, which, like her jeans, looked deceptively simple, but I'm sure had a hefty price tag attached. She exited the room again, returning with a black leather jacket. "Now, I'm biker ready."

I eased off the bed to stand in front of her. "Sexiest biker chick I've laid eyes on. Now, pick out a few things, but keep it light because motorcycle. You won't need much because for most of the time I expect to see Mussed-up Irene."

She decided in record time and looked unbelievably excited about the prospect of going on a trip without knowing the destination. I added her clothes and toiletries to the ones I'd already packed in my book bag and we headed out. She was practically bouncing as I secured the helmet on her head. I gave her a quick rundown on riding rules so she'd know to lean when I did, to not move around a lot and that, basically, we needed to maneuver as one or there'd be disaster.

Once she relied her understanding, I climbed on then I directed her to do the same, laughing when she grabbed my boobs.

"Hands around my waist, please."

"But I like this better."

"I do as well, but distractions are not advised."

She complied with my directive and her grip tightened when I cranked on the engine. "Oh, shit. Uh, Remi?"

"Yeah?"

She wiggled in her seat behind me.

"You good?"

"Yeah."

The squeal she let out when I took off made me smile. She pressed her body against mine hard, squeezing a bit too much. Once we made it out of Madison and onto open road, a sense of peace hit me. I'd missed being able to go, to ride and experience the contentment that came along with it.

It was an activity I did alone normally. Wanting the time and space to be free with my thoughts, but an extra layer of euphoria accompanied the moment thanks to the woman behind me, hanging on for dear life. The five-and-a-half-hour trip was made longer because I stopped more often to let my companion stretch her legs. In hindsight, I probably should have started her with a shorter trip, but hopefully she'd think it was all worth it when we got to the mountain resort.

"Wow. That was..." She leaned against me to get steady on her legs, but the wonderous smile on her lips drew me in for a kiss. "Mussed-up Irene would like to come out to play sooner rather than later."

I slid my hand down to squeeze her ass. "That can be arranged. But we should probably make it to our room first."

The remote location was made up of a main house but also secluded private villas, and the one I'd reserved over-looked the gardens. She loved flowers and I wanted to give her as many as possible. Irene intertwined her fingers with mine as we sat in the back of the golf cart as the concierge drove us to our location.

When she entered, Irene let out a gasp and quickly covered her mouth as she turned to face me. "Remi." She flung herself into my arms with such force I stumbled back.

They'd arranged everything I'd asked for. In the center of the bed were rose petals in the shape of a heart. In the middle of it was a tray with chocolate-covered strawberries, and on the small dining table in the corner near the fireplace was a bottle of champagne chilling along with mini bottles of Coke.

"This is a date."

"Told you you'd know."

She laughed quietly before her lips covered mine. The undercurrent of arousal from earlier quickly sparked back to life. We tore at our clothes, trying to free ourselves of as many layers we could while maintaining the hedonistic kiss. I pushed her against the door as she fumbled with the button of my pants.

I lightly sank my teeth into the side of her neck when her hand made contact with my pussy. She groaned when I was successful in doing the same. Her wetness coated my fingers, making it easy to slip into her slick opening.

We moved at a frantic pace, a tangle of tongues and hands. I pressed my thumb to her clit; she responded by pushing her palm harder against mine. Our moans danced in the air, my heart raced, and her quick, shallow breaths urged me on.

"Remi...oh god..." Her body quivered around my fingers.

I wrapped my free arm around her waist, holding us both up as my own release cascaded through me. Our movements slowed, and I shivered when she circled my sensitive nub before withdrawing her hand.

But I needed more. I always needed more of her. Dropping to my knees, I yanked her pants down and lapped at her sweetness. I pushed her thighs as wide as allowed and covered her pussy with my mouth.

"Holy shit," she cried out, gripping onto the top of my head.

The taste of her was addictive. I slid my tongue between her folds, delighting in her whimpers and pleas for more. Her enthusiastic moans, the way she rocked her hips, and the sound of my name pouring from her lips, all of it added to my own wanton need, but more, it squeezed my heart.

I loved her, and making her happy in every way possible was a new driving force for me. Closing my lips around her stiff nub sent her over the edge once again. She pounded the door and held my face in place as she released a guttural sound from the back of her throat.

After a final swipe of my tongue, I pulled her pants up as I stood. "I can't get enough of you."

She kissed me softly. "Good. The feeling's mutual."

"You know I'm hopelessly in love with you, right?"

She slipped her arms around my neck. "You damn well better be because I know I'm absolutely head over heels in love with you."

We still had the one issue between us, her divorce, but after dealing with the crisis with my father, that no longer seemed so insurmountable. She'd had my heart long before my head wanted to get on board, so there was no going back. She was mine, and I was hers.

EPILOGUE
IRENE

I WHIPPED MY CAR INTO ONE OF THE SPACES AND COULD barely contain the excitement coursing through me. Six months. Six months Derrick had held out. Tried to be as difficult as possible. And had even tried to convince me to come back to him. Six months and thousands of extra dollars he lost because he couldn't admit defeat.

He'd even used the Audi as a bargaining chip after I'd told him he could have it. I had simply wanted out. Wanted to be free. After taking a breath, I climbed out, slammed the door, and practically ran toward the bay area, clutching the envelopes in my hand.

I heard the bang and clang of tools, indistinguishable conversations, and music. When I got to the opening, I glanced around trying to spot Remi. Devon saw me and waved.

"Where's your boss?"

He pointed to the car in the last bay. He started to call for her, but I put my finger to my lips and shook my head. There was no mystery I was dating their boss, but they seemed to get a kick out of my visits for whatever reason.

I walked toward the end and saw a pair of legs sticking out. She seemed to be in her own world, totally oblivious. I adored her focus and dedication to her job. And she applied that to every aspect of her life. She didn't profess her love just through words. Every day she showed me. I'd never been so cared for, admired, appreciated, and all-around loved. Being with her had opened my eyes up to how being with someone should be. Biggest of all, I was respected.

I was finally living the life I'd pretended to have for so long, and I nearly cried from the joy of it all. Experiencing what I'd witnessed from my friends. It was life-changing. Heart bursting. And I didn't take a minute of it for granted. I kicked off my heels, then gathered up my fitted A-line skirt until it was hiked up to my thighs and lowered down to straddle her.

"What the hell?" When she rolled the little trolley from beneath the car, I had to place my hands on her stomach to steady myself. "What in the world are you doing?"

"Getting your attention."

"You could have called out my name. Knocked on the car. Either of those options cross your mind?"

"Yes, but this was equally as effective."

A frown marred her beautiful face before she lowered her eyes briefly. I knew from the angle and how I sat on her, she could easily look up my skirt. A smile pulled at my lips at the thought.

She started to put her hands on my waist but stopped. "You should move so I don't get you dirty. Then we can have whatever conversation you apparently need to have so urgently."

With more bravado coursing through my veins, I leaned forward, folding my arms across her chest. "I kinda like where I am." I inhaled, pulling in the signature scent that was Remi

Martin. The strange combination of cinnamon and motor oil. I loved that smell.

She sat up, resting her back against the car she was working on. "Okay. Well, you have my attention."

My hands shook as I fumbled trying to pull the papers free. "It's over!"

She took the papers and read over them for a minute before her sexy lopsided grin appeared. "About fucking time."

"Yes. I got home from work, checked the mail, and it was there. My official divorce decree."

This time she didn't stop herself from grabbing me, and I didn't give a damn about her grease-stained hands. I would walk out of the shop with handprints on my ass with pride as she kissed me long and deep. For a moment, we forgot where we were and that we had spectators. But it didn't matter. We got lost in our own little bubble of celebration, which would absolutely continue in privacy after she got home.

"You know they are never going to let me hear the end of this right," she whispered. "You have completely tanked my hard-ass reputation around here."

"I feel like you want me to apologize for that, but, eh, I can't."

"Nope. Definitely don't apologize."

It wasn't as easy to get up as it was down, but I managed to get back to standing somewhat gracefully. Both guys tried to look busy once I was on my feet, and Remi popped up as well.

"Okay, I'll get out of your hair, but we have dinner tomorrow with my parents. And we're spending the weekend in Atlanta so we can visit with Pop."

"Yes. I remember."

I slipped my shoes back on. "Also, I've decided to move into the main house. Axle and Hemi are happy to have me."

She laughed and shook her head. "Okay. Also noted. Anything else?"

I twisted so my back was to her. "How's my ass?"

"Marked as mine."

"Good."

Thank you for purchasing and reading! I hope you enjoyed Mechanics of Love. If you can spare a few more moments of your time, I'd greatly appreciate if you'd leave a review.

As promised you can sign up and get the bonus booty extended HEA chapter HERE.

ABOUT THE AUTHOR

Meka James is a writer of adult contemporary and erotic romance. A born and raised Georgia Peach, she still resides in the southern state with her hubby of 16 years and counting. Mom to four kids of the two legged variety, she also has four fur-babies of the canine variety. Leo the turtle and Spade the snake rounds out her wacky household. When not writing or reading, Meka can be found playing The Sims 3, sometimes Sims 4, and making up fun stories to go with the pixelated people whose world she controls.

https://www.authormekajames.com/

OTHER BOOKS BY MEKA

Fiendish: A Twisted Fairytale

please note this book tackles dark themes that may be upsetting to readers. You don't have to read Fiendish to read and enjoy Not Broken

Not Broken: The Happily Ever After

*Continuation of Calida's story from Fiendish

The Lists

*Extended HEA for Calida and Malcolm from Not Broken

Anything Once

Desert Rose Hook-ups series

Being Neighborly

Being Hospitable

Being Cordial

Being Merry

Printed in the USA
CPSIA information can be obtained
at www.ICGtesting.com
JSHW021821080624
64440JS00001B/39